THE ORDER of DUVAL

EF DEAL

NEOPARADOXA

PENNSVILLE, NJ

PUBLISHED BY
NeoParadoxa
a division of eSpec Books LLC
Danielle McPhail,
Publisher
PO Box 242,
Pennsville, New Jersey 08070
www.especbooks.com

ISBN: 978-1-956463-97-2
ISBN (ebook): 978-1-956463-96-5

Cover and Interior Design: Danielle McPhail, McP Digital Graphics

Illustrations: Art Credits - www.shutterstock.com

Copy Editor: Greg Schauer, John L. French
Interior Design: Danielle McPhail, McP Digital Graphics

Cover Art & Design: Mike McPhail, McP Digital Graphics

eSpec Titles by Ef Deal

Esprit de Corpse
Aéros & Héroes

eSpec Titles Featuring Ef Deal

The Forgotten Lore Series
A Cast of Crows
A Cry of Hounds
An Assembly of Monsters
(forthcoming)

Other Aether

DEDICATION

To my sisters Donna and Teri

1.

"Jacqueline Marie-Claire Duval de la Forge-à-Bellesfées?"

The courier read the address from the package he held, then eyed Jacqueline doubtfully. In her filthy leather trousers, quilted insulated gloves, leather apron, with dirty strands of honey-blonde hair peeping out from her welding cap, and modified safety spectacles she called "gogglers" dangling around her neck, she hardly appeared to be the intended recipient, a mistress of a petit château in the Loire valley.

When Jacqueline scowled, he proffered the package.

"Any response?"

Nothing identified the sender. She tugged off her gloves to fish in her pocket for some change and handed a few coins to the courier. He gasped with an incredulous "Merci mille fois!" before scampering away.

Jacqueline's twin, Angélique Aurélie, met her at the doorway of the château, still barefoot in her peignoir, her hair loosed, and eating an apple. Angélique was always eating these days, barely five weeks into her expectancy.

"You gave him too much for the service," she said.

Jacqueline focused on the package. "It never hurts to spend a few francs locally, as long as I have them."

"But your finances are bound by the Assizes. What if you lose to that lying, porcine piece of lard?"

"Then I'll sell more designs." Jacqueline set her gloves on the receiving table to better examine the delivery. "The lawsuit is before the King now, and I did save his life. Twice. I think he'll show clemency. I've been knighted, and all evidence in this stupid suit exonerates me. So, despite Rodolphe Armand being a friend to the King, and even though French law never favors women, the King has to see reason."

Angélique merely scoffed. "So then, what's the package?"

Jacqueline untied strings and opened the brown paper wrapping to find a portfolio stamped with the initials EG. Inside the worn leather case was a collection of designs for an updated locomotive engine for the Paris-Orléans Railroad. Curious, she set those aside and read the accompanying letter.

Angélique picked up the gloves, touching fresh globs of solder. "What are you working on?"

"I'm rebuilding your clarinetist," Jacqueline replied, still reading.

Angélique peered over her shoulder. "That doesn't look like my clarinetist." She took the designs to peruse. "You master the École Polytechnique at thirteen years of age, sell over three hundred commissions before you graduate, take first place in every exposition, and somebody wants you to make a train? That's a little beneath you, no? Or do you think you'll lose the suit and need the money?"

Jacqueline chuckled. "Ernest Goüin doesn't need anyone's help building a locomotive, mon Ange. However…"

Her brow furrowed as she reread the letter and scanned the designs again. "I think de Guise must have sent him my way." She sighed in annoyance. "Ghosts. Sorcerers. Revenants. Vampires. Assassins. Shall we add haunted trains to our list of misadventures?"

"Don't forget us lycanthropes." Angélique pointed an elongated finger to the expanded sun-glasses covering her wolf-eyes in tinted glass and winked at Jacqueline. "Does that say fifty thousand francs? Ooh! Let's have a look."

Angélique parked the apple in her teeth and took the papers from Jacqueline. She *hmp, hmp, hm-hmmped* as if reading aloud. Her eyes then widened and she pulled the apple from her mouth.

"Blood coating the machinery? The most frightful of agonized cries?" She returned the papers to Jacqueline. "What does he suppose you can do about it? You defused and rebuilt a renegade automaton, so he thinks you can resolve a haunting?"

"I have no idea." Jacqueline untied her heavy apron and smacked it down on the receiving table beside her gloves. "But I will have a little chat with dear Alain."

"Ah, no." Angélique caught her sleeve. "When you call him 'dear Alain,' I know you're charging into a fight."

Jacqueline huffed. "We never fight."

"*He* never fights. That doesn't stop you from starting them."

Angélique laughed, pressing a finger against her twin's mouth to silence a retort. With a wink, she returned Jacqueline's apron and gloves to her.

"Go finish my clarinetist. Let me broach the topic with Monsieur le Railroad Agent to learn what I can without feathers flying. Don't worry." She brushed back her black-tipped tawny hair with a coquettish grin. "I won't bite."

"Bof. Since when are you the sensible one?" Jacqueline waved her sister away impatiently.

"Since marrying a duke, becoming a grande dame of a great house in Britain, and owning the life of luxury and grace I have so richly earned."

Finishing her apple, she flung the core out the front doors and wiped her hands on her peignoir.

"Very graceful," Jacqueline said with a snort.

"I don't really need a clarinetist," Angélique said as she followed her on her way to the music conservatory. "I played plenty of concerts all over Europe without a panharmonica or an orchestrion or anyone else."

"Yes, yes, brilliant prodigy, outshining Thalberg, the favored pet of royalty and nobles throughout Europe."

"Don't forget stunning beauty," she teased.

"Of course. With wolf eyes."

"You could have those, too, if you'd join Llewellyn and me. Then we'd be twins again."

"We've had this discussion. I'm content to let you be the wolf with all your other charms."

"And I'm content to let you keep your silk armor instead of repairing my clarinetist," Angélique returned. "It saved your life. You never know when another vampire will sweep into the Loire Valley."

As they passed through the kitchens arguing, their housekeeper Marthe scowled, looking up from chopping vegetables.

"God forfend," she scolded. "Another vampire? Why not another assassin to shoot at us? I don't know how you girls get into such trouble."

The twins each kissed Marthe's cheeks and continued on past the kitchens, the pantry, and the servants' wing into the music conservatory wing, up the staircase to the concert hall, where Angélique seated herself at her beloved Érard fortepiano.

"I thought you were going to speak to de Guise," Jacqueline needled, returning to the cannibalized clarinetist of her clockwork chamber orchestra.

"I'll get there. After practice."

For the next half hour, life was as it had always been when they were children: Angélique at the piano, Jacqueline at her machines. Contentment so filled Jacqueline she didn't notice when Angélique left the hall, but eventually her thoughts drifted from happy memories to the horrors described in Goüin's letter. Each drop of molten solder evinced the gory images, while the exuberant cries of her four protégées out on the lawn drifted through the open balcony windows and resounded in the concert hall as shrieks of terror.

She gave up after a few hours and went to find Alain de Guise, the intriguingly charming man who had captured her heart and changed her world. Surely his smile could displace her dreadful imaginings.

The air was heady with the pungent fragrance of the grape harvest, which had begun in late August for the champagnes just after Angélique's wedding celebration and would continue through September. Dozens of villagers worked the vineyard from late afternoon until the next day's sunrise. At midday, a different round of workers hauled the carts of grapes to the winery for sorting before sending the vendange to the pressing room on Jacqueline's giant clockwork trucks.

She waved to the workers and watched for a few minutes. It always fascinated Jacqueline that they could strip the fruit and later cut the vines back to almost nothing, yet next year the harvest would be just as abundant or more so, and meanwhile, this vendange would produce the unique varietal wine of Bellesfées. Some ancient wisdom could likely be found in the metaphor, something about stripping away the past to have a future, growth from pain, all things in season. Jacqueline rarely wasted time searching for a philosophy; physics, chemistry, engineering, maths, logic—there were plenty of lessons to learn without digging for more.

Jacqueline found de Guise with Angélique, now fully dressed and coiffed, looking like the duchess she was, though still barefoot, seated at a table laden with a pique-nique luncheon in the courtyard of the east lawn. Jacqueline's autonomous clockwork assistant, Monsieur Claque, stood patiently near de Guise, tiny puffs of steam emerging from the top of his casque-like head every few seconds. Tasked with assisting the convalescing de Guise, the giant autonomaton dutifully tended his patient, pouring wine and slicing meats and cheeses despite de Guise's assurance his aid was no longer needed.

Angélique's intended ward Têtue stood off to the side, her brawny arms folded and her wolf-eyes sharp, watching Llewellyn train three other young women in the art of knife-wielding. Jacqueline suspected the women requested the lessons only because the duke was a handsome, exotic Welshman with his long black hair, slender but powerful frame, and the same lupine eyes as Angélique and Têtue. On the other hand, two of the young women had wielded weapons against the formidable vampire Mircalla and survived, so it made sense they would want to further their training. Jacqueline took note of Llewellyn's sword across his chair at the table. That would be Têtue's preferred weapon, and her lesson had already ended.

The oldest of the four—boyishly sturdy, rough-edged, and muscular—Têtue had experience in ironworks and punch cards, having worked in several factories in her years of wandering once she left her brutal husband. Adèle Frontenac, a slender blonde, was a bright, well-educated woman at eighteen, and had quickly caught on to the nature of draughting as well as mastering more complex formulae than the basic maths she had learned in the convent. Renée Guichet, seventeen and well-muscled from four years of house and yard work, was more facile at organizational tasks, having run her household finances for the past three years. Despite no formal education, she was a quick study under Frontenac's tutelage, and she did a splendid job of triaging and inventorying the salvage from Jacqueline's burnt-out workshop. She also had a knack for dressmaking and piecework, adjusting or redesigning Angélique's cast-off dresses to fit the four of them.

Unlike the others, fourteen-year-old Justine Montpellier had only recently risen from bed, bandaged from her head to her elbows after losing almost all the flesh on her face, head, and shoulders to the ravages of a young vampire's talons. Yet, Jacqueline was impressed by her gentle nature, her soft voice, her wide-eyed wonder, and her graceful, deliberate movements—even while brandishing a knife.

"You don't just jab or poke. Slide in, then a little slice to the side," Llewellyn told them, and demonstrated the technique. "This isn't a death cut, but it does hurt like the devil and is harder to heal."

The young women imitated his technique. While Frontenac advanced with confidence and Guichet moved with vengeful force, Montpellier applied a dancer's delicate fluidity. The women laughed at their accomplishments, surprised at the skills they acquired so quickly.

Jacqueline chewed at her cheek, however. She knew their personal talents had been sharpened by the blood they had been forced, unaware, to drink from Mircalla. The young women had yet to discover what other powers they might manifest. Jacqueline had pondered the appropriate moment to disclose the information to them and had decided to wait until they chose their roles at Bellesfées beyond "the Order of Duval," as Têtue called their little coterie.

What worried her further was the fact that Rodolphe Armand's suit against her had named Frontenac and Guichet as her accomplices in robbing him of over twenty thousand francs worth of machinery *two years earlier*. The fact she had not met the young women until a few weeks ago led her to believe the vampire's blood in them somehow factored into Armand's accusations, one of the reasons she had agreed to let the girls stay on, but she was not yet willing to accept his version of the truth. While Mircalla traveled through the aether, and likely had brought the young women through as well, people simply didn't travel back in time; that was a fact of science, and she preferred to hold fast to that.

Jacqueline came up behind de Guise and slipped her arms around his broad shoulders, resting her cheek on his unruly blond curls. The late summer sun had quickened his delicious spicy scent, and she breathed him in, satisfying some of her hunger and tempting another.

"The ladies are doing quite splendidly," he said, pointing to the martial lessons. "I'm most surprised at young Justine. She never should have survived her attack, yet there she is, ready to join the fray."

"You seem to be healing quite well too, my love," she murmured in his ear. "Has it really only been ten days?"

Ten days since Austrian assassins had shot at Louis-Philippe I, King of the French, striking de Guise instead. She didn't want to admit she was enjoying his convalescence, waiting on him, spending hours with him at cards or games or conversation, listening to harrowing tales of his exploits as an agent of the Sûreté Nationale. His deep, sonorous voice resonated through her whole body. A reticent man, he rarely laughed except when he was with her, but when he smiled, a serene warmth filled her. Their passionate nights of lovemaking had perforce become quiet hours of slow, tender movements that surprised them both as they discovered one another anew. She didn't think she could have loved him any more, but each day brought more joys and insights that only bound her closer to him.

He caught her hands and kissed both palms. "And before you ask, chérie," he said, "I did not send Goüin to you. I mentioned the haunted automaton you so cleverly managed that one glorious day in July only once, and that was on the day it occurred when I made my report. I know nothing of haunted locomotives." He shifted in his chair so he could pull her into his lap for a lingering kiss. "But I can think of no one more suited to this particular conundrum, can you?"

Jacqueline traced the lovely bow of his upper lip that had fascinated her since the day they met. "I yield to your gentle persuasion, my love." She then added, "However, I would appreciate the assistance of my sister who, apart from her skills at tempering my temper, has a nose much keener than mine at sniffing out otherworldly intruders."

Têtue, with her heightened sense of hearing, stalked over to quickly dash the suggestion. "I'll do that, Duval. Her Grace shouldn't be risking herself in adventure."

"Têtue, I'm with child, I'm not dying," Angélique said with a laugh, plucking up another slice of peach and slurping it down. "And I'm not that far along at all. Just because I've been sick every morning…"

She trailed off, then rallied again. "Although I felt pretty good yesterday and today, so perhaps that's passed."

Têtue frowned. "This early, there's always a risk. You're twenty-three years old, not a young bride. You say you're not far along, but wolf blood… Who knows how that changes things with us? Most women don't know they're pregnant until after a few months, not weeks. You're already showing. And you can't fool me, remember. I know when something isn't right."

Her brown wolf-eyes narrowed on Angélique, reminding Jacqueline of every time her twin smugly showed off her lupine skills. Jacqueline enjoyed seeing someone else challenge her, especially when the words of caution came from Têtue. Like Jacqueline, the rough woman had a quick mind and a feel for machinery. If Jacqueline could have chosen a younger sister for herself, it would have been Têtue, but since Angélique had turned her to save her life, it was more fitting the young woman join the Llewellyns' household as their ward.

"You need to be more careful, Your Grace. I lost two before I even knew I was carrying."

Angélique sobered. "I had no idea. I'm so sorry."

Têtue shrugged in the slow Parisian way that signaled indifference. "Made it easier to leave. But then, I'm sure His Grace never beats you."

Jacqueline shuddered, as she did each time she heard a new detail of one of her protégées' miserable past. "No, His Grace does not beat her."

She turned to Angélique. "Nevertheless, Têtue is right. You need to take better care of yourself, mon Ange, for your cub's sake."

"Then it's settled." Têtue folded her arms again. "Duval and I will handle the ghost train."

"And I," de Guise said. "I've been bored lounging around like a cheap bourgeois, as Llewellyn has called me. It's time I earned my keep."

A rush of anxiety prompted Jacqueline to hold him closer. "Are you sure? This doesn't sound like anything you need to worry about."

"Of course I'm sure." He kissed her again. "My time on the railroads was not merely a covert identity, chérie. If there's something endangering the security of the railroad, I'm curious to learn what it is and what I can do to help. And it will be good to see Goüin again."

"I suppose it's worth some investigation," she mused. "Since I don't have a workshop anymore, I don't know when I'll get back to any other productive work. I surrender. When should we go?"

"Go where?" Llewellyn asked, joining them. Drenched in sweat, he mopped himself down with a towel, his dark hair hanging loose from his tartan ribbon, his green wolf-eyes bright. His students flanked him, equally disheveled and aglow, gladly accepting the wine Llewellyn offered.

"Orléans," Jacqueline told him. "Têtue and I, with de Guise."

"An outing in the city? Let's all go. Angélique will be needing larger dresses soon." He winked at his wife, but she still slapped his arm.

"Ooh, and the women should have their own wardrobes," Angélique said. "It's not fair to offer them a home and only give them handoffs to wear. A full trousseau."

"I'd rather wear trousers," said Guichet, "like Duval." She ducked her head, reddening. "I'm sorry. I shouldn't ask."

"Trousers, coat, and boots," Frontenac amended. "Long coat with many pockets, like Duval's."

Montpellier added, "Leather. For sheaths."

"Yeah, sheaths," agreed Têtue. "Good idea."

"Sheaths?" Jacqueline sat up, startled. De Guise kept her from falling off his lap.

"Knife sheaths." Guichet giggled. "Not *those* kinds of sheaths. Leather ones would be uncomfortable."

Llewellyn spluttered his wine. He laughed aloud at the suggested image, then laughed harder at Jacqueline's indignant reaction. He had to sit to catch his breath, knocking his sword to the ground.

"The Order of Duval has decided they wish to wear knives strapped to their legs beneath their skirts," he explained, "either as garters or attached to their boots. I think it's a splendid idea, and Frontenac and Guichet have experience working with leather."

"Do you have the tools?" Frontenac asked.

"I think we were able to salvage a few punches and awls," Jacqueline said, "but I can't do any riveting." She rose, rubbing her brow. "And these stupid lumber strikes and secret 'banquets' are destroying my plans to rebuild the workshop any time soon."

"Banquets?" asked Montpellier.

"That's what they call the illegal gathering of the mill owners skirting monopoly laws," she explained. "But let me do a quick inventory. I'm sure there's plenty of leather and some buckles in one of the porters in the music conservatory."

"And your finances?" Guichet reminded her. "The Assizes?"

She put her hands on her hips when Jacqueline turned a sharp eye to her. "Don't pretend we're ignorant of what's going around here, Duval. It's a serious concern. You can't really afford to outfit us."

Angélique laughed in delight, halting Jacqueline's retort. "Ho, ho, ho, là! You are going to have a difficult time shepherding these little lambs, madame!"

"Ah, my love." Llewellyn wagged his finger at his wife. "Lambs are innocent, and these women are cunning, shrewd, and dangerous. Four more beautiful fairies of Bellesfées."

Jacqueline suffered their teasing, easing to a good-natured grin.

De Guise got to his feet slowly and stretched, rubbing his abdomen where the healing scar itched. He paused, gazing off to the east.

"Do you have your spyglass, Jacqueline?"

Curious, she took it from her inside pocket and handed it to him. He affixed it and focused, then said, "You have competition, chérie."

He pointed, returning the glass to her. She espied a large aerostat with a long, blunt-nosed envelope, a boxy gondola, and a single screw propeller at the rear. However, unlike her own airship *Esprit*, with a specially designed hermetic fueling system, this inelegant aerostat emitted black clouds from its engines, probably using coal as its source of fuel, as it headed southeast.

"Are those gun ports?" she cried. "Is this a new military weapon?"

He shook his head. "I'd have known of its development if it were."

She closed the spyglass and wrinkled her nose. "I'm anxious to meet the commander of this vessel. I could teach him a thing or two about flying an airship without befouling our vineyards." Under her breath she muttered, "Foute alors."

Têtue sniggered at the foul obscenity from her mentor, then stifled it as the housekeeper Marthe appeared to clean away the orts and refill the pitcher of water.

"Language, ma fille," Marthe scolded. "Working in a forge is no excuse." When she caught Llewellyn mimicking her, she raised a threatening finger at him before going back inside, passing her son Jean-Paul on his way out.

Jean-Paul handed Jacqueline a calling card, grinning at Montpellier. "How are you today, Mademoiselle Montpellier?"

She lowered her gaze. "I'm well, thank you, Jean-Paul."

The youth nodded to the others briefly, but he waved to Montpellier as he returned to the house. Guichet nudged Frontenac, and the two tittered.

Jacqueline studied the card with a frown. "Frontenac, this concerns you."

The three younger women looked at one another in alarm. When Têtue sniffed the air, she growled, ready to confront danger. Frontenac threw her shoulders back, awaiting a blow.

"You've been expecting this, haven't you?" Jacqueline noted.

Têtue leaned closer to see the card. "'Gaspard Frontenac.' Your father? How'd he find you?"

"He probably heard reports of missing girls returning from Bellesfées," de Guise answered. "Angélique certainly made the name Jacqueline Duval legendary enough from here to Chartres."

Jacqueline *tsk*ed. "I knew that was a mistake."

"It wasn't," Têtue argued. "You deserve legends and more. So, how do we save Frontenac from her father?"

Jacqueline raised a brow. "Save?" She pursed her lips. "Frontenac, do you need saving?"

Frontenac didn't seem to be a damsel in any distress, but Jacqueline was aware of the many types of distress women faced.

"Yes," Frontenac admitted quietly. "That is, I don't wish to return to my father's house." Her eyes slid to glance at de Guise before she went on. "It's not like here. I've met your father. I've seen the way he loves his daughters, unconditionally, trusting you both to own your own lives." She winced. "He'd do better cutting me off and hiring a housekeeper. Then he wouldn't have to pay a dowry to a man I haven't even met."

A soft gasp escaped Montpelier. Frontenac put her arm around the younger one's waist.

"Yes, he's engaged me to a perfect stranger, but there's something suspicious about this arrangement he's made." Her voice took on a determined edge. "Besides, I want more than marriage. I want to learn. I want — more than he wants for me. I want what you have, Duval, Your Grace: an education and the means to use it."

De Guise and Llewellyn both laughed and waggled their fingers at their respective mates. Jacqueline accepted the accusation, while Angélique feigned indignation. But the three younger women awaited Jacqueline's response nervously. The drilling of woodpeckers, chortling of larks, and woodwind warbling of thrush in the nearby woods filled the tense silence.

Jacqueline had hoped to have more time for this discussion. She met their gazes evenly, trying to reassure them. "You're all welcome to stay on as my guests at Bellesfées, of course, but legally, I can't prevent your fathers, or your husband, Guichet, from reclaiming you. You're not yet twenty-one. There's only one legal way I know to allow you to stay at Bellesfées. I can adopt you as my wards, which would mean paying off your families, or in Guichet's case, husband."

Têtue gave an annoyed "Huh."

Again Guichet put her fists on her hips. "I would work my fingers to the bare bones in the vineyards to repay you if I could be free of that lout."

Montpellier searched Jacqueline's face anxiously but made no response.

Frontenac answered her mentor's steady gaze. "Go on."

She smirked; Frontenac was a smart woman.

"As my wards, you'd be answerable to me, as I would be answerable to the law, and I'm certain to put you to work, not to repay any debt, but to make you aware of the burden of independence. I'm sorry, Guichet, but the vineyards are leased out, so I can't hire you, but you're certainly welcome to apply to the vigneron."

She winked to let her know she was being facetious. Then she sobered. "Frontenac, your father's here asking for you. How do you wish me to answer?"

Montpellier turned away and bowed her head. "Please, oh, please, oh, please," she whispered.

Frontenac hurried to lightly kiss her bandaged cheek. Still, tears also came to her eyes.

"If it's possible, Duval, I want to stay here. Maybe if you were to hire me, my father would relent, having my salary. You can teach me to work the forge or teach me to design; I'm very good at maths and languages. Hire me as your assistant, and I promise I'll be worth every sou."

"Hire you?" Jacqueline chewed her cheek. "I hadn't thought of that." She tossed the idea back and forth, then nodded. "I can do that, assuming the King decides in my favor. For my part, I'll supply you with a suit complete and a work outfit, whatever tools you require, plus three gowns and two daydresses. You'll further your education with me, receive your own room, which you must tend yourself, and I'd like you to teach all the others to read and write and do maths. You can do that, n'est-ce pas?"

Frontenac caught her breath. "Yes, I'm sure I can. Truly?" she cried. "I can stay?"

Her reply was forestalled by the appearance of a tall, portly man who came storming around the south turret, his face red with fury.

"Worthless, ungrateful snake of a daughter," he cried. "I have you now."

The man recoiled in shock when Têtue snatched up Llewellyn's sword and blocked him. The three other women of the Order of Duval assumed a crouch, brandishing their knives.

"What? What?"

He stammered, confused and outraged as the women took a menacing step toward him, poised to strike, seconded by Monsieur Claque who took a defensive position beside de Guise. Jacqueline tried to hide her glow of pride, although de Guise and Llewellyn couldn't suppress their smiles.

Angélique positively beamed. "Ooh, well done, mes filles," she cooed.

Jacqueline stepped between the women and offered her hand. "Monsieur Frontenac, I presume. It's customary to await the mistress of the château in the drawing room, as I'm sure you were asked to do."

Monsieur Frontenac stared at her hand, unsure whether to shake it or kiss it. He decided to bow his head curtly instead.

"It's customary for a daughter to obey her father." He glared at Frontenac. "Come with me, Adèle."

Jacqueline raised her hand. "Madame Frontenac does not wish to accompany you."

He curled his lip. "*Mademoiselle* Frontenac doesn't have a choice."

"Perhaps. But you do." She indicated the open doors. "The drawing room, monsieur," she said firmly. "Madame Frontenac and I have a proposition for you."

She turned to her autonomaton. "Claque, escort Monsieur Frontenac inside."

Monsieur Claque stomped forward, all two and a half meters of bronze and brass and intricate clockwork menacing the untimely visitor away from the women, then herding him into the château.

2.

Angélique shifted uncomfortably. The sudden excitement had her heart pounding, putting a stitch in her abdomen. She rubbed there gently, worried more for the young women than her own discomfort. As Adèle accompanied Jacky inside, Justine and Renée breathed audible sighs of release, though not relief. They both stared at their knives, trembling. Angélique knew they were wondering whether they'd have had the courage to use them to defend their friend.

Têtue spat. She handed Gryffin's sword back to him, and as she took up her sentry behind Angélique, her dark eyes narrowed. Her fear and anger were palpable.

Angélique spoke to the wolf in her. *"You're worried someone will reclaim you too."*

Têtue regained her usually stoic expression, but she answered, *"I don't turn twenty-one for another seven months. Will you have to pay off somebody to adopt me?"*

"Unless we can secure a divorce for you, yes."

Angélique pushed her glass of wine toward her. "Here, Têtue, have my glass. I don't seem to have a taste for it today." She sent word to Gryffin, *"Darling, can you give us some time?"*

Her husband grinned. "Come, my lady-knives," he said to Justine and Renée. "Let's go another round. De Guise, why don't you come along, get moving about, you cheap bourgeois."

Gryffin led the others off to the lawn again. With a nod and a grin to Angélique, de Guise followed. She was grateful for the friendship between the two men. De Guise understood exactly why Gryffin had called him away.

Angélique patted the chair beside her, and Têtue slumped into the seat. She reminded Angélique so much of Jacky: headstrong, as her name indicated, although Angélique preferred to say determined, ready to face any challenge.

"Têtue," Angélique said, "when Mircalla ordered you to kill Jacqueline, you took your own life instead. When you have shown such defiant courage and nobility, I have to ask what could possibly frighten you now?"

Têtue wrinkled her nose. "Not scared. Fact is, everyone thinks I'm dead. Rather stay that way. I didn't go missing from my home like the others. I left years ago, far from here. The Beast isn't looking for me."

Angélique tried to hear more than the woman was saying. "You said he beat you."

Têtue ran her hand through her short-cropped black hair. "That too." She reddened. "It was bad. I left." She shrugged. "Don't look for him, that's all. You don't have to adopt me. Can't I just stay with you? I could be a lady's maid, or maybe governess for the little one. Or ones. Foute, I've held so many jobs, I could do anything."

"Well," Angélique replied, mischief tugging the corner of her mouth, "I will not allow you to raise my cubs if you're going to use that language."

Têtue's face fell until she realized Angélique was teasing her. Then she smirked, saluted Angélique with her glass, and drank.

Angélique took Têtue's callused hand in hers. "My sister's habit of calling everyone by their family name has always irked me. It comes from her years of schooling among men. But you told us you had no family, so we called you Têtue as you asked. I would prefer to call you by your given name. Can you tell me what it is?"

The younger woman again gave her broad shrug, her eyes cast down. "I've always been Têtue. Ever since I was a kid."

Angélique leaned forward intently. "But you're not a child anymore, ma fille," she said. "Time to put away the things of childhood. I grudge you no secrets between us, but at least I would know your name so I may introduce you formally as a member of the family."

She gripped Têtue's hand as the young woman tried to pull away. After a long, uncomfortable silence, Têtue surrendered unwillingly. "Dominique," she said. "But I prefer Têtue. At least so long as we're here."

Angélique smiled. "Soit." She drew Têtue into an embrace and kissed her cheeks softly. "Dominique is a lovely name," she whispered.

Lisette, the new housemaid, came out to the courtyard trembling. The youngest of those who asked to remain in service at Bellesfées, she was a sickly child of nine. Angélique worried about the girl's constant coughing, sensing the illness that gripped her lungs.

Lisette was coughing now, her congestion exacerbated by tears. Her voice quavered. "Madame, I—I think you should see—I don't know how—"

"Ma petite, what in the world?" Alarmed, Angélique rose and followed the girl, and Têtue accompanied them. Lisette said nothing, sniffling and coughing as she took them up the back stairway behind the kitchens into the second floor of the servants' wing. She unlocked the door of the first room of the hallway.

"I cleared and cleaned up here yesterday," she said. "Today—"

Every piece of furniture was overturned, upside-down, or thrown on top of another piece. The shattered lamp spilled oil all over the floor. Shredded bedclothes and feathers covered everything. On the wall, in lurid letters, was the message, "*Pas belles fées. Les fleurs du malheur.*"

Angélique and Têtue lifted their heads for the scent of a human intruder but found none beyond the bitter stink of Monsieur Frontenac venting his spleen. Angélique, however, knew from experience humans weren't the only kind of intruder.

"Every single room," Lisette complained. "All ten of them, a mess, and paint on the walls."

"It's all right, Lisette," Angélique quickly assured the shaken girl. "I'm sure you did a fine job of cleaning. You always do. Someone's played a trick on you."

The girl lifted her red eyes hopefully. Angélique shooed her away with a smile. Lisette retreated, her head bowed.

Angélique took in the scope of the disarray, then visited the other rooms, equally ransacked. She wasn't so much puzzled as annoyed. No one in Bellesfées needed reminding of the "malheur," the misfortune that had beset them all summer, nor of the anxiety they yet faced while awaiting the King's judgment in Jacky's lawsuit in court, de Guise's return to full strength, and Montpellier's healing. And now, they had Monsieur Frontenac to combat as well. They deserved nicer "flowers" for their misfortune than tossed rooms.

Têtue set a chair against the wall and climbed up to sniff at the writing. "It's not blood," she declared. She scratched at it, but it seemed impervious to her stubby nails. "It's like it's not even here," she said.

"Perhaps it isn't," Angélique replied as she returned to the room.

"What do you mean?" Têtue hopped down. "This is an illusion?" She swatted away feathers floating in the air on the breeze from the open window. "I don't think so. This just happened."

"Oh, yes, this is fresh mischief."

Gryffin, who no doubt had sensed Angélique's dismay, came to the doorway and peered in, de Guise beside him.

"Some sort of prank?" de Guise asked.

Gryffin sniffed. "It's not what it looks like," he said, curious.

Têtue snorted. "Not some unexplainable strangeness?"

Angélique caught Têtue's arm and kept her from righting the furniture. "Strangeness, indeed, but not exactly unexplainable," Angélique said.

Têtue looked at her quizzically, but before Angélique could answer, she sensed something freshly dark on the air. Then Têtue growled as she too became aware of it.

Angélique ushered Têtue and the men out of the room and closed the door, locking it again. "We'll leave it until later. Right now —"

"Duval's mad," Têtue finished for her. "Yeah, I caught that."

De Guise gave a quiet chuckle. "Ah, Jacqueline is not getting her own way, I suppose."

"And Frontenac smells frightened," Têtue added. She hurried ahead of the others.

Angélique called after her, "Don't make things worse, Têtue."

She doubted Têtue would heed her. She linked arms with her husband as they descended the steps to the kitchen workroom and entered the halls of the château.

"Têtue asks to serve as a governess rather than being our ward," she told him. "She doesn't want us looking for her husband. She's hiding something that terrifies her, but she won't say what it is."

Gryffin kissed her head. "Wales is far enough away. Whatever frightens her won't reach her there."

De Guise *hmmed* thoughtfully. "I can't picture anything rattling Têtue. I think it's worth learning, don't you? Just in case?"

Gryffin chuckled. "Ah, the famed agent of Sûreté Nationale, of course you would get to the bottom of it."

"Only to protect her, my friend. And you."

Angélique bit her lip. "I don't want to see her hurt. Any more than she has been, that is."

"They've all been hurt," de Guise observed. "Young Justine is the only one who hasn't spoken of some underlying misery at home, but even she would rather stay here at Bellesfées."

Gryffin said, "Who wouldn't, given the choice?" He grinned. "I know I'd much rather stay here than go home."

"Naturally," de Guise retorted. "English parasite."

They reached the drawing room, a spacious chamber near the château's entrance, where Jacky faced off with Monsieur Frontenac, a man near fifty who was clearly more than a mere villager, judging by his habiliment and accoutrements: a dated cutaway, a worn silk cravate held with a pin, a much-used walking stick, and a faded tall hat set on the table beside him. Ink stained the first two fingers of his right hand, which was extended as he jabbed accusingly at his daughter seated on the couch, holding her chin high and answering his demands with a cold stare.

"Twenty thousand francs, I paid," he shouted. "Twenty thousand! You will marry Rodolphe Armand. It's done. The banns will be read beginning next week."

"Rodolphe Armand?" The edge to Jacky's voice could have sliced the man in two. "You engaged her to *Rodolphe Armand?*"

"And you, madame." He turned his finger on Jacqueline. "You will not presume to interfere with my family's business any further than you have for the past two years."

Angélique half hoped Jacky would punch the boor in the snout, but to her surprise her sister restrained herself, though she quaked with fury and her hands slowly curled to fists.

Têtue broke the tension. "Bof." She folded her arms and scoffed. "You're a liar." She drew an exaggerated sniff and sneered. "I can smell lies all over you. You didn't pay twenty anything, unless it was chickens."

Monsieur Frontenac spun on her. Before he could respond, Gryffin nodded.

"I have to agree, Dame Jacqueline," Gryffin said, emphasizing Jacky's title. "He stinks of lies."

"Lying indeed, Your Grace," agreed Angélique. "Well done, Madame Têtue."

Monsieur Frontenac's eyes bulged. His glare was met by three sets of tinted sun-glasses.

Angélique glided forward and nudged Jacky away with her hip to confront Monsieur Frontenac herself. She bestowed on him her most regal countenance. "You must admit, monsieur, you are but a mere lawyer or banker's clerk in a small town. You don't even earn twenty thousand francs a year, so you cannot possibly have paid anyone that much in dowry."

He shoved his furious crimson face into hers. "Who the devil are you, you insufferable, meddling sow?"

Angélique made a moue as she signaled the others not to flatten the man for his temerity. "Insufferable, meddling sow, Your Grace," she corrected him.

Jacky grinned, her anger abating. "Please, Madame la Duchesse, don't infuriate our guest further." Jacky sat beside Adèle and put her arms around her.

Angélique primped her hair and took center stage. "*Let the comedy begin,*" she sent to her husband.

Gryffin relaxed; de Guise followed suit. They both took their places behind the couch where Adèle and Jacky sat.

"Now, monsieur," Angélique continued, taking a seat opposite the man. "Let cooler heads prevail here, and let us speak with honesty and integrity, both of which I'm sure you possess." She eyed him up and down, then glanced away. "Somewhere. How else could you have raised such a straightforward and wise young woman?"

The man's temper shifted to nervousness as he eyed her with suspicion. He sat. Angélique smiled at the change in his scent, satisfied with the effect she had produced.

"And how else could you have come to these straits?" she continued. "Madame Frontenac, your father has by need engaged you to a wealthy prospect," she began. "Rodolphe Armand and I are acquaintances of old, although I was not as old as you are now when we met. Alas, he was older then than your father is now, so now he is even older. Old, old, old." She shook her head in scolding disapproval. "And no doubt very much fatter."

Angélique fluttered her hands as if shooing away the thought. "But he is a financier in an age of financiers, with holdings in many industries throughout Europe. That is a fortunate turn, Adèle, for he is quite rich. Or at least he was when last I knew him."

Monsieur Frontenac chuffed. "She should be on her knees thanking me for this match."

"In fact," she continued, her tone offhand, "he will be that much richer if he acquires Bellesfées next week, won't he, Dame Jacqueline?"

She returned Jacky's murderous glare with a wink. Adèle's fear intensified.

"Of course, if he loses…" Angélique fluttered her hand in the air. "However, madame, your father has failed to inform you of his reason for his choice of husbands for you. His honesty and integrity have forced him into this situation, and he owes you at least a full explanation. Badly done, monsieur. Very badly done."

Monsieur Frontenac stiffened. "I don't owe anything to my own daughter, madame."

"No? Oh, dear." Angélique *tsk*ed and shook her head. "Then allow me. You see, ma fille, your father has far too much integrity to play a dishonest game of whist. That is to his credit. On the other hand, Rodolphe Armand is a man well known in Paris, indeed, across all of Europe, as a card cheat and, in fact, keeps cards from a variety of fashionable decks tucked about his person, hoping to take advantage of an opportunity to fleece someone. Someone stupid and gullible. Thus, your father found himself twenty thousand francs in debt to Monsieur Armand, for which he set you as his gage."

The man leapt to his feet.

"Sit!" Angélique commanded. "You do not interrupt a lady, monsieur, or did you not learn that at school or church?"

Adèle lowered her head. Tears slid down her face and dropped into her lap. "I knew all along it was part of your gambling habit. That's why I refused you."

"Well, you can't refuse," her father snapped. "It's done."

"Is it?" Angélique arched her brow. She looked around the room as if searching. "I heard no banns read. I witnessed no vows taken before God and those dearly beloved gathered here today. Sit, monsieur." Her voice turned sharp. "I have not finished what I have to say."

Gryffin and de Guise glowered. Fuming, the man sat again. Angélique sent a thought to Têtue, who quickly rose to get the vermouth decanter and two cordial glasses from the sideboard to pour for the negotiations.

"Now," Angélique said, "you will agree this was shamefully done, and I will agree you felt you had no choice. I forgive you. I'm sure Madame Frontenac will as well, now that she understands the net in which you were caught." She smiled her most gracious smile. "But the solution that best suits Madame Frontenac is much simpler and involves no shame or dishonor, to either of you. You will allow Madame Frontenac to remain here at Bellesfées a while longer, and Monsieur Armand must court her properly, as a suitor seeking her hand rather than a horse trader acquiring a brood mare from a losing breeder. He will court her here at Bellesfées, and *Chevalier* Jacqueline Duval, as the mistress of Bellesfées — for now — will be her chaperone, since you have shown yourself to be incapable of responsibility to your own daughter. Certainly a knight of the Légion d'Honneur is an acceptable choice for such a role."

Angélique lifted her cordial. He glared back at her, trying to see through the tinted glasses into her eyes. She waited him out, and finally he touched his glass to hers and they drank, Angélique barely letting the liquor touch her lips. He set down his empty glass and reached for his hat, but she stopped him.

"Further, once the marriage contract is settled, you will renounce your legal rights to your daughter."

He cocked his head in agreement. "But of course." Then he hesitated. "That is, I—"

"Good."

Angélique stood and extended her hand in a peremptory dismissal. He kissed the air above her fingers, then gathered his hat and walking stick. He paused in front of his daughter. Before he could bid her adieu, Têtue ushered him out. Once he left, Adèle sobbed, burying her face in her hands.

The vermouth decanter shattered, shocking everyone but Angélique.

"Ah. Yes. I suppose I should tell you," Angélique said to Jacky. "It seems we've raised a spirit."

Jacqueline and de Guise jumped to clean the mess.

"What do you mean, a spirit? What kind of spirit?" Jacqueline cried as she gathered the larger shards of glass, while de Guise used a napkin to mop the spilled vermouth.

Angélique chuckled as she assisted them. "This is why they used to burn girls for witches. All these young women under one roof. It was bound to awaken something."

"A ghost in Bellesfées?" Jacqueline bit back a curse. Then she sighed. "Well, why not. Spirits, vampires, werewolves, sorcerers. Why not ghosts and witches?"

"Witches!" Frontenac gulped. "You think we're witches?"

"Absolutely not. I was joking," Jacqueline assured her.

"No, Jacky, not a ghost. Something else." Angélique rang for Lisette. "As you were in here arguing with Monsieur Frontenac, the upstairs rooms in the servants' wing were tossed and feathered."

Jacqueline frowned. "An intruder? Again? Why didn't you three sense it?"

Angélique shook her head. "There was nothing to sense."

Jacqueline's eyes narrowed. "You mean an esprit frappeur." She wagged her head dismissing the thought. "Throwing things around the room. Breaking possessions. Knocking and rattling about the house. There's never been any scientific proof they exist. Quite the opposite, in fact; their existence has been disproved by several—Aïe!"

Jacqueline pried a glass splinter from her fingertip and placed her finger in her mouth. "Hmm. Thtill…" She took the linen de Guise offered to wrap the cut.

"Exactly," Angélique answered. "Nothing to worry about, though inconvenient. It left a mess, and a message for us on the walls: 'Not beautiful fairies. The flowers of misfortune.'"

Frontenac sighed. "Misfortune. That describes the Order of Duval."

"Before, perhaps. See what lovely flowers you have become," Angélique soothed.

Llewellyn took a seat, content to watch the clean-up. "A tommy-knocker. More annoying than ghosts in some ways, but at least they're usually quieter."

"This one is certainly messier." Jacqueline resumed mopping the spilled vermouth. "You have noisy ghosts at Harddwch, do you?"

"To my surprise, we do," he said. "I never knew. I didn't see or hear them until my change. Eilonwy in the house, the Green Lady in the east tower, Twm in the stables, and somebody who sits and weeps and wails in the garden."

"Don't forget Biggs," Angélique added. "He's so adorable. But yes, noisy. And in some cases more dangerous. Biggs will dump you in the pond."

Frontenac giggled despite her woe. She wiped her tears but she was still shaking. Jacqueline returned to her side.

"Listen to me, Frontenac," Jacqueline said. "Angélique has a plan, we promise you. You won't marry anyone you don't wish to, and most assuredly not Monsieur Rodolphe Armand. The man is on the edge of ruin if he loses his suit against me."

"Which he will do," de Guise reassured her. "Yes, the King counts Armand as a friend. But the King himself has wandered these grounds and found nothing in your repertoire to suggest any deception, and without a contract, no one can lay claim to your designs."

"There, you see?" Jacqueline kissed Frontenac's head. "If he loses in court, I'll pay him the twenty thousand francs for you. He'll appreciate the money more than a wife."

Frontenac bowed her head. "Thank you. I know you're trying to help, and I'm grateful. I don't see any way out of it, though."

Jacqueline hugged her, holding her head to her bosom. "I said that once to Angélique. The next day, a way showed itself. There is always a way for the daughters of Bellesfées. Don't doubt the power of the Order of Duval, eh?" She patted Frontenac's shoulder. "Why don't you take the others and see if you can dig up the tools you said you needed. Everything we salvaged is in the forge. Be wearing those knife sheaths when we go to the city tomorrow, my lady-knives. You were magnificent today."

Jacqueline kissed Frontenac and let her go as Lisette came to the salon. Jacqueline sent her for a porter and a scrubber and watched worriedly as the little girl left coughing.

"Flowers of misfortune. If that doesn't describe our new family, I don't know what does. Victims of their lives, and victims of a vampire, all released from their past misery to bloom here at Bellesfées. And you think that's what raised this knocking spirit?"

"You are a powerful role model," Angélique observed. "If anyone can bring these women to a place of strength and help them blossom, it's you."

"But this kind of strength?" Jacqueline nodded to the mess.

"Put this many girls entering womanhood in one place, with the burden of all their woes, give them a sense of freedom and independence, and *poof*. It does happen."

Jacqueline brooded, still doubtful. "I've never heard of such a thing. Mensual règles aligning, yes, but levitation? Spirit writing? You never mentioned experiencing any supernatural phenomena to me, mon Ange, except the obvious one, of course."

De Guise said, "Even I've heard the stories about gathered girls, though I've never witnessed the phenomenon."

"What about the girls?" asked Têtue as she rejoined them. She frowned at the shattered glass. "What happened to the vermouth?"

"The girls are fine," Llewellyn told her, "but our growing household has awakened a knocker."

"Huh. That explains it. Hadn't thought of that." Têtue gave her characteristic shrug. "Makes sense. Bunch of girls. Hard lives. Add a bit of vampire blood. That'll do it."

Jacqueline cried, "You too?"

The lycanthropes merely smiled.

Jacqueline rubbed at her cuticles, working to connect the various lines she observed in each of the young women. The vampire had told of the power Jacqueline would gain if she drank the vampire's blood. Jacqueline had not realized the extent of such power. Naturally — or preternaturally — these very independent young women would chafe at having their power constrained and would need to find an outlet.

Who knew what other forces they would manifest?

"Does everyone know about this 'gathered girls' phenomenon but me?" Jacqueline hated being the last one to know anything, especially in the doings of the château. "Is it because of the vampire Mircalla, or is it a common occurrence?"

"You didn't have a typical girlhood," her sister reminded her. "How many other girls did you know at the Polytechnique?" She nodded when Jacqueline glowered. "Whereas I was housed with seven other young ladies in Paris when I studied with Thalberg, and our housekeeper was a termagant, harassing us unmercifully about what was proper, how to dress, how to speak, how to fold our hands and shut our mouths. Table-turning, knocking, and, mon Dieu, the things that flew across the rooms."

"You're serious? In all my life —"

"It'll pass," Angélique assured her.

"But is it one particular girl, or is it the gathering of girls that evokes the spirits?"

They all shrugged.

Jacqueline drank the last of her vermouth and tapped the glass with her bandaged finger. "It can't be just the vampire blood if it's as common as you believe. It must have something to do with magnetic forces. What did Mesmer call it? Animal magnetism."

"That sounds more like what attracted me to Angélique," quipped Llewellyn, and Têtue gave a loud "Hah!"

"Faraday did a study too." Jacqueline's face drew to a thoughtful pout. "Electro-magnetic lines of flux from charged bodies. Increase the excitation. If those fluxes were to cross… Add to it the vampire's immortality, defying the forces beyond the aether… Getting all those girls — women — to Bellesfées overnight, Mircalla may have allowed some to drink blood so they could survive the ordeal, or pass through the aether with her. Perhaps they brought something through with them? Yes, I can see this."

De Guise rolled his eyes. "We've lost her now. Next thing you know, she'll have invented a copper-and-clockwork glove so the servants can use animal magnetism to do their housework."

As if summoned by the word, the clockwork porter and scrubber arrived to gather the soiled cloths and broken glass and scrub out the carpet. Têtue loaded the automatons and set the gauges to put them to their tasks.

"Is there a possibility this is the cause of the alarm with the haunted locomotive?" Llewellyn asked. "So many young children, girls, working in the factory?"

"Hmm. Wouldn't that be interesting?" de Guise said. "We'll certainly know more in Orléans tomorrow."

"Speaking of burning girls for witches," said Angélique with a sigh.

Têtue folded her arms. "Let 'em try."

3.

Despite Angélique's nonchalance, Jacqueline was shaken by the thought of a knocking spirit at Bellesfées, particularly if she was the cause of its sudden appearance. With her head full of Faraday discs and Joule's experiments with resistance and heat in metal conductors, she paced the grounds of the château aimlessly until deciding to go to the library to find any research on magnetism as well as any reliable studies of supernatural occurrences such as esprits frappeurs. She was surprised to find de Guise at her desk, writing. He beamed when she came in.

Whenever he smiled like that, he melted her anxieties, even the inconvenience of a knocker. Love was new to Jacqueline. She felt all the silliness of girlish infatuation as well as wonder at the transcendent consummation of her womanhood. It was disconcerting at times to be both a child and a complete woman. Jacqueline had always lived by the immutable laws of a polytech. With de Guise, she had discovered within herself the lawless unbindings of passion and the unspoken bonds of devotion.

Jacqueline wrapped her arms around de Guise's neck and nuzzled his ear. "Are you very much occupied?" she whispered.

"I'm writing letters for each of the girls' families," he told her, "so we're not taken off guard again. We should have done this as soon as Mircalla was vanquished. Their families should know they're safe and secure."

She straightened. "Should they, though? Lisette's family can't afford a doctor, and you know they'll only send her back to the mill that destroyed her lungs. Geneviève loves helping Jean-Paul with the animals, and she's so happy here. So are Guichet and Montpellier."

He held her hand. "Do you remember the fear that gripped you when you thought Angélique was dead?"

Jacqueline's breath hitched. Which time? When Angélique died in Saint Petersburg and returned from the dead as a shapeshifting wolf? When she hid herself in the bowels of Paris for four months, pursued by the préfecture for obscenity? When she ran off with one of her many lovers to Italy? When she was arrested for two months in Clermont-Ferrand—Jacqueline still didn't know the story of that debacle. Or when she was shot by the sinister Count Draganov?

When Jacqueline didn't answer, he kissed her fingertips. "They deserve to know their daughters are alive and thriving, and they deserve to learn it from you."

Jacqueline released him reluctantly. "You're right, of course. I just don't want to see them hurt again."

"You still blame yourself," he observed. He swiveled around in the secretary chair Jacqueline had designed. He hugged her about the waist. "You're not the one who made them victims."

Jacqueline pouted. "No, but if I had killed Mircalla that night aboard *Esprit* instead of merely crippling her, she wouldn't have had to feed on so many."

"If I recall, you were under her spell," he reminded her. "You couldn't have killed her, so you could not be responsible."

She freed herself from his arms, unwilling to admit he was right. Lisette may have risked her life toiling in a mill, but sick or not, she had earned income for the family. Geneviève worked a farm with her parents; she made a contribution to the family's well-being. Who was Jacqueline to side against the law for the sake of the girls, who had no legal recourse that supported their requests to stay at Bellesfées? She should at least make some financial restitution to the families of those two who worked in her service.

That is, unless she lost Bellesfées to Rodolphe Armand.

Bitterness colored her tone. "Compose the letters, my love," she said. "I'll sign them and see they're delivered."

"Jacqueline—"

"I said I'll sign them."

Jacqueline left the library, annoyed at the world and the unfairness of the law. Men selling daughters or beating child brides. Men lying bald-faced to the Assizes. Men looking down their noses at women who sought to better their station and find independence. Couldn't they all be as sensible and open as de Guise and Llewellyn?

When would women finally be seen as human beings without being accused of trying to be men?

Whenever Jacqueline felt out of sorts, she had always gone to her workshop, but the workshop had burned to the ground in the battle with Mircalla. The clarinetist for Angélique still awaited completion, but that too reminded her of the vampire. She decided to take another look at Goüin's portfolio, which she had left in the courtyard.

As she gathered up the documents, Jacqueline caught sight of Montpellier standing at the far edge of the lawn, gazing out over the vineyard. With bandages covering her head, neck, and upper body, she resembled King Tutankhamen's mummified remains. Her head moved gracefully from side to side, as if tracing the flight of distant birds.

"Montpellier?" Jacqueline called.

The young woman turned and nodded to her. From between strips of gauze, her blank eyes seemed to gaze on something far away. "Duval. So many colors in motion down there. You built the carts, n'est-ce pas? I can see you in them."

Jacqueline joined her to watch the workers. "I did. We don't profit from the vineyards, but I cultivated a grape for this soil as a school biology project, and I automated some of the machinery for harvesting as a mechanics experiment. In return the vigneron gives us sixty cases. I think it's a fair arrangement."

Montpellier put a hand to her bandaged face. "You made the unguent for my skin, too. The surgeon said I should have died of my injuries, but instead, I'm healing. You make so many wonderful things."

Jacqueline kicked the grass, shifting uncomfortably. "Things, yes. I know how to make things."

Montpellier fixed her strange white eyes on her, her head still dancing to some inner music. "Did you make things better for Frontenac? I hope so. I want to learn to read and write."

"You and Frontenac are close, aren't you?" Jacqueline smiled, but worry tightened her jaw. She took Montpellier's hand. "What about you? What have you decided?"

Montpellier didn't answer right away. She again looked out over the fields of Bellesfées, resuming her inner dance. Finally, she murmured, "I can't go home like this." She pointed to her face and shook her head. "I can't. I don't belong there. I'm not really sure where I belong, but I am happier here."

Jacqueline's heart broke for the girl. She herself had spent her life avoiding the mirror. She was never pleased with her strong features, her muscular arms and legs. Her self-deprecating regard had made her prey to Mircalla's lusts.

But Montpellier had no doubt been a lovely girl, probably the darling of her village. Mircalla's minion had torn the flesh from the girl's face and shoulders, leaving her near death from shock and exposure. It was a miracle she was alive at all, yet that seemed to be no comfort to her, with her ravaged scarring, lurid and mottled, and her damaged eyes, ghostly pale peering out from the bandages. *I can't go home like this.* Jacqueline didn't know what made the girl believe her parents wouldn't want her back safe, but she was willing to accept her decision.

Jacqueline put her arm around her. "Then stay as my ward, if you think your parents will allow it."

Montpellier once more searched Jacqueline's face. "Maybe you can make another fair arrangement?"

Jacqueline hugged her. "I'll try."

When Guichet didn't come down to dinner, Jacqueline excused herself to see to her health and bid the others start without them. She tapped at the young woman's door and entered at the muffled response.

Guichet lay curled on her bed, hugging a pillow, wearing only her chemise. She had been crying. "Oh! I'm sorry!" She sat up suddenly, rubbing at her puffy eyes, when she saw Jacqueline. "I thought it was one of the others."

Jacqueline sat beside her on the bed and caressed her unpinned auburn hair.

"I wish there was more I could do to reassure you," Jacqueline said. "Têtue says her husband wouldn't come looking for her. Will yours?"

Guichet sighed. "I don't know. He married me so he could have a son. So far, I've failed him. No children."

"And how do you know you failed him? You're young. You have years ahead of you to bear children. Besides, it's just as much the husband's part to be able to produce an heir."

Guichet grinned wryly. "I doubt he would accept the blame."

Jacqueline had to acknowledge that likelihood. "I think you're too quick to accept the blame. We could attempt to file for a legal separation."

"On what grounds? Failure to produce a child isn't grounds for divorce."

Once again Jacqueline railed silently against the injustice. "Sadly, it's not. Laws are made by men and do not favor women in any fashion. Come the next revolution, women might have a bit more freedom again. The King of the French had best heed the cries of the oppressed instead of his bankers and industrialists."

She saw Guichet's confusion and set her political rant aside. "In the meantime, let's proceed with abandonment as a first step. It worked for Madame Sand; it may work for you. Write to your husband and explain you have no wish to return to him. You should state your reasons privately but explicitly to him. And we shall make a copy of the letter so you might later provide evidence of your intentions to the court."

Guichet shook her head. "If I tell him where I am, he'll come for me. If I list my real reasons—" She shuddered. "I'll be punished. If I simply stay quiet, he can assume I've left him."

"Unfortunately, as we saw today, you don't have the legal right to leave. Of course, you don't have to tell him where you are, and I certainly won't, but like Monsieur Frontenac, he may learn of your whereabouts. Unless you can prove cruelty on his part, he can have the prefecture reclaim you if he does find you."

Guichet's eyes filled with tears again. "I can't prove his kind of cruelty. Not anymore. Not since…"

Hugging the young woman more closely, Jacqueline waited until Guichet spent her tears on Jacqueline's shoulder.

When her quiet sobs stilled to sighs, Guichet whispered, "He called it pleasuring, but it hurt so much. Sometimes a riding crop. Sometimes his belt. But since I've been here, the scars are gone. And there's—other things." She could not hide the flush of shame that colored her face.

Jacqueline trembled with fury. "How is this not proof? Oh, Guichet."

"I wasn't an ideal wife either." She seemed on the edge of confessing some great misdeed. Then she simply said. "I—I made him angry." She shrugged.

"I killed a vampire for less cruelty than this." Jacqueline caressed Guichet's head again. "All right, I'll do as you ask and say nothing. Unless this animal shows up at my door. Then, I think, I will have much to say." Jacqueline drew Guichet from the bed. "Come to dinner. Enjoy the company of people who love you, and of good men who care about you."

Guichet protested. "I'm not dressed."

"Then I'll help you. And I *will* help you. I promise."

If nothing else, she would make certain Monsieur Guichet never touched his wife again, even if Jacqueline had to cut off his hands.

Evening set in, and Jacqueline went to check the systems on her airship, making certain they had enough fuel for the engines and hydrogen for the canopy. Monsieur Claque assisted her in her preparations. Like the airship, he was a remnant of Count Draganov's diabolical plot, but Jacqueline had repurposed the bronze automaton using the discoveries of the Countess of Lovelace, Jacqueline's adorable friend Ada King. With countless tiny punch cards and a complete sensory system, Monsieur Claque was almost intuitive. Adept in the forge as well as in the kitchens, he had proven indispensable over the past several weeks, especially caring for de Guise and guarding the château.

After securing the gauges, Jacqueline headed for the gangway. She stopped when she noticed lights in the second-floor windows of the servants' wing. Shadows moved across the curtains. Piqued, she told Monsieur Claque to batten down the ship while she trotted back to the château and slipped up the back stairway, hoping to catch the culprits.

All was silent in the hallway. Light shone under the doors. Before she inserted the key in the lock of the first room, the knob turned on its own and the door slowly opened. Her heart thumped against her breast as she edged forward and peered inside.

The argand lamp on the mantel was lit, all furniture was in place, and not a single feather floated on the breeze. The lurid message, however, remained on the wall.

Angélique came up the hallway from the other end. "I smelled your anger, and then your fear. What is it?" She peeked in the doorway. "Ah.

You see? All fixed again. Nothing to be afraid of. I wonder if all the rooms have been redressed."

Jacqueline wrinkled her nose. "Bof. I have to wonder if it isn't me doing this. Some hidden power of vampire blood. Some sign of my life being turned upside down the past two months."

She slumped on the bed and put her head in her hands. "What am I doing? I could lose Bellesfées, and I'm adopting wards? Negotiating marriage contracts and separations? Keeping girls under my roof without their families' approval?"

Her sister sat and wrapped her arm around her shoulder. "You're afraid, silly. You think you'll lose Bellesfées, and you think you've lost me now that I'm married and expecting a child."

Jacqueline swallowed the lump that rose in her throat. "Haven't I?"

"And," Angélique continued, "you've spent the past five years taking care of me, and you want to be sure you have someone else to take care of when I leave."

Jacqueline leaned to Angélique. Exhausted by the day's worries and the work ahead, she savored her sister's calm, the scent of her lavender soap, and the familiar touch on her shoulder.

"Don't leave," Jaqueline murmured. "I've only just found you again. And I feel like I need you now more than you ever needed me."

Angélique hugged her, and they rocked together.

"Don't worry," Angélique said. "I don't plan to leave before Christmas, and then you're coming with me."

Jacqueline chuckled. "Along with the entire Order of Duval?"

Angélique laughed too. "If they haven't found their way by then, yes. Besides," she added, "you have de Guise. If he's stayed with you through all of this, you know he'll never leave you."

The very mention of de Guise sparked a need in Jacqueline to see him, to be near him, to hold him, and more. The twins left the room, locking the door behind them, and went down for evening brandies.

Llewellyn was teaching Frontenac cribbage while Montpellier and Têtue watched. Frontenac had quickly caught on to the subtleties of the game; she was about to skunk her teacher. De Guise and Guichet sat off to the side discussing the legal ramifications of her options. Jacqueline was heartened to see her cheerful again.

De Guise and Llewellyn stood as they entered, and the way de Guise's eyes lit up stirred Jacqueline's heart, she had to wonder how she had lived so long without this joy. She embraced him, intimating her desire. He responded in kind, but whispered, "Later, chérie. I'll be all yours."

Content for the moment, Jacqueline accepted a brandy from her maid, Marthe's niece Gaudin. "And you, Gaudin," Jacqueline said. "Are you happy here?"

Gaudin blinked at her the way Marthe would blink at the twins when they did something foolish. "Do you doubt it, madame?" she replied. She waved her hands in a gesture imitative of her aunt's dismissive nature. "Really, madame."

Jacqueline and Angélique both chuckled, recognizing Gaudin's mannerisms. Jacqueline sipped her brandy, satisfied that all had settled down into routine, at least for the night.

Later, in their afterglow, Jacqueline asked de Guise, "Am I childish?"

De Guise caressed her arm, sending a warm thrill through her. "No, not at all. A little naïve. I think you are, in some ways, inexperienced."

She giggled. "I certainly was about—this." She touched him, and he sighed with a groan. "You taught me well," she murmured. "But that's not what you meant, is it?"

He turned to his side and gazed into her eyes as he brushed her hair from her brow. "It would be naïve to send these young women back to their homes when they object so strongly. You've seen the cruelty of Renée's husband and Adèle's father. You and I are both aware of evils beyond crazed despots, beyond necromancy and vampires. One needn't build a thermal airship or an army of clockwork soldiers to bring ruin upon innocent young lives. You fight the evil that presents itself, just as I do. It's why we belong together."

She stroked his cheek, tracing his jaw, then his throat. "Alain, when I'm with you, I want the rest of the world to go away."

He caught her hand and kissed her palm. "And when you're not with me, you face the world and try to fix it. There's nothing wrong with that."

"But is it enough?"

He kissed her neck. "It's never enough, but it must be done."

Her leg crossed over his. The embers of their afterglow stirred and brought up a new flame.

4.

Jacqueline rose early to inflate the envelope of her airship and ignite the boiler to power up the engines. As a young polytech, she had always dreamed of building her own aerostat and had even studied Pauly's work at the Polytechnique ten years earlier. His efforts, however, lacked any precision or amenity, and the image of Pauly's fish-shaped balloon put her off her plans. She'd turned her energies to mechanics and engine systems, which proved more lucrative than flights of fanciful aerostats. The defeat of the evil Count Draganov had garnered her possession of his colossal airship designed in the conceit of a seafaring galleon and rendered virtually invisible at night by a reflective coating. Jacqueline had modified the ship to her own tastes, so she now commanded the most elegant transport in all of Europe: *Esprit*.

Aboard *Esprit*, Monsieur Claque managed the crown lines for the envelope as it filled, but he was fully capable of navigating the aerostat himself.

"Ohé, ma capitaine!" de Guise called as he strode up the gangplank. "Luc is unmooring us. And Marthe insisted on sending a basket of food along, of course."

He set down said basket and embraced Jacqueline, then kissed her as if he hadn't spent the night kissing her just so. Warm and deep and soft. The fragrance of his shaving soap blended with the scent of his worsted coat and his own spicy taste awakened a rush of renewed desire through her whole body. She hummed in delicious contentment and broke off reluctantly.

"Let me lay in the course, mon amour," she murmured.

"No."

He kissed her again. What else could she do? She returned his ardor until they were interrupted by Angélique and Llewellyn.

"Fine example you set for these girls," Angélique scolded with a twinkle in her eye.

But the girls were preoccupied, giggling and batting one another's light bustles Angélique had insisted they wear, all but Têtue, who had eschewed any feminine trappings in favor of Jacqueline's formal work costume.

With a final caress of de Guise's face, Jacqueline headed to the captain's wheel and the gauges that would set the keel. She sang out, "Weigh anchor!"

Frontenac replied, "Weigh anchor, aye!" and initiated the capstan controlling them. "Anchors a-weigh."

The first time the young women had boarded *Esprit* a week earlier, they had huddled near the companionway door as Jacqueline flitted from capstan to capstan, clambered up rigging, and swung between upper decks clinging to a cable. At first they watched in disbelief, but soon Têtue and Frontenac were keen to follow Jacqueline's movements and the workings of the ship. Frontenac caught on quickly to the navigation systems. Têtue was more interested in the machinery itself, so Jacqueline had Monsieur Claque teach her some basic maintenance as they sailed on their first star cruise. Jacqueline had quite a crew working the ship as *Esprit* lifted off.

Montpellier, understandably, had no memory of the ship where she had been dragged and tortured near to death while trapped in the vampire's hypnotic spell. She gazed about her with the curious dancing motion of her head.

Guichet went up to the fo'c'sle rail at the bow, gazing at the vista before her, the entire Loire valley to the east. Jacqueline joined her there. They could make out domes, towers, and spires of Orléans in the distance, as well as the stacks of factories and mills spewing clouds of smoke and soot that half obscured their view.

Jacqueline slipped her arm around Guichet. "Does this still frighten you?"

"A little. How can this entire vessel be lighter than the air?" Guichet said. "What if we fall?"

Jacqueline grinned. "Do I look like I'd let you fall?" She leaned back, hooking both elbows over the railing. First gazing up beyond the rigging, she then looked back along the beam of the magnificent *Esprit*. "What, and risk my ship?"

Laughing, she took Guichet's arm and led her back down to the main deck, checking to make certain Frontenac had set the gauges correctly. She was pleased to see Frontenac had mastered the skill.

"Show Guichet how it's done, Frontenac," Jacqueline told her. "You're ready to take on a second mate."

Montpellier, meanwhile, fretted over how she would be received in the city, covered in bandages with just a narrow slit to see through. Angélique demonstrated the subtle drape of a shawl and pinned a veil around the brim of Montpellier's bonnet. Angélique then taught her how to use a fan to conceal her face. Jacqueline was again struck by the young woman's natural gracefulness as she manipulated the fan in a few limited gestures.

"And no tapping your lips or stroking your cheek," she called down to them from the aft deck. "No ward of mine will be a coquette."

"Spoilsport," Angélique returned.

Montpellier whispered something to Angélique.

"No, Justine, there's no secret language of fans. It's only a myth, or perhaps a marketing technique," Angélique told her. "If you're warm, you fan away." She demonstrated, setting Montpellier to giggles.

De Guise and Llewellyn joined Jacqueline on the aft deck as *Esprit* approached the industrial edges of the city.

"I don't recall Orléans being as bad as Manchester when we were here a few weeks ago," Llewellyn said as the grey haze enshrouded them.

Jacqueline wrinkled her nose. "Nor I. I can't believe I missed the opening of any new factories in so short a time. I hope it never gets as bad as Yorkshire. We can't afford heavy soot choking out our vineyards." She nodded toward the airship they had seen the day before, now moored above a factory engulfed in the pollution spewed from its stacks and descending from the airship.

Llewellyn also wrinkled his nose, but for another reason. "It's not just soot," he said with a frown. "There's an odor of burning flesh."

"Perhaps a house fire?" de Guise suggested. He scanned the skyline for signs of conflagration.

"Very sad," Llewellyn said.

"I'm all in favor of industry," Jacqueline said, "but not at the expense of lives." She coughed in the foul air. "I hope I resolve this locomotive problem quickly."

When they landed in the field just beyond the Gare d'Orléans, Angélique took the three younger women to the mercantile district of the city to find corsetières, milliners, shoemakers, and dressmakers. Only after placing the necessary orders for well-fitted stays, corsets, dresses, gowns, and accoutrements would they be allowed to visit the tailor for coats and suits, and the cordonnier for boots.

Têtue wore Jacqueline's business outfit of a chemise and cravate, trousers, knee boots, a waistcoat, and a redingote. She also sported one of de Guise's tall hats rather than the leather welding cap Jacqueline wore. Têtue's brown-tinted sun-glasses, like the Llewellyns' blue-tinted glasses designed by Jacqueline, hid the strangeness of her wolf-eyes. With her stocky build, muscular arms, and short, unadorned black curls, she fit right in beside Jacqueline, de Guise, and Llewellyn.

Jacqueline was accustomed to the oily smell of coal-fueled factories and the constant and deafening *thrum* and *whir* of engines. The forge and her workshop had always been her comfortable nest. But crossing the city toward the trainyards, Jacqueline's unease increased. Some darker, noisier shroud smothered the city, clinging to her skin and pounding at her thoughts with muffled blows. She couldn't shake the sensation despite the pleasant warmth of the day. Sun didn't pierce the heavy smoke. The unnatural fog unnerved her; she hoped it wasn't a portent of the day. Casting about, she located the other airship floating above a foundry, making note of its provenance.

No one questioned the "gentlemen" who entered the Paris-Orléans factory and asked to see Monsieur Goüin. They were ushered to the ground floor where he was supervising an incoming shipment. Ernest Goüin was a tall, energetic, youthful looking man with a receding hairline, full blond whiskers down to his chin and broad moustaches, and piercing eyes. Only four years older than Jacqueline, he had the appearance of a middle-aged businessman with all the freight that position carried. He immediately shook hands all around, disregarding gender etiquette. The deafening thunder of factory machinery forced them all to shout their greetings.

"De Guise, Duval, thank you for coming. This is — ?"

"His Grace, Monsieur Llewellyn," Jacqueline replied, "and Têtue, my associate."

Goüin acknowledged them, then said, "Come, I want to show you something." He led them to the far end of the warehouse where crates were being opened and parts separated onto conveyors. He held up a steam shut-off valve, then another, then a third. He handed one to Jacqueline and one to Têtue.

"They look normal, don't they?"

Jacqueline and Têtue both nodded. Then Goüin dropped them back into the crate and went to an open crate shoved back into a corner. He handed a valve to Têtue. She immediately threw it back with a growl as if it had burned her. Jacqueline and Goüin both raised a brow. Llewellyn picked it up and sniffed it. He too tossed it back.

"Tainted," Llewellyn declared.

Goüin bristled. "Tainted how? The weight is the weight, the quality is solid. Good iron. The best, in fact."

Têtue shrugged. "Stinks. Something in the puddling, maybe?"

Goüin pressed his lips. Then he sighed. "We used the materials from this crate, and others in the same shipment, for this project, and I cannot see how they produced the effects we've noted."

"Show us the locomotive engine," Jacqueline said. "We'll be able to tell more."

"But you agree this isn't a natural occurrence?" he said as he led them out to the construction bay.

"Of course it isn't natural for iron to bleed. The question is whether it is supernatural, or if there's more at play." She hesitated to use the word magic or necromancy to the engineer. "You're building the one-one-one, I assume?"

"Yes. Two-two-two in Manchester."

Jacqueline explained to Têtue, "The English count wheels; the French count axles."

In the next bay, the bright green engine with its candy-red pistons and polished brass-trimmed black smokestack and dome looked exactly like the locomotive that arrived from Paris every early afternoon and departed Orléans an hour later. Jacqueline had been on site when the first "Sharpie" engine was built several years earlier, so she was familiar with the structure. The designs Goüin had sent indicated only a few changes to the dimensions of the tiny firebox. She examined the exterior of the locomotive, her hand hovering above each line, each seam, each pipe, each bar to delineate her scrutiny. The machine was built to specifications as best she could recall. She gripped the rail and mounted the engineer's cabin to view the firebox.

Every surface dripped with blood.

Horrified, Jacqueline swallowed her fear. "Têtue, come see."

Têtue hoisted herself up to the cab. She uttered her quiet "huh" and explored the grisly gauges, valves, water pipes, and controls. She whispered, "More than one person, Duval. Dozens, maybe. Flesh, too."

Têtue drew a handkerchief from her vest pocket and wiped the pressure gauge clean. Jacqueline did the same for the two steam valves, keeping the stains separated. They both jumped down again, and Jacqueline pocketed the evidence.

"Is it blood?" Goüin asked.

"At least," Têtue said.

"I'll analyze it to verify, but it seems to be, yes," Jacqueline said. "What about the noises you mentioned?"

Goüin shook his head. "I haven't heard anything myself, but my men are so terrified, they won't work on the thing. What can I do? Systems still need connecting, and I have deadlines to meet."

He handed her his own handkerchief, and she wiped her hands.

"When did this phenomenon manifest itself?" she asked.

"When we put the final bolt on the firebox," he said, "about five days ago, when we got that last crate in from the Marteau factory. I wrenched it myself for a bit, and I had no trouble, but my workers swear—"

"Let me talk to them," offered de Guise, "have them describe it."

Têtue folded her arms. "Got a better idea. Let us finish the work."

Jacqueline beamed. "Excellent." She loved watching the fire of industry grow in Têtue's quick mind. "We can sort this out for you."

Goüin looked from one woman to the other with consternation. The pounding of engines around them could have been his pulse. "You'll want some assistance, surely."

"Oh, they have assistants," Llewellyn said with a grin.

Goüin rubbed his hand up his high forehead and blew out a breath. "I don't know. I'd rather—which is to say—"

"You'd rather work on it yourself? Or you'd rather the mystery had not presented itself?" Jacqueline drew out her watch to check the time. "Têtue and I can begin the work now, and Llewellyn and de Guise will round up our assistants, who can be here this afternoon." Jacqueline snapped the watch closed and met Goüin's dubious gaze. "Or we can leave you to your deadlines."

De Guise said, "After we collect the others, I think I'd like to nose around the quarter and see if any other factories have been disrupted."

"That's a good idea, de Guise," Jacqueline said. "I'm especially curious about the new ironworks. And look into this Marteau manufacturer as well."

"Ah," Goüin said, "they are one and the same."

Llewellyn growled. "I will wager that's also the source of the pestilential exhalations."

Jacqueline exchanged worried glances with de Guise. He nodded, and the two men left.

Within the hour, Jacqueline was brought the remaining necessary specifications, parts, and tools. Têtue hoisted these to the cabin.

"I'm going to take a look inside first," Jacqueline called down to her as she tugged her welding cap on and placed her gogglers, affixing the secondary loupes for further magnification. She opened the tiny firehole door and peered down the coal chute.

"Need a lamp?" Têtue handed up a lit Mueseler.

Jacqueline passed it into the chute and set it on the base sheet of the firebox. She pressed closer to peer down the chute, but the door was too narrow. Reaching her arm down, she groaned.

"It's everywhere," she said. "Coating the whole bin. Let me see…"

She patted herself down but couldn't find a spare cloth in her pockets. Dropping her coat off the cabin, she checked her waistcoat pocket.

"Got an extra handkerchief?"

"Sorry."

"Fetch a rag for me?"

Têtue trotted off.

Jacqueline again tried peering into the chute, and to her surprise she found she could fit her head snugly inside. The door suddenly gave way to her, and she went head and shoulders through the firehole door to get a better view of the front flue sheet. Grimacing, she set her hands down onto the bloody bottom sheet.

A low moan rose up. It sounded like Têtue.

Jacqueline froze. "Was that you? What's wrong?"

No answer.

"Têtue?"

When Jacqueline tried to back out, she found her hands stuck fast, glued in blood. Her heart pounded and beads of sweat broke out on her brow as she called again. The wolf in Têtue would hear her call, would sense her growing fear.

The moan repeated, louder this time. It *was* Têtue!

Then a second voice joined in, then a third, then—

More. Many more. Quiet moans of uncountable numbers of children in agony, muted as if across a vast distance.

"Who are you?" Jacqueline murmured. Then she called, "Where are you?"

Their answering cries broke her heart. They grew louder and louder. Children groaning in pain, wailing in distress, weeping in deepest grief. Jacqueline tried to shake the sound of their cries from her head as the echoes reverberated through her.

"How can I help you?" she shouted.

As if seized by a thousand hands, she lurched into the firebox, and the firehole door slammed shut.

5.

Renée Guichet passed her rough hand over the bolt of peach-colored silk, thrilling to its soft texture, before pulling back guiltily. She looked around the shop in wonder at shelf after shelf of luxurious fabrics, but came back to the peach, eyeing it wistfully.

"Beautiful," Madame Llewellyn commented. "That would bring out the highlights in your hair."

Guichet flinched, searching the duchess's face for deception. "You mean I can have a gown of this?"

"Of course. I said three gowns and two daydresses each." The duchess smiled. "You've never worn silk?"

Guichet shook her head. "Before I came to Bellesfées, I never wore anything but muslin or wool. Monsieur Guichet squeezed blood from every sou he earned. Or that I earned, for that matter."

"What work did you do?" Madame Llewellyn asked as she selected another bolt of fabric.

"Piecework, patchwork, lace, crochet. Whatever I could find, when I had time. There was the house, the chickens and ducks, the garden, the goats and sheep… Oh!"

She gasped, reaching but not daring to caress the lilac gown draping the dressmaker's model. The neckline fell off the shoulder, the bodice was modestly draped, the waistline made a lovely V, and the bell of the skirt featured so many folds it dizzied her to think how much fabric had gone into it. "What I could do with this!"

"You wouldn't have to do anything, Renée," the duchess said softly, "but wear it proudly and with honor as a daughter of Bellesfées." The duchess signaled to the dressmaker to add the lilac to the order.

Everything inside Guichet wanted to laugh. At the same time, tears sprang to her eyes. Frontenac hugged her and whispered, "I know."

"Now you, Adèle." Madame Llewellyn summoned Frontenac to her. "Hair like cornsilk, big, blue eyes… I think dark blues and deep reds, don't you?" She pointed to an array of bolts and let Frontenac decide for herself. "Justine, let's have a look at you."

Montpellier ducked her head and fanned herself.

"Over here, Justine," Madame Llewellyn insisted. She took her by the hand and led her to a series of patterned fabrics, mostly florals on pale yellow. "These will give you such an exotic appearance. With your black hair, mysterious eyes—"

"Ugly eyes, you mean." Montpellier sulked. "Blank and scary and…" She groaned.

"Be glad that monster didn't blind you," Frontenac reassured her. "You can always wear tinted glasses like Têtue and Madame Llewellyn if you're embarrassed."

Guichet wandered from the argument. She had harbored one thought for the past day, ever since defending Frontenac from her father: *The Order of Duval*. Why hide their knives beneath skirts when they could boldly proclaim themselves with arm sheaths? She whispered to the shopkeeper's assistant, who quickly fetched her a selection of satin ribbons in blues, golds, and pinks. Selecting the three closest in hue to the tri-color of Bellesfées, she set them aside, not wishing to add them to the bill without permission. She also perused a tray of buttons and selected three large gold ones. Guichet returned to the others to hear Montpellier's quiet pleas to be excused from being measured. The young girl was backed into a corner with the dressmaker demanding she be amenable.

"I'll do it," Guichet told the dressmaker, tugging the tape measure from her. "My sister is very shy."

She hooked arms with Montpellier and led her to the fitting room, where the younger one collapsed in a chair with a deep sigh of relief. Guichet took care to undress her without disturbing her bandages and was gentle in applying the tape measure.

"You're an angel," Montpellier told her. "Me, I grubbed on a farm. I don't see the sense of owning a gown. It's not like I'll be presented at court."

Guichet grinned. "I grubbed too. You never know. Monsieur de Guise is a good friend of the King, and His Grace is a favorite of the Queen of England. You needn't wear it décolletée if you don't want to."

Montpellier shook her head. "Never. But I may need to wear a mask."

"Why, because of scars? None of us is unscarred or unchanged, Justine. None of us. But aren't we in a better place now? I know I am. Away from my husband. Awful, awful man. Stand, let me measure your hips and waist."

"Is marriage really so bad?" Montpellier asked.

Guichet shivered with disgust. "Mine is bad." She shook her head. "I was fourteen, he was almost sixty. I was so terrified of him, and he wasn't gentle. Isn't gentle. When I couldn't produce an heir in the expected amount of time, I was made to earn my keep in ways—you don't want to know about. And afterwards, his snores and noxious flatulence in bed with me."

"I'm almost fifteen," Montpellier said. "My father said it was past time to marry, but we have no money. No one wanted me. He found a boy, but—"

Guichet snorted. "No man who marries you for money is worth having anyway." She rolled the tape measure around her finger. "All finished. Let's get you dressed again. Then I'll teach you how to take my measurements."

They emerged from the fitting room as Frontenac emerged from hers. They grinned at one another, initiated into a new and higher level of society than they had ever expected. Guichet took Madame Llewellyn aside and explained the ribbons and buttons, asking more than telling, and the duchess was delighted to be in on her secret. As Madame Llewellyn settled the orders with the dressmaker, and Frontenac and Montpellier gathered all their previous purchases, Guichet caught sight of Messieurs de Guise and Llewellyn coming toward the shop.

"Why are they back so soon?" she asked, her worries returning. "Has something gone wrong?"

Fear for Duval uppermost in mind, Guichet hastened from the shop to meet them. They startled her when they both bowed. *Bow?* That's what men did for ladies when they met in public. No one had ever bowed to Guichet before. Blushing, she remembered she was then expected to curtsy. It felt wonderful to behave like a lady of society, the way she had been taught by her parents, a way she had not practiced since marrying.

"I'm afraid we must hurry you along," Monsieur Llewellyn told her and the others as they joined them. "Madame Duval needs your assistance."

At that announcement, the women all decided they could come to the city another time to visit the tailor and cordonnier. If Duval needed them, they were hers to command. Guichet took Montpellier's hand, and de Guise escorted Frontenac.

They crossed the Place Jeanne d'Arc while Frontenac filled them in on the story of "La Pucelle d'Orléans," the maiden no older than sixteen when she began her military campaign. Guichet listened with rapt attention to the story of a girl nearly her own age who faced down armies. Shame gnawed at Guichet; she couldn't even face down her husband. When Frontenac recounted the trial and grisly sentence, Guichet shuddered.

"They burned her for dressing like a man?" she said in disgust. "Like Duval does?"

"They burned her as a witch for claiming to hear voices," Frontenac corrected her. "But transvestism was one of the charges against her. Frankly, I think they burned her for knowing more than the men did, and religion was just a good excuse, as is so often the case with men and war."

Madame Llewellyn snickered.

Doubt still gripped Guichet. "Witchcraft is hearing voices, then?" She shivered. "Or is it more?"

"In those days, my dear, any intelligent woman who spoke her mind and used her gifts was called a witch." Madame Llewellyn's contempt filled her voice. "We would all of us still be burned for witches if ignorance ran the world. There's no greater evil than ignorance, if you ask me."

"So, she didn't have any magical powers?" Guichet pressed.

"If she did or didn't, who cares?" Montpellier squeezed her arm. "Seems to me the only thing she did wrong was win battles against men and get caught by the English."

Guichet clamped her mouth shut rather than push her argument. She wanted to remind Montpellier that they had all been caught by Mircalla. They had all heard a voice telling them to fight, to kill. Guichet wondered if the others also shared her so-called gift.

As they strode the streets toward the trainyards, Guichet tingled every time a passing gentleman bowed or an officer tipped his cap at them. Her husband had never so much as stood when she entered a room, as Monsieur de Guise and the duke did, nor bowed, nor took her arm to escort her. She never realized how hungry she had been for such consideration.

The aromas that wafted from pastry shops, bakeries, crèmeries, and charcuteries filled her head and aroused another hunger. The duchess must have sensed it too because she steered Monsieur Llewellyn into a bakery and picked up meat tartes for all of them, along with a few baguettes. She then stopped to pick up cheese and pastries for later.

"I told you we should have brought the basket," Monsieur Llewellyn teased his wife. "You're eating for two now."

"Or maybe three or four," she retorted. She bit deep into a flaky religieuse, getting crème Chantilly on her nose.

Guichet breathed in the air of the city and grinned. Yes, there was the stink of animals and garbage and the trenches, nothing worse than there had been at home other than the choking grime of the industrial spewage, but there were also the noises of carriages, the smells of intriguing foods, the chatter on the streets, and the scents of many people surrounding her, especially the pleasant male presence of Messieurs de Guise and Llewellyn and the lavender, citron, or rose-water fragrance of her friends, her sisters in misery.

But not misery, not anymore. Duval had reassured her; she believed Duval.

How curious that a simple stroll along a city street could feel as grand as a dance at a ball. Seventeen and free and valued. Guichet had never known such happiness. It frightened her, the way standing on the deck of *Esprit* that first time had frightened her—thrilling and terrible and wonderful and entirely out of her control.

"It occurs to me," Madame Llewellyn said, halting suddenly. "I have the girls' measurements now, so I could go to the tailor and the cordonnier myself to have suits and boots made. If you ladies wouldn't mind my choices?"

"Suits and boots." Montpellier laughed. "Sounds so funny."

"Well, Jacqueline did say Frontenac was to have a suit complete," Madame Llewellyn said, "and I'm guessing you others will want the same." She pursed her lips. "I wish I had Têtue's measurements, too, so she won't have to borrow Jacky's clothes." Then she brightened. "Oh, but Laval will have Jacky's, so they'll be the same."

Guichet was torn. Duval had summoned them, but she wanted to explore the tailor's shop to see if it held the same magic as the dressmaker's. Her heart leapt when Frontenac said, "I know, Guichet can help you, madame. She's very good with fabrics."

The duchess beamed. "Marvelous. Come, Renée. Let's see what we can find."

The two of them backtracked to the mercantile district. The number of shops dizzied Guichet.

Madame Llewellyn passed several tailors before entering the establishment of Monsieur Laval. Two young men assisted a gentleman at the mirror. A short, older man in shirtsleeves and waistcoat came out from the back to greet them with a tape draped around his neck and his silvery hair disheveled. His eyes widened in delight.

"Mademoiselle Laforge, it has been so long since I've seen you. How is your father?"

"He's well, dear Monsieur Laval," the duchess answered, kissing his cheeks. "But I am no longer a 'mademoiselle.' I'm recently married."

"Felicitations, madame. I adore your tinted glasses. Très bohé. What brings you to me today?"

"A rather sizable order, monsieur, for four suits complete."

"Four? Is Madame Duval contemplating a trip, to need so many?"

The duchess took a copy of the dressmaker's measurements from her reticule. As he looked over the numbers, a sly smile came to his face.

"But these are not for Madame Duval."

"Madame Duval is hoping to take on four apprentices, who will need appropriate attire to join her in her particular work," the duchess told him.

"Of course, of course." He turned his gaze to Guichet. "Is this lovely demoiselle one of them?"

Guichet gulped and nodded.

"Show Madame Guichet your fabrics, dear Monsieur Laval. She has quite the eye." Madame Llewellyn smiled at her and nodded encouragement. "Madame Duval trusts no other tailor, Renée. I'm going now to the cordonnier, and I'll return soon to collect you. Enjoy yourself."

Again she embraced the old tailor. "Take good care of Madame Guichet, monsieur."

Guichet watched in disbelief as the duchess swept out the door, leaving her in the keeping of the little stranger. Hesitant, she looked into his crinkly eyes. He smiled and indicated the far wall stacked with bolts of fabrics.

If Duval trusted him to dress her, what could Guichet have to fear?

Monsieur Laval showed her Duval's preferred fabrics and explained the purpose of each. She listened, but at the same time her eyes wandered to the lighter colors, thinking of blonde Frontenac, and the browns for herself to match her auburn hair. She hesitated, but in the end she dared to ask. The tailor's beaming smile showed he was impressed with her line of thought. Before long, she found herself thoroughly engaged with talk of tweeds, twills, stripes, checks; worsted versus cloth; morning dress versus evening dress (which the Order of Duval would likely eschew); silks and satins; matching or contrasting; the appropriate application of a touch of velvet.

"Keep in mind," Monsieur Laval said, "Madame Duval's choices reflect not only her craft but also her business affairs. Perhaps you would need two suits each?"

Guichet startled. "Oh, I couldn't. That is, it's not my place to make that decision."

He acknowledged the sense of her response. "Perhaps if you could tell me what roles you will fill?"

She straightened and tried to look confident. "Whatever she asks of us."

He hummed, amused. "Can you be more specific?"

Guichet pondered. "One of us will be in the workshop learning designs. She's the blonde. Another is very strong and will probably work in the forge. So will Justine, I think, once she recovers."

"Recovers?" He blinked in curiosity.

Guichet glanced away. "An accident. She was badly wounded, but she's doing well."

"And you?"

Guichet sighed. "And I. I would do anything for her. I owe her so much."

Monsieur Laval sat back and gave her a long, assessing look. "I think you would do very well managing her estate. Keep her business affairs in order. Once you learn business skills, you can manage a fabric shop of your own. It's clear you know much already." He slapped his thighs and stood. "I think I have an idea of the order, madame. Let's drink to our agreement."

He reached behind the cutting counter and brought out sherry and two glasses. Guichet suppressed her laughter. How could she have gone from drudge to businesswoman in so short a time? She accepted the glass, sipping with quiet joy. She had negotiated her first business transaction—more or less—and was now literally the toast of the town, or at least of the shop. She had never felt so powerful.

Take that, Monsieur Guichet!

A yelp from one of the assistants in the front room caught them off guard. When they came out front, they found the two young men holding up a set of shelves that had toppled forward. Bolts of fabric were strewn in piles on the floor. Their customer in his chalked fitting suit lay stunned with four bolts of wool on top of him.

Guichet's heart punished her mercilessly. *Not again!*

All the joy she had felt vanished in a wave of guilt. She rushed forward to lift the bolts off the gentleman while the assistants wrangled the shelving back against the wall.

"I'm fine," the gentleman said, catching his breath. "Surprised, that's all."

"Please, rest a moment," Guichet insisted. She knelt and held his head, examining him for any bruises or lumps.

He caught her hand in a tight grip and gazed up at her. "Aren't you a sweet thing? Mon Dieu, have I died and gone to the angels?"

She reddened with an uncomfortable fire. "I assure you, you have not."

"Come, madame," Monsieur Laval said, offering his hand. "We'll see he's cared for. Monsieur Blanchet, I am so sorry. Let me help you."

But Monsieur Blanchet refused to relinquish Guichet. "No, no, I feel faint, Laval. If I might stay right here with this delicious young creature—" He held her hand to his breast.

A shudder of revulsion ran through her. She yanked her hand away and got to her feet, stammering. "Thank you again, Monsieur Laval. I look forward to receiving my order." She ran out of the shop before the tailor could reply.

Guichet peered up the street. She knew they hadn't passed a cordonnier, so she continued on, hoping to espy Madame Llewellyn through a shop window or along the pavement. When she reached the crossroad, she halted in dismay. Where now?

Only then did she realize she was crying. People stared at her in disapproval as they passed. She drew a handkerchief from her reticule and dabbed her face, breathing deeply to restore some sense of herself. She bowed her head to her hand, but she smelled something foreign— Blanchet's soap, perhaps, or maybe just his sweat on her glove or—

"Mon Dieu, Renée, what happened?" cried the duchess, suddenly next to her.

Guichet threw herself into her arms, trembling. She couldn't breathe. Madame Llewellyn patted her head gently and held her to her shoulder. Guichet didn't know what to say, how to tell her what she'd done, how to describe what she'd felt, the wave of nausea filling her head.

Madame Llewellyn steered her down the cross street to a café where they took an outside table, she then gripped Guichet's hands tightly. The duchess ordered two coffees and croissants, holding Guichet all the while.

Shame, embarrassment, disgust, despair, fear—Guichet was torn in so many directions she didn't know where to begin.

"I'm sorry I left you alone," Madame Llewellyn was saying. "I'm so sorry."

But it was Guichet who needed to apologize, beg forgiveness for— something, she wasn't sure what. She just knew it had to be her fault. It was always her fault. *Not enough dowry, her fault. I'm so sorry, monsieur. No children, her fault. So sorry, monsieur. Leaking roof, a lamb dies in birth, the artichoke crop fails, her fault. So, so sorry, monsieur. Pots flying off the kitchen shelves —*

"Renée." Madame Llewellyn lifted Guichet's chin until she looked up. The duchess removed her tinted glasses to meet her gaze. "Did someone hurt you?"

Hurt her? Hurt *her*? The duchess's golden wolf-eyes reminded her this was a woman who would understand what it meant to be different.

"No, madame, no one hurt me. But—" Tears threatened again. Guichet whispered, "I think I hurt someone just now. And not just today. I think I may truly be a witch."

The duchess pressed her lips tightly. That usually meant she was annoyed but not by the person she was listening to.

"What did we say about witches? You're a woman of intelligence who can speak your mind. There's no shame in that."

Shame. That was the word. Years of shame.

The duchess's eyes didn't condemn her. She waited patiently for Guichet to voice her fears. When the patron brought their coffee and croissants, Madame Llewellyn released Guichet's hands and sipped from her cup. She then sat back at ease and sighed.

"I know how difficult it is to discover you have something no one else can understand," she said. She replaced her tinted glasses. "When I discovered what happened to me, I confided in my sister."

Guichet nodded. "Duval."

"I knew she'd accept my change because she too had been different. No, not in that way, or in the way you describe." The duchess smiled wistfully. "Oh, Renée, imagine having a mind like Jacky's in a world dominated by men. Engineering, of all subjects. There are still those who think her devices are somehow infernal and demonic. Whereas I," she said, spreading her hands, "truly was infernally enchanted. I managed to overcome my base re-creation. I'm sure you can overcome your fear."

The duchess casually dipped the tip of her croissant into her coffee and took a bite. "So tell me what enchantment you suffer from."

The duchess's soothing manner stilled Guichet's trembling. It was true, she had believed herself cursed with a dreadful power, but the duchess had found power beyond the curse. Perhaps Guichet would as well.

"I hate my husband," Guichet confided. She gripped her cup with both hands and sipped. "I didn't realize how much I hated him until one day, a few months ago. I was exhausted from the day. I suppose—" She squeezed her eyes closed. "I guess that was the first time Mircalla had visited me. I felt weak, confused. Monsieur Guichet called me a terrible word. I don't know how, but I sent an iron skillet his way. But I didn't throw it!" she quickly added. "It just—flew." She wagged her head, staring into the coffee. "He punished me, of course." She sipped again. "Another time, he criticized my cooking. That night, an entire shelf of dishes came down."

She glanced up and was surprised to see the duchess's eyes dancing in amusement.

"I didn't think anything of it except they were two very odd incidents," Guichet said, her anxiety returning. "But then they kept happening. He blamed me. I didn't know why or how they happened, but he blamed me. But today, in Monsieur Laval's shop..."

She was quick to reassure the duchess. "Oh, no, Monsieur Laval is wonderful. He made me feel like a grown woman for the first time in my life. We talked about fabrics and cuts and styles. I saw myself becoming a successful businesswoman, and it was thrilling. I wanted to gloat over Monsieur Guichet. Instead, I made a cabinet fall on the head of a stranger. I don't want to hurt anyone, madame. I didn't even know him, and I could have killed him."

She flexed the hand Monsieur Blanchet had clung to, and she shuddered.

Madame Llewellyn tapped the table. "Go on," she urged quietly. "Because that's not the part that really bothers you."

Guichet shook her head. "No, it isn't."

She squeezed her eyes shut. She couldn't even explain to herself the revulsion at the touch of the stranger's hand. The disgust at his hungry, predatory gaze. He had done nothing wrong. *He* hadn't ripped her clothing from her and tossed it into the garbage. *He* hadn't called her hideous or unnatural or that word. *He* hadn't forced himself on her night after night, or struck her with riding crops and whips, or choked her unconscious while —

"Renée, stop."

Guichet gasped. She opened her eyes. Her coffee bubbled up in the cup.

Yet, Madame Llewellyn smiled at her, even chuckled, thoroughly pleased.

6.

ADÈLE FRONTENAC GAZED LONGINGLY BEYOND THE TOWERS OF THE magnificent Basilique Cathédrale Sainte-Croix d'Orléans to the mansard roofs at the edge of the city, the halls of the Université d'Orléans. In all her years of schooling, no one had ever spoken of such a place as a university, where even more could be learned beyond the history of France, beyond geometry, beyond Latin, beyond Catholicism and the endless litanies of the saints—beyond the walls of a convent. She'd always assumed boys went to seminaries and learned the same way, the same subjects, the same fate of a life of joyless obligation.

Duval had attended the École Polytechnique de Paris. And at thirteen.

At thirteen, Frontenac was defying her father's plan for a marriage for the first time, gaining her another two years at the convent, after which she defied him a second time. Her father thought her rebellious and unmanageable. He had no idea his daughter only fought with him so she could remain in school. No idea she had a brain that hungered for more, always more. Who wrote the books from which she had drawn all her knowledge? Surely there were other books, other writers? Was there no more to learn, nothing more to explore, no new frontiers to forge?

"It's not good to fill your head with useless knowledge," Sister Donald scolded.

Then she made Frontenac memorize the entire Gospel of St. Jean. What good was that to her, imprisoned in the walls of her father's house? It was St. Luc's words that resonated with her: "... *you must hate your father and mother.*" She had no mother, but she was content to hate her father enough for both.

The only time there was peace between them was hunting season. The mutual understanding—they had to thin the herd; they had to eat—

brought with it an acknowledgement of each other's more basic need: to regain a sense of power over a defiant world burgeoning around them. In essence, to kill something.

That he had gaged her as one might a pocket watch only proved how desperate was her need to be free of him, to find someone who would value her.

"Madame Frontenac, you seem preoccupied," Monsieur de Guise broke into her thoughts.

Frontenac liked Monsieur de Guise, mostly because of his manner with the women around him. Respectful, but not overly solicitous. Deferential, but not patronizing. He honestly appreciated the women of the Order, too, if not as equals, at least as people who might one day be his equals. He had his secrets, which he guarded well, and Frontenac never pried. But his tender, passionate devotion to Duval gave Frontenac hope one day she might also meet such a man.

Not that she listened to his thoughts on purpose. She couldn't help hearing anyone's thoughts anymore. And Monsieur de Guise's love was loud.

"I was wishing I'd had the opportunity to attend university," she told him.

"It's not too late for you to apply."

And he meant it. Frontenac appreciated his encouragement, but she demurred. "Duval started when she was much younger. I think I may be too old now."

Monsieur de Guise put his hand on hers to reassure her. "Madame Duval did most things earlier than usual. She is brilliant, after all."

"Many students wait to apply until they're much older, and many others apply and have to wait to be accepted," the duke commented. He pointed to a gathering at a bar-tabac across the street. "Those young men aren't that much older than you, and they're students."

"Trust me," Monsieur de Guise said. "If you wish to attend the university or the Institute, Madame Duval will make certain you'll be accepted."

"But please don't go before you teach me to read and write," Justine protested. "Maybe it's not too late for me too."

Justine's sudden wave of fear in Frontenac's head drowned out the noise of the conversations on the streets of Orléans. Frontenac relinquished Monsieur de Guise's arm and took Justine's hand from the duke.

"Don't worry. I won't leave you."

Her gesture pleased the men, but more importantly, it calmed Montpellier's fear.

Justine Montpellier awakened in Frontenac the kind of compassion the sisters had described in the Christ, a compassion she herself had never understood. Give money to that poor man? She sensed he was going to gamble or drink it away. Make clothing for that widow with seven children? Everyone knew the woman sold the dresses they made at the convent and kept the money for herself and her lover. The sick they visited had brought their diseases on themselves, in drinking and debauchery. The prisoners… Frontenac shuddered, recalling the miasma of murderous hungers and rage. Were these truly the "sick and afflicted" for which they prayed the Mass? She gave a silent prayer of thanks her odd talent had not yet been refined by Mircalla's blood while she was in the convent because she was certain she would have gone mad.

Justine, though, needed her. Frontenac gave her hand a little squeeze and intertwined their fingers. Unlike Frontenac, Justine adored her father and had a wonderful mother who doted on her. She had enjoyed working their little wheat farm in a village near Châteaudun. The arrangement of marriage to a cretin named Jacques Cezet had devastated her not only for the choice in partners, but also because she would leave behind the home she had loved to be with someone she didn't love and who likely wouldn't love her.

That was one fear that plagued Justine: to never be loved again. The vampire Mircalla had caught her on the road, just as she had caught Frontenac — trying to run away from home in the middle of the night. That was how the two fugitives found themselves at Bellesfées, where one of Mircalla's minions left Justine disfigured and hanging on to life.

A second fear haunted Justine as well, one Frontenac couldn't see, but which filled the girl with dread. Frontenac felt every drop of despair and terror in the younger one's soul.

This was the kind of person the Christ wanted Frontenac to redeem: the kind who couldn't find redemption for themselves.

They left the city gates and arrived at the train yards. Monsieur de Guise led them beyond the station to a square building with the "P-O" mark of the Paris-Orléans Railroad company. The noise of the huge machinery was overwhelming, as was the stink of coal smoke, soot, and oils. They passed through several workshops and warehouses until they came to the factory floor. The ambient roar of machinery nearly deafened Frontenac and the pulse of pistons drilled through her bones. Suddenly, Frontenac drew up short, almost tripping the men. A wall of dread blocked her.

She instinctively wrapped her arm around Justine's waist. "Shh."

The men were confused. Frontenac tried to listen past their questions. Beyond the thunderous motors and pistons, a low hum of tension obscured the shouts that circled her thoughts.

"Something's wrong," Frontenac said.

"Jacqueline must have fixed the locomotive," Monsieur de Guise observed. "It's not here."

"Neither is Jacky," the duke said.

Monsieur de Guise strode toward the group at the end of the floor at the open bay. Têtue detached herself from the group to meet him, followed by a tall man. Têtue held Duval's work coat, glowering fiercely.

Fear, anger, confusion, worry—all the flavors Frontenac detested. She kept hearing "gone, gone, gone, gone," everyone's head calling out the word. Frontenac gripped Justine so tightly the girl pulled away.

"Something's very wrong here," Frontenac said.

"Ah, you heard that too?" The duke ushered them to join Monsieur de Guise and Têtue. "Let's find out what we can do to amend it."

As Monsieur de Guise introduced the two young women to the stranger, Monsieur Goüin, his voice conveyed none of the anxiety that coursed through his thoughts. "The engine has somehow vanished, along with Madame Duval," Monsieur de Guise said.

"Say, rather, Duval has vanished with my locomotive," said Monsieur Goüin, clearly someone in charge. "I know the woman is a devil of an engineer, but it takes a lot longer than two minutes to build up enough steam to move the thing. And it wasn't even completed yet. Parbleu, I want to know what is going on. How the devil did she manage to steal my engine?"

Monsieur de Guise bristled. "She would not steal your engine, Goüin."

"Well, they've both disappeared together," the other argued. "Damned suspicious to me."

The duke sniffed the air, then coughed. "And yet—"

Têtue nodded. "Exactly. That's what I've been telling them. She's still here."

The tall man rubbed the back of his head. "You said that before, Monsieur Têtue, but it makes no sense. How do you deduce it? Do those glasses of yours give you special sight?"

As the duke began some pretextual explanation, Duval interrupted. "Someone tell me where I am. I know you can hear me."

Frontenac jumped. A glance around the circle let her know no one else had heard Duval's voice, and the woman was nowhere in sight. Frontenac shook her head. What could she say? That she heard voices? Here in Orléans?

Têtue watched her curiously, twisting her mouth to the side. Frontenac grabbed Têtue's arm and led her to the track. Frontenac pointed.

"She's here," she said in Têtue's ear. "She's right here."

"I know that," Têtue rasped back, glaring at her, "but how do you know that?"

Frontenac bit her lip. "I don't know how, but I hear her. Don't tell anyone else. I don't want them burning me at the stake."

Têtue smirked. "What's she saying?"

The duke joined them, keeping to a low voice as well. "What is who saying?"

The others were right behind him. Frontenac fretted. She knew she could trust the women of the Order and the men of Bellesfées, but the stranger in their midst disturbed her. His thoughts were so busy, a hundred questions, a dozen numbers, names flying around. He was grounded in mechanics; he wouldn't understand.

"I only want to help you," Duval said.

Frontenac focused on just Duval's voice.

Duval shouted, "I won't hurt you. Won't you please, please, help me?"

To whom was she shouting? Was she trapped somewhere, begging for release?

"Have you searched the crates, monsieur?" Frontenac asked Monsieur Goüin.

His eyes fixed on her sternly. "Do you think Madame Duval disassembled the engine and put all the parts away in the two minutes it took Monsieur Têtue to remove his cravate?"

Despite his words, the man felt concern for Duval. The perplexing problem of a disappearing locomotive overwhelmed all his other thoughts, but Frontenac did hear Duval's name flying around in his mind.

"I meant that someone may have closed her up into one," Frontenac said, "or —" Duval's voice had sounded like an echo. "Perhaps locked her into a piece of the machinery inside a crates."

"Mon Dieu." Goüin spun about and hastened away, calling out names of other workers and barking orders to have all the crates searched.

Once he left, Têtue put her hand on Frontenac's shoulder with a nod. "Go on. You can tell them."

The men waited on her words. Monsieur de Guise's calm face seemed so out of place when she could hear his dismay so strongly.

Frontenac released a quavering breath. "Duval is still here," she said. "I mean, right here." She pointed to the tracks. "She's far away, shut up somewhere, locked in, and she's pleading with someone to help her."

 Monsieur de Guise's brow furrowed. "Far away, but right here?"

The duke shook his head fiercely, as if ridding himself of an annoying fly. "It doesn't make any sense, but she's right."

"Ouf! I thought I was going crazy." Têtue sounded relieved to have her suspicions confirmed, but no less upset they were true.

"Tell us what happened, Têtue," Monsieur de Guise suggested. "Maybe we can put our minds together and sort this out."

As Têtue began, Frontenac drew a deep breath of amazement. No one had questioned her. No one had accused her of delusions. No one doubted her. Why weren't they shocked? Why weren't they surprised she could hear what they couldn't? She didn't want to pry; they had treated her with respect and she didn't want to take advantage of her ability to learn what they weren't saying.

But of course, these were men and women who had faced down a vampire and assassins. Monsieur de Guise and the Duke of Singlebury had been spies; surely they had seen more worldly wonders than a country girl with an inner knowledge of secret things.

Someone, though, was still emitting confusion, nervousness, terror. Frontenac looked around and saw Justine standing apart from them, quaking.

"Tell me what it is you need," Duval pleaded. "I'll do whatever I can for you. Just please, tell me where I am. Let me come to you."

Frontenac winced at the anguish in Duval's voice, matched by Justine's sudden blur of panicked thoughts. She reached for Justine's hand. "Justine, what is it?"

Through the opening in the bandages that covered her face, Justine gazed back with her empty eyes. "I don't understand," she said. "Why can't anyone else see the train?"

Frontenac's heart raced. She met Justine's even gaze and listened. The girl was confused, but also terrified. Oh, how she knew that feeling! Frontenac heaved a huge sigh of relief and began to laugh. The men and Têtue demanded an explanation, although they said nothing. Frontenac chuckled again.

"Aren't we the pair?" she said to Justine. "Show us where it is."

Justine was offended. "Don't laugh at me," she cried. "Do you really not see the train engine right there?"

The others looked at the empty track and back to Justine.

"No, we don't," Frontenac said. She turned to the men. "And you can't hear her voice, but I can."

"Please let me out," Duval called again. "Please, I won't hurt you. Help me, so I can help you."

Monsieur de Guise rubbed his jaw. "This is a bit more than table-turning."

"Indeed," the duke agreed. "But if Mademoiselle Montpellier can see the locomotive, and Madame Frontenac can hear her voice, we may be able to find Jacky."

Justine's elation was a rush of cool air in Frontenac's fevered mind. The girl strode confidently to the track and put up her hand. Before anyone could stop her, she grabbed hold of something, put her foot on air, and pulled herself up. She vanished.

De Guise cried out in alarm, but the others knew Justine was present.

"Montpellier?" Têtue called. "You're there?"

Frontenac listened. "She is," she said, a new fear taking form. "But she's not here anymore."

"Where did you go?" Justine cried.

"We're still here," Frontenac called. She looked to the others; they had not heard Justine's voice. "I'm here with you."

Têtue started toward the spot, but Monsieur de Guise restrained her.

"Mademoiselle Montpellier, what do you see now? Describe it." He looked to Frontenac for an answer.

Frontenac recited, "Standing where the engineer stands… There's a large glass thing like a clock at the upper right, and the needle is pointing to the right… two horizontal valves above the tank… two valves on… glass pipes?" She shook her head and shrugged. "Two little doors."

"That's it," said Têtue. "The upper door. Can you open it?" She turned to Monsieur de Guise. "Duval was examining the firebox when I left. Maybe someone shoved her in there."

"That would be difficult," Monsieur Goüin said sharply.

He had returned, and Frontenac felt the force of his anger and frustration.

"Shh!" Frontenac held up her hand as if she could silence the man's thoughts. "The door's handle won't budge."

"What is she talking about?" Monsieur Goüin demanded.

Monsieur De Guise tried to explain.

"You're talking nonsense. A human being cannot possibly fit inside a firebox. And there is no train!"

The duke removed his sun-glasses and met the engineer's angry glower with his green wolf-eyes, sending him back a pace at the lupine ferocity of the duke's gaze.

"Don't presume to tell us what we can and cannot know, monsieur. We know the locomotive is still present, although none of us can see it except Mademoiselle Montpellier, who is now trapped aboard. We know Madame Duval is also trapped within it, although only Madame Frontenac can hear her. There are many things in this world that are possible, however improbable they may be."

Monsieur Goüin didn't argue with the duke. "Mademoiselle, can you deboard?" he asked.

"She's afraid," Frontenac told them. "She can't see us or this place any more than we can see her. She's — she's terrified."

Têtue grumbled. "But she is here. She needs to take the risk and jump."

Frontenac chuckled despite the tension. "She says you would say that, Têtue."

Monsieur Goüin wiped his broad forehead. "It's possible she can't open the firehole door because she's not strong enough. I'll take the risk. I'll board."

"No, Goüin," Monsieur de Guise insisted. "You called us here to help. So, let us."

"It's my damned engine. And if it's gone, I may as well be gone too." He walked over to where the engine had sat, waving his hand through the air, finding nothing solid.

"Please stop crying," Duval called. "Please let me help you. Tell me where you are. Tell me where I am!"

Monsieur de Guise came to Frontenac and put his hand on her shoulder. "Adèle, are you all right? You look pale."

Frontenac caught her breath. She wasn't used to a man caring for her welfare. She nodded, but then shook her head.

"So many voices. Duval's frightened. So is Justine, but not for the same reason." Then she suddenly felt Justine's excitement. "Oh! She's opened the firehole door," she relayed. She strained to listen. Failure overwhelmed her. Tears filled her eyes. "Duval isn't there."

"What?" Têtue cried. "She has to be. I can feel her." She paced a circle.

"Monsieur de Guise," Frontenac whispered. "Duval. She's crying. She's weeping now."

His jaw tightened. His mind turned red. He gave a short nod and patted her. "Hold on to her for me, Adèle."

Duval's sobs saddened her until Justine's rising courage lifted her spirits. "Justine is going to jump," Frontenac announced.

The duke cried, "Wait. Tell me where to find you, and I'll catch you."

Frontenac guided him with Justine's help, and the duke braced himself. Justine popped out of the air and landed safely in his arms.

Têtue rushed to her. "Montpellier, was there blood all over the cab?"

Justine shook her head as she regained her feet. "It was new, shiny, beautiful. So many colors moving. It was—peaceful. I—I need to sit. I feel as if I've been running a terrible distance."

The duke wrapped his arm about her and led her to a crate to sit.

Monsieur Goüin again wiped his brow. "I must admit, I am confounded. I rather counted on Duval to resolve this, but—"

Monsieur de Guise pursed his lips. Duval always called them his 'pretty bowed lips,' Frontenac recalled with fondness.

"There's no 'but.' Madame Duval will resolve it," he told Goüin. "We must give her time to figure out what 'it' is first. You can be certain she'll discover it before we do."

Frontenac wondered at Monsieur de Guise's easy manner. The man was absolutely torn apart inside. How could he be so calm?

"Madame Frontenac," Monsieur de Guise asked her, "can you hear the noises the men complained about? The frightful cries."

Frontenac brushed her tears away and shook her head. "Just Duval."

He handed her a handkerchief. She smiled gratefully.

Têtue snapped her fingers. "Frontenac, come with me. I've got an idea." She stalked toward the warehouse door.

Frontenac followed, feeling the hope and trepidation Têtue felt. Têtue took her to a crate shoved away at the back wall, where she picked up a valve.

"Take this. Listen."

"Listen? To what?" Frontenac said. As if metal had thoughts or feelings.

Têtue placed the valve in Frontenac's hand. The screams of a thousand children welled up within her.

7.

Jacqueline huddled shivering beside the small wooden door locked against her in the dark. The air was close, oily, filthy. She had wrapped her cravate around her nose and mouth, but after so many — how many? — hours, that too was now befouled. She managed to pull the stitching from her chemise enough to tug off the sleeve and replace the cravate.

She had called. She had roared. She had pleaded. She had plugged her ears with her fingers, but still the tortured children moaned and cried. She'd wept, too, not for herself but for them, catching tears in her gogglers and wiping her nose on her knees. She'd knocked, then banged on the door. She had kicked at it, and still it hadn't yielded even though she knew by its thin resonance it was veneered wood no more than four plies thick.

Exhausted, Jacqueline closed her eyes. The cry had managed to clean some of the dust that had slipped in behind her gogglers, but her eyes still burned. She pulled the neckline of her chemise up to double the mask over her face, tucking her head between her knees. She wanted to sleep, but she didn't want to fall asleep in this coffin of a hole, wherever it was.

This was the question plaguing her. She knew she couldn't possibly be in the firebox. Spiritual forces of some kind had beckoned, found someone who would listen, and dragged her across the aether to here. But where was here? She knew it was a coal mine, although there were none in the Loire valley between Orléans and Chartres. The Loire Basin in the Rhône-Alpes, yes, but not the valley. It wasn't logical — if logic could be applied — that she'd traveled upriver into the Massif Central. Logically, everything about the little locomotive had its source in

England, the engine parts having come from the workshops of the Sharp brothers in Manchester.

Zut! That was it. She had to be in England. Jacqueline thumped her head against the hard wall of her trap. If only she'd applied logic sooner.

"Hello," she called, this time in English. "Can you let me out?"

The wooden door flipped up. Jacqueline tipped over, her head out the door. Dim light from a tiny candle blinded her momentarily. She blinked up into the blackened face of a child covered in coal dust, holding to a rope that had opened the door. The child grinned.

"Art awlreet?" The boy — or girl, Jacqueline couldn't tell — chuckled at her. "Po fagged, th'art."

Ah, Lancashire.

Jacqueline gulped the relatively clean air. "Lenda hond, mon?" she croaked, her throat drier than the coal dust she breathed.

The child hitched the rope on a hook above the door and gripped her waistcoat at the shoulders. "Wossup withi?"

With his or her help, Jacqueline wriggled out the tiny door and got to her knees. She was in a narrow horizontal drift, but there was the literal daylight at the far end of the tunnel, some thirty meters away.

"Mon Dieu, merci." She coughed and spat mud. "Where am I?" she asked in proper English.

"Owdonabit." The child unhitched the rope and the door slammed shut. "Art addled?"

Parbleu, she was more than addled. "Yes. Very addled. What's your name?"

"Cawed Walmesley."

"I am called Duval." She saluted as best she could in the cramped drift.

He or she whistled, then laughed at her again. A jerk of his or her thumb meant, "Off you go."

"Thank you, Walmesley."

Jacqueline flattened herself on her belly and crawled with her hips and elbows. Her arms ached from the hours on end of being folded against her chest. She inched forward up the slight incline, trying not to breathe too deeply the coal-dusty draughts. She came out of the drift onto the side of a shallow hillside in heavy woods, just above a tiny stream no less black than her spit. Still, she slid out and dipped her cravate and her sleeve into it, wrung them both out, and tried to clean herself with the dirty rags.

Standing eluded her; her legs had been bent tightly for too long. The woods were silent, but she heard the distinct rhythmic *chunk* and *hsss* of a steam engine, likely over the hill behind her. The day was hot. The child was no doubt better off in the cool of the drift, even if it was filthier. As she peered through the forest to the vale below, she saw nothing but black in the expansive mining scape, a small mountain range of cinder and coal. The soiled green of the woods surrounding her was the only indication of life.

Jacqueline kicked a stone in disgust. Walmesley couldn't have been more than seven or eight years old. Life in the industrial fields was harsh and unsparing, but to force one so young down into the bowels of the black earth was outright cruelty. She wondered how many others worked beyond that door, further down the drift, down the shaft being drilled by the engines she could hear, or the many other drifts that regulated the air in the mining shafts and the various levels of the mine. How many children were dragged out of bed at two or three in the morning to descend into the darkness, harnessed to shuttles like dogs, crawling on their bellies as she'd crawled, to reach the crevices the grown men couldn't? How many worked until five or six at night, dropping exhausted to bed only to rise again in the dark, to work in the dark, to come home in the dark? How many—

Jacqueline paused. She no longer heard the wailing of many children in her head.

She held onto a branch and pulled herself to her feet. The stream trickled along a yellow-brown stony bed, easy to follow as it wound around the hillside. When she got to a clearing, she basked in the sunshine, appreciating the glow on her face despite the heat. Judging by the position of the sun, it was close to two in the afternoon. Of what day, she couldn't say, but hot in England usually meant July or August.

Below her lay the colliery. A Stephenson *Rocket* was chugging its way out of the ore house hauling a dozen cars of coal, probably on its way to Manchester. A tramway snaked away from the ore house toward the far side of the hill, presumably to access the shaft. The steady *chonk-wheeze-chonk-wheeze* percussion of the steam engine grew louder. Jacqueline peered up to the hilltop, where black billows of smoke indicated the location of the main shaft.

She also saw the cobalt billows of thunderheads bearing down on the hilltop, the colliery, and her.

Jacqueline plunged back into the woods to find a heavy thicket where she could sit out the storm. She didn't want to risk getting caught in a mudslide. Her stiff legs argued, but she strained to climb higher to the area of stronger trees and heavier brush. Finding a spot that presented some measure of security, she plopped down and waited. Drenching sweat formed muddy streaks through the coal dust that coated her. She was actually looking forward to the cold rain cleaning her skin and clearing her burning sinuses and throat.

Thunder soon eclipsed the sound of the steam engines as clouds swallowed the sun. Wind hit suddenly and with force. Jacqueline ducked her head under her arms to keep cinders and forest detritus from flying into her face. As the clouds cleared the hilltop, hail fell, striking her hands and arms hard enough to cut her skin. She wriggled out of her waistcoat and used it to shield her. Hail fell steadily for a quarter of an hour.

Then came heavy rains. She lifted her face, but what water fell from above was too foul with soot to drink. She stretched herself out, nonetheless, and let rain wash over her. Lightning slashed the sky and thunder deafened her, but after the dreadful hours of darkness and filth and children's cries, she was grateful for the air and the water and the drone of rain.

The steady shower suddenly exploded into a torrential downpour. Jacqueline was forced to shield herself again just to breathe. It beat down on her like the Grand Cascade of Mt. Dore. A tenor-pitched roar beyond the pounding rain warned her. A moment later a flash stream shot down the hill about ten meters to her left, dragging rocks and branches with it. She gasped in amazement at the violence of the storm and the forces it had unleashed. Above the fury, however, another sound reached her:

Laughter. Hoots of joy. Happy shouts of children and young teens.

Jacqueline grinned, soothed, the memory of the horrific wailing washed away as with the rain. The children who worked the mines had emerged from the drift. The rain had probably extinguished the boiler for the steam engine that worked the shaft lifts. With drilling stopped for the day, the young workers took advantage of the break. She imagined them dancing in the rain, clearing their young bodies of the filth of the mines. She wished she could see them, pouring out of the black earth, freed for the moment from their misery.

Only, shouts turned to screams. Then shrieks.

Jacqueline's horrified cry died in her throat as the little ripple of stream below her swelled within seconds to a raging flood more than a meter deep. Deep enough to flood the drift. Vicious enough to sweep young bodies down, down thirty meters or more. To hurl them against the little wooden door, against one another, against the stone ceiling and walls.

Water struck Jacqueline's back and lifted her. She barely had time to hook her arm around a sapling and latch on as a flash flood swept beneath her. Rocks pelted her back. Water engulfed her. She dug in her heels and pressed her knee against the bole of a hemlock, lurching upward to gulp air. When a loose bough struck the side of her head, she lost her grip, stunned. The flood slammed her down the hill, striking trees, whipping through bushes that tore at her face and hands. She curled into a ball and tumbled until she landed face down atop a rhododendron bush that held her securely. Barely conscious, bleeding, she lay splayed in a hammock of purple flowers.

The rain poured for at least another hour. The screams faded, to be followed by angry bellows that swept east along with the thunder and the rain.

Jacqueline wept until she lost consciousness.

When Jacqueline opened her eyes, she was encased once again in impenetrable darkness. She blinked to make certain she was awake. When she tried to move, her head struck a metal ceiling. She couldn't bend her legs or shift her arms. She lay as she had landed, though she was no longer in the woods, or on the hillside, or anywhere she could sense. The air didn't stink of coal but of machinery grease and sweat. The children were gone.

In the ventilation drift of a coal pit, children had crashed against the air door with the violence of the sudden summer flood. Jacqueline knew exactly where and when she had been: the Husker Colliery, England, 1838. When the storm shut down the pumps, forty young workers decided to ignore the orders to gather at the bottom of the pit. Instead, they crawled out to daylight, twenty-six of them to their deaths. The oldest was seventeen, her own age at the time, but most of them were only eight or ten.

Jacqueline wondered if Walmesley had made it out alive, or if he — she? — had held the door for the others and died, crushed at the bottom of the drift. She wanted to cry again, but her body had exhausted itself with weeping. Once again, she was between worlds, flat on her face in a coffin of metal. Was she still in England?

"Hello?"

The floor suddenly opened. She stood in a doorway to be greeted by a tall man with deep-set hazel eyes, a receding hairline, but a full head of brown hair, a long, square beard, and a thick mustache. Jacqueline pitched forward, disoriented, and he steadied her.

"By the stars," he said, "Duval?"

Jacqueline was in a small draughting workshop set above a factory floor. The little office had broad windows separating it from the factory, and five different draughting tables with stacks of designs on each. Locomotive engine designs, she realized. Her thoughts whirled.

"Y-yes," she stammered. "Duval. I'm—addled."

"It's good to see you in England again, Duval," he said as he helped her to a seat. He then knocked on the window and called, "Sam. Tea, right away."

By the time he returned to her, she recognized him: Charles Beyer, a masterful young German draughtsman she met when she toured the Atlas Works while still at the Polytechnique. Part of her was relieved to see a familiar face. Another part of her despaired. How could she explain her presence, her condition, mon Dieu, her age? She was only fourteen when they'd met. If she was still trapped in 1838, she should only be seventeen.

Beyer pointed to her welding cap. "You work here now? What a wonderful surprise."

"Ah." She did a quick inventory and found she was attired as she had been on the engineer's cabin before being dragged across the aether. Her clothes were intact; she was no longer soaked from the storm, if ever she had been in the storm at all. "No, I—Oh dear, I don't know any way to explain myself."

Before Beyer could comment, the door opened again. Jacqueline gulped as Richard Roberts himself entered the workshop, carrying rolls of draughting sheets. Roberts was the only man in Europe who rivaled Jacqueline for inventions and patents. A driven man, he rarely attended the various exhibitions on the continent, but they had met once in the past three years—her past three years. He hadn't known her in 1838, but was she still in 1838? Would he recognize her now?

"Sorry, Beyer, didn't realize you were occupied," he said. He nodded to Jacqueline as Beyer made the introduction. "A pleasure, sir."

"It's 'miss,'" Beyer corrected him with a grin. "Visiting from Paris. The Polytechnique."

Roberts wasn't impressed. Thankfully, a boy came in with a tea service, distracting them all. The men then began a discussion over a draughting table while Jacqueline fixed herself tea and sought a clue as to when she was. She paced the room slowly, trying to appear casual. She glanced over a sheet on another table, and there was the date: 1840. She relaxed then, feeling a little more secure about meeting Beyer and Roberts both.

"That would take weeks," Roberts was arguing.

Beyer answered, "I see no other way." He realized Jacqueline was listening, so he turned to her. "What do you say, Duval? You've done this sort of thing, yes?"

Had she? She approached and quickly saw they were debating one of Roberts' huge machines. It would require a lot of plate punching, a laborious and time-consuming process in 1840, and she did indeed know the solution to the problem because Roberts had invented it a year ago. Or rather, next year.

Jacqueline swallowed and waited for the room to stop spinning again. Now she knew how Monsieur Claque felt when she tinkered with his machinery, gears whirring and going nowhere.

And Monsieur Claque's machinery was the answer to Roberts' conundrum on the table before her. How much should she give away? Jacqueline needed their good favor because she had to fashion a way to return across the aether. If she gave Roberts his answer, he might look kindly on her request to build her own machine using the same process.

"The Jacquard system," she said at last. "I would use punch cards to control the systems."

She turned away quickly to avoid Roberts' keen gaze. *Mon Dieu, what have I done?* She hoped the Countess of Lovelace would forgive her if she somehow destroyed linear time and all of history's future by divulging Ada's work before Ada even knew of it. She suppressed a grin to think she, not Roberts, had come up with the idea all along.

The men were silent, studying the design. After a moment, Roberts re-rolled his sheets. He bowed to Jacqueline and left without a word.

"Well done, Duval," Beyer said with a shake of his head. "I don't know how you arrive at your solutions so swiftly." He poured himself tea with a drop of milk and a small cube of sugar. "So what brings you to England, then, and ready to roll up your sleeves?"

Jacqueline heaved a trembling sigh. She could not lie to a man like Beyer, but she was not sure how much of her story he would believe. She decided she couldn't reveal the whole truth, not at once, but he was a good enough engineer that he would soon ask questions, and she had time for answers.

"Beyer, I'm in need of a foundry where I might build a design I've been working on for Goüin. My workshop in Bellesfées was lost in a fire, and the fact is, this is the finest locomotive factory in all Europe."

"I believe it is as well. What is it you need? You have the specifications?"

Instinctively she reached for her inside coat pocket before remembering she'd left her coat on Goüin's factory floor. She groaned, lost once again. She tapped her temple. "In here."

He laughed. "Such an impulsive woman."

"So I'm told. Hand me a pencil." She quickly jotted a list, and as he read through it, his eyes widened.

"So much electricity? What is it you plan to do?"

Tears sprang to her eyes. "Get home."

8.

Têtue picked up Duval's coat from the floor where it had been tossed and began to fold it, forgetting Duval used her coat as a repository for money, notes, tools, whatever. Sous, écus, and louis d'ors went rolling and spinning across the floor. Pincers, screwdrivers, pencils, the spyglass, and a friction igniter dropped and clattered, as well.

Foute, you clumsy oaf. Têtue picked it all up again and tried to find the right pockets for them. In the inside vest pocket, she came across a wad of pages covered in numbers, arrows, shapes, and diagrams, and on the final page, a design for a machine.

"De Guise, what are these, do you think?"

Têtue handed them to Duval's partner to examine. A grin slowly came to his lips.

"I think it may have something to do with animal magnetism," he murmured to her. "Goüin," he called, "what do you make of this design?"

The industrialist strode over and took the notes. At first he leafed through them. When he got to the last sheet, he perused it. After a few minutes, he looked around, headed to the wall to sit down on a crate, and continued to pore over the page with the finished design.

Têtue folded her arms. She'd never been patient, and her wolf blood only worsened her temper. Two hours since Duval vanished. Têtue was hungry, frustrated, and anxious to resolve the mystery and retrieve Duval safely, but the men didn't seem to be doing anything about it. Montpellier could see the train, but not the blood. Frontenac had lost contact with Duval, whatever contact that was… her disembodied voice? Where could Duval have gone, if not into the aether? Yet, Têtue still had her scent, so close.

She put Duval's coat on. She reached into the side pocket and brought out the stained handkerchiefs. As Frontenac joined her, Têtue handed the linen to her. Frontenac cried out in shock and shuddered.

"These must be the noises the workers heard," Frontenac said, pressing her fingers to the stains. "Children crying, calling for help, screaming like someone is beating them, screaming in fear. Oh, it's too horrible." She gave it back to Têtue. "If that's what Duval heard, no wonder she went to find them."

"What children?" the duke said as he came up behind them.

"We don't know," Têtue replied, "but this must be their blood, if Frontenac can hear them."

Frontenac rubbed at her temples. "I can't—that is, I've never heard the thoughts of people I wasn't near. This—it's all new to me."

At the far end of the factory, the duchess and Guichet arrived. The duchess must have smelled the fear in the air because she quickened her step. She also put up a scent Têtue didn't recognize.

Têtue relieved her of the packages with the food and looked her up and down. "You all right? Anything wrong?"

"No, no," the duchess said. "It's just that something's wrong here, isn't it?"

Têtue blew out a breath. "Oh, yeah." For a moment, she'd feared for the duchess's baby.

She began setting out the bread, cheese, and pastries for them while the duchess went over to speak with the duke. The three younger ones pounced on the food. Têtue waited for the Llewellyns, but they were absorbed in discussion with de Guise and Goüin about the designs, about Duval's whereabouts, and about the young women's newly manifested powers. She listened with interest and gave an amused "huh" when she learned of Guichet's ability to throw things around. She tore off a hunk of baguette and stuffed it with cheese so she could munch and listen and think.

"It's a device to generate electro-magnetic force of some kind," Goüin said. "I don't recognize any of these formulae, but I have a clever fellow upstairs who should be able to understand them. And this—" He indicated the sheet with the machine's design. "It looks like a Faraday cage, but the generator…" He fell silent, his expression a mixture of awe and doubt.

De Guise clapped his shoulder. "That's my Jacqueline. The question is, can you put it together?"

"Let me talk to Coquelet. He's my brightest." Goüin left with Duval's papers.

De Guise bowed his head and stretched his body again. Têtue could tell his gunshot wound bothered him. She admired the fact he never spoke of it. Duval's strange disappearance had put more strain on the man. The new papers only complicated things. His usual agreeable scent was tainted with anguish and fear, two things she had never before associated with de Guise. She joined him and the Llewellyns.

"So what was all that?" Têtue asked de Guise.

He collected himself and smiled. "I think she was trying to harness that animal magnetism we discussed last night." He looked at the young women and gave a quiet chuckle. "And that was assuming you were all just simple girls from some small village."

Têtue caught on to the source of his humor. "We have three women with incredible powers, thanks to Mircalla."

"And then there's the three of us," said the duchess. "Six against the aether."

Têtue held up her hands. "No. You're not going anywhere. Not this time. Not with child."

The duke agreed. "Not this time, fy nghariad. You need to rest. I know you're not feeling well." He, like Têtue, tapped his nose. "Têtue will go with the girls."

De Guise raised a finger. "And I."

"No, you're not listening." Têtue gave a loud snort of annoyance. "She designed this for *us*. For us four. And that makes five against the aether. You don't think Duval's just sitting on her ass, do you?"

De Guise rubbed the back of his head. Probably a tension headache. Têtue had one as well. All the noise, the constant shouting to be heard. Plus the stink in the air. She doubted de Guise recognized the odor, but she did, and it filled her with anger. Charred flesh, blood, and bone.

The duchess frowned, watching the three younger ones devour the tit-bits she had provided. "I thought we'd be dining chez Jules, but I suppose no one wants to leave the factory. Let me go fetch us a more complete meal. Something tells me we'll be here quite a while."

Têtue's stomach grumbled almost as loudly as the duchess did.

As the duchess left, Goüin returned with Coquelet, a man about Duval's age who was breathless with excitement. "Designed by Jacqueline Duval," he gushed. "This is an honor. Yes, yes. I can see what she's done here. I never saw such elegance in physics. Never seen electro-magnetism used this way. I understand the concepts, but, monsieur," he said to Goüin, "it has never been combined like this. She uses the word 'subject,' but she's talking about the impact of these flux lines on people."

"Not exactly," Têtue said. "She's talking about the impact of the four of us on flux lines."

Coquelet regarded her with disdain. "Do you even know what you're talking about?"

Têtue sneered. "Yeah. We're talking about Duval's life."

Coquelet considered her, then measured de Guise's stern face. Têtue folded her arms and raised a brow, and Coquelet backed off. "The simple answer," he said, "is yes, we can construct this. I just don't know what the outcome will be."

"Duval designed it," Têtue said with a shrug. "The outcome will be brilliant. Let's get started."

"Monsieur Têtue, I don't think you understand."

"You're right," Têtue snapped. "I don't understand why you're arguing." She pointed to the track. "Do you see that train?" When he shook his head, she said, "Do you hear the children crying?"

"What children?"

"Can you smell the blood?"

"Mon Dieu!" Coquelet gaped at her.

She pulled off her tinted glasses and met his gaze. He recoiled with a look of disgust and swallowed any further argument.

Goüin put his hand on Coquelet's shoulder. "Enough. Get your team together. As you said, it's an honor. It's also our only solution to recovering Madame Duval. And the locomotive."

Têtue snorted her satisfaction that Goüin had also put Duval first. As Coquelet walked away, Têtue followed, with a nod to de Guise. Coquelet wrinkled his nose—a typical Tourangelle—but kept silent. They went up a flight of steps to a large open room with dozens of draughting tables in rows. Coquelet signaled to four men who followed them into a private office.

"Michel Simon, Raphael Sançille, Donat Bardît, Léon Vincent," he told her, indicating each.

"Têtue." She shook hands firmly, refusing to give any indication she had no idea what she was doing. Têtue had worked in mills and factories across the past four years after leaving the Beast. Machines weren't new to her. They made sense. This pushed that, this tooth fit into that cog, these cards told those strings when to move. Nobody had ever put machines together like Duval, with her clockwork porters and ingenious Monsieur Claque. But as Duval would say, "It's just a machine."

So, what machine had Duval designed this time?

Simon and Sançille argued. Vincent was shaking his head. Bardît spoke enthusiastically with Coquelet. They used words she hadn't heard before but were easy to guess: flux, capacitator, radiation, excitation, metrometometer. They threw in names she didn't recognize: Ørsted and Ampère and Coulomb and Volta. Têtue leaned back against the wall, her arms crossed to hold in her urge to turn wolf and thrash these men into action. She nodded now and again, but after half an hour of back and forth, yes and no, does or doesn't, she straightened and leaned her fists on the table.

"Messieurs, Duval is languishing in the aether. Stop discussing the philosophy of this design and start building it! If you aren't down on the floor of the factory in ten minutes, you'll answer to the Order of Duval."

Borrowing a move from the duchess, she spun on her heel and walked out.

What was it about men that they couldn't just do? They talked in high-blown language, showing off to one another, probably quoting somebody else anyway, trying to justify their existence through words. And the odor they put up—Parbleu, she just wanted to bite them.

Têtue stalked out of the building into the street. She needed to breathe air that didn't hold the odor of the men, though the pervasive stench of burning flesh and bone that befouled Orléans almost made her retch. How could anyone stand it? Couldn't they sense its wrongness?

It was mid-afternoon. A shift of workers was leaving the factory. Têtue followed them, and as she suspected, they led her to a good bar-tabac across the square by the station with a clear view of the factory. She sat outside with a bowl of mussels and a pint of 1664, waiting for Madame Llewelyn to return. She hoped Duval wouldn't mind her spending a franc or two if it meant forestalling a lupine rampage.

Têtue hadn't had mussels in months. After getting fired for fighting—again—from the Denière foundry in the spring, she'd begged her way to the Loire valley, where she knew she could get some work helping in a vineyard somewhere. So long as she kept her hair short and stayed in small villages to the south, no one recognized her, usually didn't even notice she was a woman. Sheltering in haystacks, sleeping in fields, avoiding conversation… Parbleu, it was lonely. Then the work dried up in late June, so it was back to hiding, begging, sometimes stealing, always small. Like her life.

Then Mircalla caught her.

Less than two weeks since being bitten by the merdique vampire. Since awakening aboard *Esprit*, footsore, exhausted from walking almost fifty kilometers without food or water. Since landing on her feet in a house—a château! —that offered her much more than food and a bed: honor, dignity, respect… and a chance at vengeance. Since throwing herself on the stake meant for Duval and reviving to discover she was a wolf, no longer a homeless fugitive. Less than a week since accepting the offer of the duke and duchess's care. She would be governess to the duchess's child, or children, but more than that, she would be part of a family. She would have a legacy after all. Têtue marveled she was still alive, and she ached to recover the woman she owed for it all.

Têtue sniffed a familiar scent on the air. Vincent headed her way. She greeted him with a handshake and offered a seat, then called for a beer.

"You know this is madness, don't you?" Vincent complained. "The amount of power she wants us to generate could kill them all."

Têtue shrugged. "You don't know Duval."

"Well, I know *of* her. Yes, it's stunning in its scope, but mon Dieu—"

"It's a machine."

Vincent welcomed his beer and drank half of it in two gulps. "Thanks. I'm Léon. They're gathering parts now. We'll probably be here until midnight, maybe later."

"Zut." Têtue huffed impatiently. "The last we heard from her, she was crying. Don't know why. If she's hurt…"

"They said one of the girls could hear her voice, right?" Léon said. "And the other one can see the engine. The invisible engine. Even climbed aboard. Crazy. I've never come across anything like it, have you? I mean, they're just girls, really, aren't they? A pair of witches. And the other one's a mummy. What is that?"

Têtue growled.

Léon didn't seem to notice. "What's Duval doing with girls like that? Well, obviously, she's planning an electro-magnetic miracle machine. And these girls are willing to throw themselves into it."

Têtue finished her beer and ordered a second one. She held her temper until the beer arrived, and by then the urge to snarl had passed. "Léon? Ever love a woman so much you'd give your life?"

He straightened, concerned. "Hold on, man. I'm sorry. I didn't realize you and Madame Duval—"

Têtue shook her head. "No, you don't understand. It's… She's worth the risk. Look, I watched her build a suit of bullet-deflecting armor in two hours, out of gowns and solder. She invented a flying device for a clockwork man. She built a whole orchestra out of brass and leather. I'm telling you, you can trust her designs. Whatever danger you think there is, Duval's already mapped it out in her head. This'll work. It has to."

Léon studied her, and she shifted uncomfortably under his gaze. He raised his glass and tapped it to hers. "Well, then, here's to Duval and her electro-magnetic trans-aether teleporter," he said.

They drank and grinned at one another.

Têtue said, "Is that what we're building?" She got up and fished in her pocket for change.

"Let me," said Léon as he dropped two francs on the table. "It's not every day a man can say he's building a Duval."

They strolled back to the factory, Léon chatting about working with Goüin as if Têtue understood the complexities of manufacturing huge machinery like locomotives. She nodded and said, "absolutely" and "I know" and she decided she liked this fellow. He wasn't particularly attractive in a romantic sense, with hazel eyes, a pointed nose like a ski slope, and a wide, dimpled chin, but he was open, he loved his work, and he had a nice smile beneath his bristling moustaches. It was reassuring to know there were good men besides de Guise and the duke.

Têtue caught the odd new scent of the duchess, as well as roast chicken and vegetables. She turned to wait for her. The duchess struggled with ten packages. The two hurried to help her.

"Why do you wear those sun-glasses?" Léon asked Têtue as they headed to the duchess. "You, your friends?"

"They hide our eyes. We're part wolf," she answered, finding no reason to lie to him. "Hard to explain."

Léon laughed at her. Together they unburdened the duchess.

"Her Grace, Madame Llewellyn," Têtue introduced.

"Léon Vincent," he said, bowing. "Your Grace."

The duchess sighed with relief. "Thank you, Têtue, Monsieur Vincent. How goes the project?" She winced and rubbed her front.

"Vincent says it'll be done by midnight." Têtue frowned at the duchess. "Are you sure you're all right?"

The duchess waved her off. "Are they up to Jacky's plans?"

Léon hastened to say, "We are. I just hope the girls understand what they're getting into."

"It's women, not girls," Têtue said. "I keep telling him, we don't have to understand. We trust Duval."

The duchess bit her lip. "We do." She blinked away tears. "But this goes far beyond anything we've met before, Tetue. Ghosts. Sorcery. Vampires. Revenants. Knocking spirits. I don't even know what to call this."

Têtue glanced at Léon. He cleared his throat and tried to hide his astonishment.

"Yeah," Têtue said, "she's not lying."

Léon twitched his moustaches. "I was on the construction site when… mon Dieu, the cries. And Monsieur Goüin says the engine is still there? It's madness."

The duchess sighed. "Well, madness or not, it's our only key to getting my sister back."

"It's not madness," Têtue said. "It's electro-magnetic trans-aether teleportation."

Léon juggled the packages to get the door for the duchess. Têtue then held it for him. They made their way to the factory floor, and Frontenac and Guichet rushed to assist. They both embraced Têtue, and she kissed their brows.

"This is Léon," she told the others. "Léon, these women haven't eaten the whole day except for some pastry and cheese. Is there a table we can set this on?"

Léon stared at her, then at Frontenac and Guichet. "You're a woman," he said to Têtue.

Têtue smirked. "Yeah, I know. Table?"

Léon straightened, reddening. He bowed and went off to find a table.

"He thinks you're strange," Frontenac whispered.

Têtue scoffed. "You say that like he's wrong. We're all strange."

She slid Duval's coat from her shoulders and gripped it tightly to her chest. Frontenac brought her a pastry and took the coat. After a few steps, Frontenac halted. She turned back to Têtue.

"She's talking again," Frontenac said. "She keeps saying, 'they're dead.' I think she means the children."

Têtue shuddered. "Makes sense. You heard their spirits, screaming. She must have met them." She bit into the pastry, frowning. "Foute, that could be anywhere. Mills, factories, coal mines, iron or tin mines. They work kids to death. I mean really little ones. Four, five, six years old. They don't feed 'em. No time to themselves, so they just piss or poop where they are. Beat 'em like dogs on the street. Kids get tired, or they get too weak to stand, they fall into the machinery. Saw a kid get chewed up and spat out in pieces at a mill. They don't care. Just go buy another one from the church."

Montpellier gasped. "But aren't there laws?"

"Laws are no good if no one cares to see they're enforced," said the duke, coming over to them. "Adèle, what else does she say?"

"They drowned," Frontenac answered.

Têtue's thoughts wove about like yarn on the loom. "This machinery is from a railroad factory. How do children drown in a railroad factory?" She wished she had Duval's quick logic. "Track it back. The factory runs on steam. Boilers need coal. Kids drowned in a coal pit, and the coal from that pit fueled the factory when it made these parts. I can't think of any other connection, can you?"

The duke stiffened. She smelled his disgust and dread. "What is it?"

He beckoned to de Guise. "I'd say it's impossible, but we all know better. Lancashire, 1838," he said to de Guise.

De Guise put up the same scent of dread.

"Is Duval safe?" Têtue demanded. She felt the center of her inner self collapsing and she fought to keep the wolf at bay. "Where the hell are those men?"

"Language, ma fille," said the duchess. "This is good news. We know where she is."

De Guise ran his hand through his hair. "Where and when. How does that help us? We can't go back in time."

Léon returned with Bardît, carrying the requested table. The three younger women and the duchess picked up the packages of food and set up what amounted to supper at that hour. This time, Têtue didn't stand on ceremony. She helped herself to chicken, pork, and fried potato slices, eating with none of the delicacy of the other women. She joined the men again, and the young women followed a few minutes later with their food plated on paper and napkins over their hands.

"Chronological displacement?" Léon said, furrowing his brow. "Adding to the madness?"

Têtue growled, but she was too busy eating to reply.

Frontenac leaned toward Léon. "Adding to the witchcraft, monsieur."

He blushed, his temper rising.

Frontenac smugly returned to her food. Têtue snorted; Frontenac must have heard the man's thoughts. Têtue was not surprised when a spoonful of crème fraîche smacked Léon's cheek. Guichet gulped, wide-eyed with guilt. The duchess laid her hand gently on Guichet's head, then handed Léon a napkin, her eyes twinkling. Têtue loved the way the duchess viewed the world as a stage for everyone to stand in footlights.

Frontenac cocked her head. "Duval just said 'hello.'"

The duke raised a brow. "In English?"

Frontenac nodded. They waited. Frontenac shook her head. "She's gone again." She caught her breath as de Guise stormed off. Her eyes welled. "He's so broken," she whispered. Then she lifted her gaze to Têtue. "You are too, n'est-ce pas?"

Têtue let Frontenac lay her head on her shoulder and patted her. "I swear, Frontenac, if I don't let the wolf out soon, I'm going to explode."

Léon looked confused. "What wolf?"

"Patience, Têtue," said the duchess. "Here come the men now."

Coquelet and his team drove through the bay doors in a horse cart crammed with the materials listed in Duval's designs. Têtue had been listening for them indoors and missed the cues. She shoved the last of her frites into her mouth and wiped her hands on her trousers, then helped the men unload.

"This can't be all of it," she said.

"It's not," said Coquelet. "Goüin is out scavenging the train yards and mills and other foundries in the province. Don't worry, it will be here in time."

"Why the mills?" she asked.

"Punch cards," Simon said. "Never saw such genius with punch cards. Do the work of a hundred men." He grinned at her. "You are one lucky devil, working with Duval."

Têtue shrugged. "More devil than you know."

She lifted a huge disc from the cart, grinning at the men's surprise. Then she dropped it to the floor with a roar and a curse. "This is from

Marteau, isn't it?" She kicked the disc. "F—" She stopped herself, lest she lose her chance at being governess.

9.

Justine Montpellier fretted in dizzy confusion as she followed the colors of those busying themselves with the heavy machinery. She didn't belong here. She was useless to all of them. The thousands of hues in the dressmaker's shop still spun in her memory, on top of the swirl of shades comprising the city and the factory.

Her healing body also burned after the long day. Knife exercises were one thing; Justine could push past the pain of raw scar tissue on her arms and shoulders for a short time. But so many emotions twisted her new facial skin. Frowns pulled at her cheeks, and her racing pulse throbbed in her neck. Terror foremost kept knitting her brow.

Terror was a relatively new sensation to Justine. For fourteen years, her life had been pleasant, content, and utterly blank. Born blind, she'd never questioned her dark world. Maman taught her to work by touch. Justine could sew, she could cook, she could clean. She fed chickens, pushed the harvest carts, and threshed wheat. Papa insisted she had no limitations, and as far as she knew, he was right.

Why then had he tried so hard to get rid of her? Sunday after Sunday at Mass, talking up her virtues to various men of the village, inviting young men to supper, inviting old men to come watch her complete her chores like a prize pig at the fair. Her heart died when he announced her engagement to Monsieur Cezet's son Jacques, the one boy of the village who tormented her most. When they were children, he'd pulled her hair, poked her with sticks, thrown garbage and muck and stones at her. He thought she didn't know it was him, but she recognized his laugh when he ran off. Four years older than her, and in his own father's words, worthless. That's the future Papa had chosen for her? She couldn't bear it. She wouldn't bear it.

Justine wasn't wanted at home. She didn't belong with Jacques Cezet. She didn't belong here.

Frontenac left the group of workers and came to her side. "This has been a long day," she said to Justine. "Did you bring your unguent?"

Justine nodded and held up her reticule, something she had never heard of before coming to Bellesfées. Reticule. Nor chatelaine, corset, bustle, stays, or tucker. Certainly not décolletée either.

Frontenac grinned. "Come on, I'll take care of you."

Justine took Frontenac's arm gratefully.

Frontenac's was the first face Justine had seen when she had awakened at Bellesfées, the first *anything* she'd ever seen. She had slept in a daze of pain and numbing unguents and drugs and the new sensation of sight. She couldn't make sense of Frontenac. She had stared at her, a phantasmagoria of colors, shapes, motion, shades of light and shadow, swirling and scattering and pulling other shapes and motion with it. Where was her familiar blank world? Where was she?

Frontenac had seemed to know what Justine felt. "It's all right," she'd told her, "you're safe now."

Safe? Safe, where? The last thing Justine remembered was leaving the farm in the middle of the night. She had walked the road from her village, carefully probing the path ahead with her walking stick as she was accustomed. Had she fallen asleep? And why was she in such pain!

Frontenac then told her everything, the story spilling out like water rushing from the pump, the words in colors that billowed and splashed. Justine had never heard of a vampire. She didn't understand what it meant to be bitten by one. She did understand she'd been mauled, which explained the pain. None of it explained the miracle of her newfound sight. Père Garien had always said the Christ could make a blind man see, but the Christ had never bothered to do the same for her despite her prayers. Had the demon vampire done this to her? Was her soul now damned?

Justine had spent her days healing in terror they would learn her secret.

Now, terror set in once again. The strangeness of her ability to see the locomotive overtook her, and again Frontenac was there for her, like a sister with a kind of love Justine had not known from her parents, wrapping around her in dozens of vivid hues for which she had no words. Frontenac led her to an office away from the factory floor and the jumble of images and motion. She tenderly removed Justine's bandages, and even more gently applied the cooling ointment Duval had devised for her ravaged skin. Justine sighed and groaned.

"You're exhausted, aren't you?" Frontenac asked. "You should find a place to rest. Maybe go back to *Esprit* and sleep. We can come get you when we're ready."

Frontenac tucked the ointment back into Justine's reticule. She pursed her lips thoughtfully as she began the task of bandaging. "Your skin is looking a lot better today. You may heal much better than you fear."

When Frontenac smiled at her, Justine's entire body filled with the same cooling sensation the unguent brought to her face and shoulders.

"Could you always hear thoughts?" she asked Frontenac. "Or is this because of Mircalla?"

"Not exactly. Maybe." Her colors grew ragged and frayed. "I've always had an intuition of what people were feeling. It may be stronger now. Why?"

Justine clamped down on her response. "No reason."

"*Hmph*. The only thing Mircalla gave me was a place to grow. With Duval, at Bellesfées. I'm not letting anyone take that from me."

"Yes." But Justine wasn't convinced Frontenac was telling the truth, any more than she was convinced of her own answer.

Frontenac finished the bandaging. "What about you?" she asked. "You can see into the aether. Could you do that before Mircalla?"

Justine wanted so much to tell her the great secret Frontenac had no way of knowing. At the same time, she didn't want to lose her as a friend, as a sister. She gripped Frontenac's hand. "I wonder…"

Frontenac squeezed her hand in return. "What? What is it?"

Justine felt blood rush to her face. She needed so much to share her fear. "Gaudin told me Duval had been badly battered, even shot. But when she drank Mircalla's blood, she healed. Completely. No scars." She shuddered at the implication.

Frontenac held both her hands. The colors surrounding her calmed their frantic motion. "Maybe you did. Maybe I did, too. It doesn't matter. And now I can hear Duval, and Guichet can move objects with her mind, and you have a gift of trans-aethereal sight. Guichet and I were bitten by the wolves, and we bear no scar. Who knows? Maybe your skin will be fully restored too."

There was so much strength in Frontenac's hands, Justine had to smile, then laugh. Terror faded. Frontenac lifted her to her feet and embraced her, and the world was bright again. Together they returned to the floor. As Frontenac rejoined the workers, Justine examined the locomotive. She kept wondering: if she could see the engine, why couldn't she see Duval? She set her hand against the piston.

Madame Llewellyn was suddenly beside her. "What is it, Justine?" The duchess had an uncanny sense of when to seek out her company.

Justine said, "I'm wondering why I can see it."

Madame Llewellyn patted her shoulder lovingly and said, "Because you're gifted."

Justine shook her head. "No, that's not what I mean. If you can't see the train, the men say, it's because it's in the aether. But it's right here. If I could see things in the aether, I'd be able to see Duval."

Madame Llewellyn was quiet for a moment. "That is a shrewd observation, Justine. Let's push that a little further."

"What do you mean?"

"Adèle can hear Jacky, but only when she's lost in the aether. She was trapped there, and Adèle heard her calling for help. She went silent for a while, and when Adèle heard her a second time, it was after she had witnessed the disaster and was trapped again."

"Then she said 'hello' and went silent again, so she must be somewhere." Justine patted the locomotive. "Just like this train is here. I think…" She gulped. "Your Grace, Frontenac said Mircalla could vanish and reappear. I wonder if…"

When she couldn't finish the thought, Madame Llewellyn finished it for her. "You think Mircalla may have imparted the mastery of the aether to you young women. I wondered the same thing myself. Well done, Justine."

Justine hesitated. "Têtue said she was looking into the firebox when she vanished. What if I try to follow her?"

"Then you might be lost as well," Madame Llewellyn said. "Besides, didn't you say she wasn't in the firebox?"

"She wasn't. But perhaps the firebox can send me where it sent Duval."

Madame Llewellyn's colors darkened. "Monsieur Llewellyn says we must take precautions."

Justine still wasn't sure. "I—I don't know if I'm strong enough anyway." She flushed, blinking rapidly. "When I went up the first time, it drained me. I don't want to disappoint anyone."

"I can understand that," Madame Llewellyn said. "We'll think more about it. Monsieur Llewellyn believes she's still in England, perhaps at the Manchester locomotive factory, as Têtue suggested." She hugged Justine's head to her bosom and kissed her hair. "Rest up, Justine. We'll need you to be strong later, once the trans-aether teleporter is built. Then we'll see what you can see."

Justine nodded. Madame Llewellyn led her back to where the pieces of Duval's machine were coming together. They sat side by side on a crate, and Madame Llewellyn coaxed her to lie down, cradling Justine's head in her lap as she stroked her hair. Justine closed her eyes and smiled. Her mother had often held her just this way, a place of safety.

"Madame, may I ask you a secret favor?"

Madame Llewellyn chuckled, light dancing up from her. "It's quite a day for revealing secrets, Justine."

Secrets. Frontenac and Guichet had told theirs. Could Justine do no less?

"In the shop, the dress shop, you talked about all the colors," Justine said. "I could see them all. But before, at home, my home, before Mircalla, I couldn't."

"You were color-blind?"

"No. Just blind."

That was it. Simply saying the words aloud freed her. Justine felt light, airy.

Madame Llewellyn *hmm*ed. "And what is the favor?" she asked, as easily as if she hadn't heard of a miracle.

And why should the duchess be surprised? This was a woman who could turn into a wolf at will. Justine relaxed even more.

"I want to know the colors I can see now," Justine said. "I don't know their names, what they're called."

Madame Llewellyn laughed. Justine trembled, worried she had made a fool of herself again.

"Oh, dear," said the duchess. "I'm afraid you have an advantage over me, Justine. Wolves don't see colors the way people do. In fact, we can't see most of them." She sighed. "Ah, I do miss rich, vibrant blues, greens, reds, and golds."

Justine relaxed again. "I don't know what those words mean. But back at the shop, you could name the colors there."

"I had to teach myself," Madame Llewellyn answered, "and it took a very long time. Many things I remembered, and so I could figure out which was my favorite purple gown or recognize the deep crimson of a good Bordeaux. I miss the familiar bleu-de-France, amaranth, and gold of Bellesfées. Every color to me is washed out to pale blue, yellow, or shades of white and grey. My sister tells me Monsieur Llewellyn's eyes are a lovely olive green, yet to me they look silver, though I remember when they were a beautiful blueberry blue. At least that's how I saw them." Her eyes glistened, and though she smiled, her colors deepened, then suddenly lit up again. "But I have the advantage of a very good memory of how colors are laid out in a fabric shop, so I do make good guesses."

Justine covered her mouth, giggling. The duchess sometimes seemed as girlish as she was. "Can you still see them move at least?"

"Move?" This time the duchess was surprised. "Tell me more."

Justine caught her breath, confusion and embarrassment building again. "Move. I mean, the way colors have a way of folding into each other or pushing each other away. Or how when people talk, they spread out into other colors and make new colors. Or the way they swirl up and around when you play the fortepiano. And right now, I can tell you don't feel well because you have little dark flashes in your lightness."

"Oh, Justine, you are truly wonderful. No, no." She patted Justine's trembling hand. "I'm beginning to understand."

Monsieur Llewellyn and Monsieur de Guise turned abruptly from the work site and headed to them, as if summoned.

"Monsieur Llewelyn and I can hear one another's thoughts when we need to," the duchess explained quickly, "and I've called them. De Guise," she said, "I believe we've just gained another advantage. Mademoiselle Montpellier can see the flux lines of the aether."

Justine's heart raced. She sat up. She had no idea what Madame Llewellyn meant, but she sounded happy about it. At the same time, fear enveloped Justine. For fourteen years, blindness was normal. Sight was new and dazzling and fantastic, but to everyone else, sight was more normal than blindness. "The flux lines of the aether," she knew, was not normal. She could read it on their faces. Once more, she didn't belong.

A dark hue in Monsieur de Guise's colors deepened. "Seeing them and knowing what to do with them are two different matters," he said. "I'll talk to Coquelet."

Monsieur Llewellyn chuckled. "And here we were afraid of a haunting."

The men returned to the machine they were building. They obviously told the others what they'd learned, as Frontenac and Guichet laughed and clapped their hands. Têtue leapt down from atop the machine to join Justine and the duchess.

"Tell me something," Têtue said, pointing to the huge disc of the Faraday generator. "That big round thing, what's it look like to you?"

Justine hesitated. "I'm not sure what you mean."

The duchess said, "Justine never learned the names of colors. Let me try." She put Justine's hand on her own skirt. "This is the color orange, like the fruit. This," she said, touching Justine's daydress, "is brown. Do you see a distinction? Are they different to you in any way?"

Justine nodded. She touched Têtue's trousers. "This is brown, right?"

"Yes, very good. What else is orange?"

Justine looked around the bay and came back to the duchess. "Your hair is almost orange. It's not brown exactly."

The duchess laughed. "That's close enough. Now, what in here is the same color as the disc?"

Têtue shifted. Justine could never understand why the motion of Têtue's colors was so edgy all the time, like the frayed end of an old towel in the breeze.

"Well," she said finally, "it is the same as the valves and the firebox door on the train."

"Huh. Thought so. Marteau's factory." Têtue sniffed. "I bet that's what's stinking up this city, too."

"It's also the same colors as Têtue," Justine added. Her fingers knotted around each other. "So odd."

Justine saw a cold, grey blade sweep through Têtue and slice her heart.

"Huh. I'm going to have a look."

Têtue trotted toward the open doors of the bay, into the deepening evening. As she passed the workers, Léon broke away and followed her.

"Wait!" Justine cried. "I know what to look for."

She slid down from the crate and ran after Têtue. Guichet and Frontenac swiftly caught up to her, and together they overtook Têtue.

Frontenac asked, "Justine, are you sure you're up for this? You're still healing, after all."

Justine did wish Têtue would slow their pace, but she said, "I'll manage. Please, I think we have to work together. I think—I think I need to be with you all. We've all touched the aether. I think I do belong."

"I think you're right," Guichet agreed. "Léon, you're the one who should go back."

Léon's colors puffed from him, in the same way Monsieur Claque would sometimes puff steam in tiny clouds. "Mesdemoiselles, you seem to be aware of flaws in the machinery that I can't detect, so I'm coming with you to discover their source. Besides, I know my way around Marteau's factory."

Têtue grunted. "Just don't get in my way," she said. "I know a thing or two about factories myself."

Justine glanced up at the sky, at the monstrous void that floated above the factory at the edge of the city. Darkness poured from the envelope, spilled over the gondola, and billowed down, folding into the sooty smoke that bloomed from the Marteau factory's stacks. Nothing wholesome would be found where they were going. She hoped some good would come from their endeavors.

But now she had learned orange and brown. Something like orange but much darker emanated from Guichet. Justine tried to take in some of the signs in bar and café windows. She tugged Frontenac's sleeve and pointed.

"What's that color?"

"Red."

"And that one?"

"Green."

"And there?"

And so Justine swiftly learned that Guichet's flux lines were mostly red, Frontenac's mainly purple, Têtue's all gold like the duchess's except where streaks of grey sullied it, and Léon's dark blue with narrow ribbons of yellow, pink, and gold. She couldn't see her own flux lines. She hoped it was because she was inside them. She hoped it was for the same reason she could see the train.

Têtue, in the meantime, talked with Léon about what he knew of Marteau's ironworks. As they spoke, Têtue's gold lines would flash with bursts of red, and Léon's would slip between the frays to soothe them back to gold again. In the same way, Guichet and

Frontenac interwove one into another and swept around Justine like a comforter.

Justine marveled at the variety of colors that surrounded the people they passed on the street. As they drew closer to the factory, however, colors deepened, darkened, and ultimately compressed to an impenetrable grey. At the same time, the varied smells and sounds of the city sank under an oppressive gloom of heavy, greasy smoke, the odor of burnt meat, and the thunder of machinery, a constant, deafening roar. Têtue sneezed and gagged. Justine fanned herself to little avail.

"I've never smelled ironworks like this," Têtue grumbled. "More like an abattoir."

"A knacker's yard," Guichet agreed. "Blood, bone, and flesh; crushed, ground, and cooked down."

"There's no end of hard labor being done," Léon said. "It's harsh work."

"What do you know of labor? You push a pencil around pieces of paper," Têtue retorted. "Duval doesn't just design; she does the work herself. She punches cards, welds joints, melts iron or silver or copper. She doesn't ask six-year-olds to fetch burning rods from a furnace, or pluck dust out of kerfs, or crawl under fly-wheels."

Léon didn't answer. After a long thoughtful moment in which his colors wavered between blue and gold, he said. "Mon Dieu, I envy you. To watch Duval at work."

"Pouah." Guichet held up her reticule. "Look at the filth on this. And on our dresses."

"I'm sure an engineer as accomplished as Duval has the necessary sodium-bicarbonate soap to clean it," Léon assured her. He wiped his hand across his own shirt and showed her his soiled hands. "We have soaps at our shop as well. You ladies are probably accustomed to the more refined Pears, but ours do the job."

Têtue snorted. "Pears!"

Justine chuckled at the way Têtue's flux lines made miniature explosions of green when she did that. But she then whispered to Guichet, "What do pears have to do with soap?"

Guichet shrugged.

Léon indicated a narrow alley between the main floor and the foundry itself. Justine couldn't see past the first few meters. For a moment she felt her blindness reaching for her as it filled the alleyway in smokey clouds. As the others turned down the passage, Justine halted. She trembled before the void that had swallowed her companions. It roiled. It beckoned to her. It wanted her. She struggled to breathe, as one in a dream trying to call for help only to manage inarticulate gasps.

Frontenac returned quickly to her side. "Tell us what you see."

"Don't go in there." She gulped. "It's—dark."

As the others emerged from the complete darkness and rejoined her, she tried to find the words. "Earlier today, after the dress shop, you were hungry, Guichet."

Guichet cocked her head and blinked. "You could see that?"

Justine nodded. "Usually, your lines are a pale red color, but you began puffing out dark red in little—" She wiggled her hand. "—ripples?—that went away when you finished the meat tarte. I'd never seen it before; we've never been hungry at Bellesfées. But that's what I'm seeing down there." She shuddered. "Hunger. Something about this factory is very hungry."

Frontenac nodded. Guichet blew out a trembling breath.

"We've faced a vampire," Têtue reminded them. She put her hands on her hips and looked down at the sidewalk. After a tense minute, she bent down and began removing her boots.

Frontenac took Léon by the shoulders and turned him away. "Léon, please be so kind as to grant a bit of privacy."

Léon sputtered protests, then insistent "I'm sorry, but—" apologies, but the others understood what was about to happen. They shielded Têtue as she stripped and stuffed her clothing into her boots.

Justine always enjoyed watching Têtue turn from sturdy, muscular woman to a sleek, lithe, black-haired wolf with a luxuriant, black-tipped bright tail. Her body seemed to fall into itself. Fur swiftly, fluidly emerged from her skin as her squarish face reshaped around her wolf-eyes to present a bright lower mask and throat, and her ears lined in velvety light as well. Yet, throughout her transformation, her flux lines remained a brilliant gold.

Léon couldn't speak. He looked from one to another, but they all solemnly nodded. Têtue nosed his leg, then trotted down the alley. Guichet and Frontenac followed.

Justine took Léon's arm. "Please, monsieur, I may need your support."

Léon hastened to provide assistance but remained silent as they proceeded into the rapacious void of the Marteau factory. His dark blue flux lines gained a new stripe she couldn't identify.

Têtue stopped at the workers' entrance. When Guichet opened the door, Têtue balked and herded them back. Cautiously she sniffed about the doorway and ventured inside. The others slowly followed, descending a short stairway. Frontenac winced and Têtue whined as they reached the floor.

Justine clung tightly to Léon, but as she stepped from the bottom step to the concrete, blindness consumed her. She dropped into a well. Swallowed by the dark, Justine screamed. She could no longer feel Léon's arm.

She was falling, falling upward into an interminable darkness. She couldn't breathe. Hot white flashes flew past like shooting stars, but she was the one hurtling through the icy vacuum of night. She choked for air; there was none. She would die.

The flashes became a glowing white tunnel with an incandescent sun at its end. As Justine closed her eyes, surrendering to death, there was nothing but light.

Then silence. Peaceful. Soothing. Dreamlike.

Justine drifted on a cushion of stars and placid waves of colors. Fear vanished. Newness and wonder vanished. A nightmare ended, and she dreamed serenity, familiarity, home.

Yes, home, where she belonged. Not the farm. Not even Bellesfées. Here, wherever here was, she belonged with her whole being. Colors surrounded her, embraced her, caressed her, nourished her like a womb from which she hoped never to be birthed.

Peaceful silence was then broken by a ragged voice. "Montpellier?"

"Hmm?"

"Montpellier, how are you here?"

Piqued, Justine opened her eyes.

Jacqueline Duval stood before her, hands on hips, gogglers on her brow, and a welding torch at the ready.

10.

Montpellier gazed about at the factory bay and the machinery that surrounded Jacqueline. "I was in the Marteau ironworks," the girl said in surprise.

Jacqueline was too tired to question anything anymore. She pulled her gogglers down and bent to her welding.

The ghost of Montpellier persisted. "Where and when are you?"

"Sharp's Manchester factory, 1840. I'm trying to get back to Orléans, but I don't know when I'll manage to finish this."

The apparition floated above the machine, examining it. "It looks like what Têtue is building," Montpellier said. "She found your plans. They say it'll be done by midnight."

Jacqueline sighed. "Of what day? How long have I been gone?"

"Just today, one day. It's evening now. How did I get here, Duval? Why can I see you?" Montpellier put out her hand as if to feel the air. "And why don't your colors move?"

"Colors don't move."

"Your flux lines. Nothing moves. But the metal does. Your machine. It looks like Têtue."

Montpellier reached for her, but she seemed stuck, as Jacqueline had been stuck, first outside the drift, then in the metal coffin.

"You're not really here, are you?" Jacqueline groaned. She'd been working ceaselessly for days with too little sleep, afraid to close her eyes and find herself somewhen else. "Flux lines, eh? You know about those?"

"Madame Llewellyn said I could see the flux lines of the aether."

At the thought of Angélique, tears burned Jacqueline's eyes. She set the torch down again and lifted her spectacles. She dried her eyes on an oily rag and blew her nose.

"Frontenac said you were crying, before," Montpellier said. "She could hear you when you were inside the aether, but not now, or at the coal pit."

Jacqueline shuddered, fighting her desire to flop down and have a good cry in the company of a familiar face. She lifted her gaze to Montpellier, studying her appearance with doubt.

"Your face," Jacqueline said. "Is that really you?"

Montpellier covered her bare face with her hands. "I fell. My bandages fell off."

Jacqueline stared. "No, here, wherever you are, your face is healed. It's perfect."

Montpellier took her hands away. Her pink round cheeks reddened, and she cocked her head.

Jacqueline chewed the inside of her cheek. "Zut."

Could Montpellier have healed so quickly? She suspected the girl survived her torture because of Mircalla's blood, but her skin had remained ravaged with scar tissue that Jacqueline assumed would take weeks, maybe months to heal. Yet, here she was, fresh-faced, sprayed with a few freckles, with no blemish.

It was just a dream after all. Bitterness returned.

"Mon Dieu, I've gone too long today." Jacqueline sagged against the machine, her arms spread along its surface in a cold embrace. "I'll find you, my love," she whispered.

Jacqueline closed the blow lamp, slung her gogglers over an exhaust pipe, and stalked off the factory floor with Montpellier's voice echoing in her ears, calling her, begging her to come back. Come back to what? Delusion and disappointment. Hope where none could exist.

As Jacqueline got to the exit, Beyer met her on his way in. "I came to see if you needed anything to eat," he said. He offered her a packet.

Jacqueline could smell the meat pasties wrapped within. Her hands trembled as she accepted gratefully. "I'm starting to hallucinate," she said. "I thought I'd better put dangerous tools away before I blow something up."

While Beyer looked over her progress, Jacqueline sat on a crate and ate, uttering appreciative *mmms* as she savored each satisfying bite.

"It's almost complete," Beyer said, nodding in approval. "I pray to God it doesn't kill you."

"I trust the science," Jacqueline replied, "which is not to say I don't appreciate your prayers."

"God is faithful." Beyer hesitated. "I must tell you, however, this science is beyond me, and that's admitting quite a lot. I don't care to work with electricity, and what you're building goes far beyond just electricity. What do you hope to accomplish with such an endeavor?"

Jacqueline took a moment to swallow the last bite. "Well, the original idea was to create a magnetic field around another field of organic electrical forces to combine and focus them, be able to direct them. But as I began to work on it, I realized I had to find a way to interweave the fields to create a concentrated force that would pierce the surrounding aethers, so I can get back to my time and my place. In my original plans—"

Jacqueline halted. "But wait," she said. "How did Montpellier know about my plans?"

What was it Montpellier had said? Têtue was building a machine in Orléans. But the plans in her pocket were not completed. How then? Oh, she should not have dismissed Montpellier! What were those women up to? Did Goüin have anyone on his staff capable of finishing one of her designs?

Beyer's moustaches twitched. "Who is Montpellier? Someone was here?"

Jacqueline's brow furrowed, pressuring her nagging headache. "How could Frontenac hear me when I wasn't anywhere? How did Montpellier see me when she wasn't here? I'm not hallucinating. I'm not hearing voices. How did they find me in the aether? Or *through* it?"

Beyer studied her worriedly.

Jacqueline stood. "Beyer, I realize tea is the national drink of England, but is there any place that has good, strong coffee?"

"Coffee? Why, yes. Quite good, in fact, at the entry of St. Anne's Square. I'll take you there."

"No, I can't leave the floor. I need to finish this quickly, tonight, if possible. Could you—?"

"Of course."

Jacqueline gripped his hand. "You've been so good to me, Beyer. I hope one day soon to return your kindness."

Beyer smiled. "Kindness is not for the returning, but for the turning, to others."

Her shoulders drooped again. "If I get home again," she said. Then she shook off her melancholy. "*When.* When I get home."

Jacqueline watched him leave, then hurried back to the machine. The huge disc she had connected to the cage would not be sufficient to generate the energy she needed to create a large enough counterforce field. She needed more power, or a way to keep the counterflow from siphoning away what was generated.

But Montpellier's crossing had given her a spark of an idea: two discs, parallel to one another, with opposite magnetic polarization, so the flux alternated from one to the other, providing energy without loss of power. She'd need twice the amount of inventory she'd already appropriated, plus a metal belt that would drive them relative to each other to balance the magnetic flux. It should work, providing a far more powerful, consistent current to the cage.

Better still, use a series of smaller paired discs. Smaller discs would rotate faster, but how many would it take to surpass the output of the larger discs? She would need more electrical current than—

Ooh…

Electro-magnets. Driving the power into the rotors. A constant rotation of electro-magnetized discs in opposite directions, creating electricity to power the greater parallel discs in opposite directions, transferring power to a belt that would be wired to the cage. The output could be enormous, certainly enough to generate excitation within the cage itself and intensify the animal magnetism of the subject.

Subject?

Person.

Jacqueline.

Jacqueline waggled her hands and stamped her feet to quicken her circulation. Têtue was building a machine in an attempt to accomplish the same goal: crossing the aether. Jacqueline wondered if she should be concentrating on receiving the flux from the 1843 site. If Goüin and his team stayed within the parameters of her original design, it would only enhance the basic magnetism of one of the women. Certainly not enough to cross the aether.

Not that Jacqueline knew what was required to cross the aether, other than the needless and horrific deaths of children, it would seem. She rubbed her brow, trying to erase the heart-breaking memory of Walmesley's friendly grin.

But if Jacqueline wasn't hallucinating, Montpellier had crossed the aether upon entering the Marteau ironworks. It could not be coincidence; the "source of the pestilential exhalations," as Llewellyn had so eloquently phrased it, figured in the sudden appearance of two separate portals.

Jacqueline was sure the ironworks had not been in Orléans ten days earlier, when she had flown *Esprit* to retrieve the guests for Angélique's wedding reception from the Orléans train station. There was something diabolical in so swift a construction, so mephitic an excretion within the soot and smoke. *"Burnt flesh,"* Llewellyn had said. *"Blood and flesh,"* Têtue had said.

What connected it all to the Husker disaster?

Coal; yes, that much she could see. Coal from Husker fueling the factory in Manchester, perhaps? But she was three years removed from the disaster, and two years away from the Marteau ironworks. Something else held her here in Manchester.

In the short week at the Sharp factory so far, she had seen terrible accidents and gruesome deaths befall child laborers, grisly enough to make her glad she operated her own forge. Enough to make her question taking on apprentices like Frontenac, Guichet, and Montpellier. She could not risk another's life or limb for her own ambitions.

Angélique believed the esprit frappeur had been raised by the release of the girls' combined history of distress, but Jacqueline now believed it more probably was the result of Mircalla's meddling with the girls' magnetic resonance within the aether. Somehow the vampire had dragged more than twenty girls with her to Bellesfées across a hundred kilometers. How else could that be accomplished except by transporting them through the nebulous space between time and space? That's why Mircalla had forced the girls to feed on her: so they could transverse the aether as easily as the vampire did.

Jacqueline, too, had crossed through twice now. Montpellier had crossed it, and she said Frontenac could hear Jacqueline when she was lost. Where was the logic path? Jacqueline had followed the ghostly cries of the victims of industry. If the aether was the continuity of energies in constant flux binding reality with animal magnetism, why was the torture of children the secret to unraveling its bonds?

"God forfend," Jacqueline muttered.

She pulled off her welding cap and massaged her aching head. She had almost become inured to the pain after a week of constant stress, but it felt good to stir the cells, as if tapping internal voltaic piles to charge her own engines.

Jacqueline sat up with a sudden spark.

Of course! Electrical energy. Pain was the noxious stimulus of the nerves, like an electrical charge. Jacqueline had been so focused on engineering, she had overlooked the biochemical sources of electricity. Animal electricity, as Galvani and Volta had proven. That must be the electricity generating animal magnetism. Tightly connected cells, like copper coils around iron. In effect, it was animal electro-magnetism.

That explained all of it. Ghosts might be souls galvanized to this life because of their pain. The esprit frappeur, with the force of a thunderbolt, had its source in the tightly wound pain of the abused girls released from the aether. The agony of the children drowned and crushed in a coal drift touched the pain their cries evinced in Jacqueline's heart. Montpellier's psychic ability to sense the flux lines had somehow crippled her in Marteau's factory, enabling her to cross the aether to touch Jacqueline's desperation.

Jacqueline's mind raced with excitement. If only she had the means to test her theory before applying it to her design. How much pain could one endure before producing sufficient animal electro-magnetism? Was pain the only stimulus the aether accepted?

Questions flew up, snapping at pieces of thoughts for their answers like seagulls snapping at yesterday's fish. Were fish — No, wait — pain. Bof, she was tired. Was noxious stimulus necessary? Could salubrious stimulus, even pleasurable or erogenous, produce the same output of energy?

Erogenous stimulus she had not felt in what seemed like forever.

That last night — just last night, if Montpellier had truly visited her — in de Guise's arms. In de Guise's bed. Pleasure that coursed through her and quickened every nerve in her body, making every cell tingle with breathless ecstasy. Enough to light all of Paris. The very memory kindled fire in her innermost parts and in her breasts, stiffening her nipples. Jacqueline pressed her knees together to still her sudden desperate urge.

But it was 1840. Jacqueline would not meet de Guise for another two years. She could not have known such pleasure yet, and unless she succeeded, she never would again.

The pain of that prospect could also light all of Paris.

The boy who had brought her tea a week ago returned and set up a large silver coffee pot on the table beside her worktable. "Milk and sugar, miss?" he asked.

"Just milk, Varney."

"It's 'Sam,' miss," he said with a chuckle. "Varney's my older brother. It's terrible to have a name from the blood dreadfuls, yeh?"

Yet another vampire tale. Jacqueline smiled as he handed her a cup. "I have a sister. I miss her." She blinked quickly. "I miss—everyone."

"Yer far from home, yeh?"

"Farther than you know, Sam. And shouldn't you be home in bed by now? You were here at six this morning. That's a long day."

"Long enough, miss. It's a job, yeh?"

Jacqueline frowned. The boy couldn't be more than nine years old. She suspected Beyer had set him the task of tending to her needs, and he would rest when she rested. She finished her coffee in a single gulp and looked woefully at the delicate porcelain cup, less than two hundred milliliters. "I don't suppose you have something bigger than this?"

Sam grinned. "I'll fetch a pint mug." He trotted toward the door.

Jacqueline held up the odd ring-shaped doughy pastry he'd brought with the coffee. "What are these?"

"Mum calls 'em dimsdales," he said on his way out. "Fried sweet dough boiled in hog fat, but they cook through nice with the hole in 'em. I like 'em 'cause they're easier to hold when you dip 'em in your coffee."

Jacqueline stared at the toroidal treat. Once again, the seagulls started diving.

If she were to use an iron torus…

Jacqueline finished tightening the last nut. She straightened and was startled to realize she was at least fifteen meters from the floor. She scratched her head. As usual, she was not sure how she'd got there.

Jacqueline surveyed the project, from the elegant Faraday cage of fine copper mesh, with a velvet sling that would suspend her comfortably within the electro-magnetic field, to graduated echelons of discs, cogs, sprockets, cables, coils, tubes, tori, and brushes. Her eyes traced the route of power from the initiator through the Jacquard trans-coordinator, up into the para-rotators. Static transducers would then take electricity from the alternating magnetic fields generated by the para-rotators to the augmentationary coils that drove the two hundred tertiary discs, sending it two-hundred-fold into the automatonic re-binders that lined the cage and refocused the power through dynamic coils into the subject's own magnetic field.

If that didn't excitate animal electro-magnetism, she couldn't fathom what else could.

Jacqueline sat at the edge of the exhaust flume and wiped her brow. When she closed her eyes, sine waves flickered behind her eyelids. She could no longer remember de Guise's pretty bowed lips, his smile, his face, what he felt like pressed against her body. She could no longer remember what it was to ache for him; she just ached.

Jacqueline slid down the flume and out the open hatch at the bend near the bottom. She was too tired to go back to her rooms. It was almost four in the morning. Almost time for shift change in the other bays, maybe another three hours before Beyer reported for work. She had time for a short nap. She yanked her boots off and emptied her pockets into them. Then she climbed into the sling inside the cage and curled up, settling into a position that accommodated her stiffness and strain. The steady *whirr* of shafts and wheels spelled the song of crickets and nightbirds of Bellesfées. She slept.

"Madame Duval."

Jacqueline scratched her nose and snuggled back down into the sling. She swatted the hand that shook her arm and rolled over.

"Madame Duval?"

"Go away," she mumbled.

"Madame Duval, réveillez-vous!"

Jacqueline startled and sat up so suddenly she tipped out of the sling to land on the cement floor.

"Aïe!"

She rubbed her hip and glared up at the man who had awakened her. Corpulent, close to sixty years of age, she guessed, with a bulbous nose ruddied by dissipation, and more wattle than neck. He was dressed in a suit complete of fine wool; not a workman then.

"When am I?" Jacqueline said, allowing him to help her to her feet. "You speak French. Who are you?"

She blinked about, trying to orient herself. Beyer and Sam stood apart, near the coffee pot. Neither looked happy.

"Madame Duval, do you mind explaining yourself?" the rude man demanded. He waved his arm at the massive construct surrounding them. "We make locomotives here, not whatever the hell this is."

Jacqueline pushed past the man and lumbered unsteadily toward the coffee. "You make haunted locomotives," she said. "I'm here to fix them." She opened the spigot and sighed blissfully as fresh steaming coffee filled her pint mug. "Bless you, Sam. Any more dimsdales?"

"Oh, yes, miss." Sam left, glad to be escaping the brewing storm.

Jacqueline lightened her coffee and gulped some down. She had to admit, the man showed patience with her. She relented.

"I'm working the Orléans side of the rail," she replied, which was not untrue. "Some of the parts that came in showed irregularities, and Goüin asked me to look into it. Unfortunately, my own workshop was destroyed in a fire, and so I came back to the source to see what I could do." She drank more coffee. "Your turn. Who are you?"

"What sort of irregularities?" he asked. "Goüin said nothing to me."

"Not yet." She rolled her eyes and answered, "He consulted me first because I was close by, and he trusts I can resolve the issues. I'm very good at what I do." She set her mug down and folded her arms. "And at my own expense I traveled to Manchester to attend to it first-hand. I've been working on the solution for days now, and I've just completed the mechanism that will set Goüin's mind at ease."

"She also gave Roberts a key bit of insight for his piece," Beyer volunteered.

The man's mouth twitched. "Did she?" he sneered.

Jacqueline's eyes widened. Then she grinned. "You don't know who I am, do you? Well, monsieur, it would seem we are even. I don't know you either."

"In brief, I own this factory, Madame Duval. I'm—"

"Oh, so you're the one who hires little ones to work to death," she snapped. "Pays too little for them to feed themselves. Sends them to tend machinery that crushes fingers and breaks their bones and slams them into grinding wheels. Yes," she cut him off again, "I saw it yesterday. Another Mary Richards chewed up and spat out in a bloodied heap. The whole damned child population of this town looks like your soldiers returning from Afghanistan. How do you justify their deaths and maimings, monsieur? How do you face yourself in the mirror?"

Jacqueline took up her coffee again. "Answer that, and I'll justify my actions to you. Meanwhile, I fight the evil that presents itself." She picked up her boots on her way back into the cage. "Come bother me again after I've saved the Paris-Orléans."

"Mademoiselle!" he shouted. "The railway to Orléans hasn't even been built yet. I insist you cease this work and leave the premises. Beyer, this woman deceived you. Get this charlatan out of there."

Jacqueline felt guilty she'd put Beyer in an awkward position. The rude man was obviously his superior at some level, at least in rank. She shut the cage door and strode to the control panel of the machine.

"Work has already ceased, Monsieur Whoever-you-are. I suggest you clear the floor, gentlemen," she called. "Once the initiator commences, the capacitator will begin the charge, and you do not want to be in this bay when that happens."

Beyer cleared his throat. "Please, Mr. Armand, the woman knows what she is about, and she does have Roberts' blessing. Her work is highly regarded throughout the continent."

"We're not on the continent," the rude man retorted. "There must be at least fifty thousand pounds' worth of machinery here."

"Send the bill to Bellesfées," Jacqueline said. Then she halted and whirled to glare at the man. "Armand? Rodolphe Armand?"

The man who had accused her of stealing machinery from him and laid a lawsuit at her feet two years ago. This year. 1840. She grinned, wicked mischief filling her head.

"Oh, monsieur, I beg you, come to Bellesfées to collect your fifty thousand pounds. That's twenty thousand in francs, isn't it? I will be pleased to pay whatever I owe once you come to Bellesfées."

Still chuckling, Jacqueline dumped out her boots and put them on. She stuffed her pockets again, then donned her cap and gogglers before beginning a final inspection, determined to ignore the rants of Mr. Armand, although at least now she understood a piece of his delusional lawsuit against her.

His accusations of deceitful apprentices, however, worried her. How could the women of the Order be involved in her plans here in 1840? How had Montpellier crossed the aether?

Jacqueline tried to dismiss the obvious, that Têtue's efforts in 1843 would bring them all here and to Armand's attention, but the suspicion nagged at her as she continued her systems check. Marthe had once, long ago, warned her, "One day you'll have a daughter just like you, and you'll wonder how I put up with you." Now Jacqueline had four such daughters. She sighed.

Armand bellowed, "Are you going to stop her or not, Beyer?"

Jacqueline laughed. "I tell you, there's nothing you can do to stop me."

She hoped the financier would not take any immediate retribution against Beyer or the Sharp factory. She'd hate to return to a future where there was no Paris-Orléans Railroad. How then would she ever meet de Guise? Or rather, how would she have ever met de Guise? Will she have met… Will meet…

"Zut!" she roared. With a furious shake of her head, Jacqueline went back to the machine.

Sam returned with a plate of dimsdales. He watched wide-eyed as Jacqueline once again traced the elements that would serve to conduct the power through to the Faraday cage.

"Beyer, you may be Roberts' pet engineer, but this is beyond outrage," Armand warned. "I'll see you shipped back to Saxony if you don't put a stop to this."

Jacqueline came to the cage door and nodded to Sam. The boy brought her dimsdales and took her empty mug.

"Good luck, miss," he said.

"Thank you, Sam. I hope to see you again in a few years." She bit into a pastry and *mmm*ed. "Gentlemen, last chance. Once I finish my salubrious stimuli, I'm initiating. If you respect electricity as I do, you'll take yourselves out of here. Now!"

Armand gripped his grizzled hair in fury. "Madame Duval, I will have you in court!"

Yes, you will. And if this works, you'll lose.

Jacqueline savored a second dimsdale. If all went according to her design, she'd be safe in de Guise's arms again within the hour.

De Guise!

Jacqueline had to focus on de Guise to initiate the right stimulus deep within her most intimate part. The sugary dimsdale set her on the path to delight, but she had to heighten physical pleasure, intensify stimulus in her erogenous regions to create enough animal electromagnetism to interweave with the Faraday field. She downed the last dimsdale and wiped sugar from her hands. Sugar was sweet, but de Guise was salty, spicy.

Alain.

In bed, together, skin to skin, she called him Alain. Her legs wrapping his, her body quivering in waves, she would cry his name: *Alain.*

"Initiating!" she cried.

"I am warning you, Madame Duval."

"No, my dear Mr. Armand, I'm warning you. Those children's blood is on your hands. If you don't fix it, you will be ruined."

Jacqueline pulled down the cover of the initiator and cranked for ignition. Sparks flew from the panel. The engine ground, then buzzed to life. As coils transformed to electro-magnets, discs spun like mill saws. Arcs of electricity clutched at the perimeter of the cage, lunging upward and falling in a cascade of lights. Every hair on Jacqueline's body rose in response. She climbed into the sling and nestled down, hidden from view by the massive engineering.

Beyer hastily bustled Sam and Armand out of the bay. Good. She didn't want anyone witnessing the next phase of the plan.

11.

FRONTENAC CRADLED MONTPELLIER IN THE ALLEY, AND GUICHET STROKED her hair while Léon stood watch. Têtue paced around him despite the scent of fear he put up, pausing to check on Montpellier and occasionally whining.

"Shouldn't we go back?" Guichet asked anxiously, but no one answered her, and Têtue wasn't about to concede.

Frontenac sighed, exasperated. "I could hear her when she was on the train, when we couldn't see her. I can't hear her now. She has to be beyond the aether."

Têtue shook herself. *"Like Duval. Maybe they're together,"* she mused.

Frontenac gasped and turned to her. "I heard that," she said in surprise. "The duchess said you wolves could speak to one another, but I never heard her do it."

Têtue licked her maw, disturbed at the thought. *"Huh."*

Léon muttered to himself.

"I heard that too, Léon," Frontenac said, frowning. "No, your comfortable world is not so small as it was yesterday. We are the Order of Duval, and you're very fortunate we're on the side of Good."

Têtue raised her head. De Guise was coming. She trotted to the end of the alley and paced a circle. When he caught sight of her and Léon, he hastened, and she drew him to where Montpellier lay.

"Justine! What have you girls been up to?" He crouched beside Frontenac and put his hand to Montpellier's brow.

Léon scowled. "That's all you have to say?" he demanded. "With a wolf in our midst?"

"Tell me what happened," de Guise said.

"She fainted." Léon shrugged.

Têtue gruffed at him.

Frontenac raised her hand to calm Têtue. "She said it was dark down this alley, that she couldn't see anything, and that the factory was—hungry. She felt blind. She leaned on Léon as we entered, but she no sooner set foot inside when she collapsed."

"You've been gone two hours," de Guise said. "How long—"

"Almost an hour," Guichet answered.

"I want you all back at Goüin's."

De Guise took Montpellier into his arms and stood. She moaned. Her eyes fluttered open and she smiled weakly.

"Sharp's Manchester factory, 1840," she said with a sigh. Then she caressed de Guise's face and traced his jaw. "I'll find you, my love."

Têtue shook herself and her ears twitched forward. She nosed de Guise.

Montpellier nestled against de Guise's chest. "Sharp's Manchester factory, 1840," she repeated as if lost in a dream. "I'll find you, my love."

"That was Duval," Frontenac whispered, "not Justine."

"I realize that," de Guise said through clenched teeth. "But is she here, within Justine, or is Justine there with her?" He gazed up at the devilish airship overhead. "I need to learn what's behind this Marteau fellow. Vincent, summon a fiacre." He glanced around. "And Adèle, grab Têtue's boots."

Têtue waited in the alley while de Guise bundled the others into the fiacre. Léon gave her one last look. Têtue shook herself. She was not leaving de Guise if he was going after Marteau.

De Guise knelt and gently combed back her ears and scritched them. "Têtue, the machine. It's designed for the four of you. You should be with them."

Têtue bared her fangs, glaring with fierce brown eyes.

De Guise grinned. "I didn't think so." He closed the fiacre door. "P-O factory," he told the driver, handing him some coins. "Hurry."

The fiacre took off. Têtue padded back to the back entrance alley.

"All right," said de Guise. "Let's see what trouble we can get into."

The duke and duchess greeted the fiacre. The duke took Montpellier inside while Frontenac explained to the duchess. Léon stood aside. His pinched expression saddened Guichet. She hesitantly laid her hand on his arm, fearful she would sense revulsion from him as she had in Laval's shop. She was thankful to feel nothing but the man's turmoil.

"She said they were half-wolf," Léon said. "I thought she was mocking me."

Guichet had no answer for him. "None of us is what we appear to be, Monsieur Vincent, and I am sorry."

"For what?" He waved, his frown bitter. "In a world where locomotives can vanish and women can turn into wolves, what have you to apologize for? You're not to blame for anyone's presumptions, Madame Guichet. I'm a polytech. I should know better than to make them."

He sighed with regret, but he offered half a smile. "Let's see to your friend. You must be worried, and I shouldn't be distracting you." He rubbed the back of his neck. "As I understand things, if you become too upset, objects tend to fly about the room. Not a safe skill in the middle of construction."

Guichet blushed and looked away. "I'm sorry," she murmured again.

"Talents are a kind of power, and one thing we learn at the Polytechnique, power is something to be mastered. The duke tells me you learned of your skill only today, so all you lack is training." Then he shrugged. "Not that I know anyone who could train you. But it's worth some research, don't you think?"

Guichet nodded and smiled back at him. "Please don't hate Têtue for who she is," she said. "Like all of us in the Order of Duval, she's suffered a most horrific assault. But you must believe me, she's a selfless and generous soul."

He released her and kissed her hand. "As are you, madame."

He rejoined the work crew. Guichet breathed a sigh of relief. She had hurt no one in the exchange, and no one had hurt her. Guichet hastened to where the duchess and Frontenac were trying to ply Montpellier with water. Frontenac wept, pleading quietly to Montpellier to waken, while the duke argued with the duchess.

"If he wanted you with him, he'd have said so," the duchess insisted.

The duke fumed. "But he wouldn't, fy nghariad. He's accustomed to working on his own. That's his nature."

"Then he must be sorely vexed that Têtue remained at his side. I know I am." She grabbed his arm as he turned to go. "Please, my love. Be careful."

The duke kissed her. Guichet observed with a mixture of admiration and envy. His tenderness and the duchess's concern for him signaled a conjugal passion she could never have imagined possible between man and woman.

When he left, the duchess groaned quietly, shaking her head. She buried her face in her hands, then wrapped her arms around her stomach. Guichet felt a twinge of jealousy; she understood the duchess was uncomfortable, but oh, to be with child… Guichet sighed.

Montpellier suddenly sat up and blinked about. "No. No, that's not right," she said. She pointed to the construct. "Duval's is much bigger. That's not going to be enough."

Madame Llewellyn gave a cry of relief. "Justine, where have you been?"

Frontenac hugged her friend as Montpellier took a moment to orient herself. "I fell into a tunnel. I thought I died, but then I found Duval. She's building her machine as well, but it's quite different from ours."

Guichet ran back to tell Monsieur Vincent, who in turn relayed the news to Coquelet.

Coquelet whirled on her, angry.

"Bigger?"

A one-meter pipe clanged across the floor.

"Sorry! I'm sorry!" Guichet wrung her hands.

The workmen looked at her in confusion; she was nowhere near the pipe.

Coquelet strode over to consult with Montpellier, followed by Monsieur Goüin and Léon. "How much bigger?" he asked. "Show me what we need to do."

Montpellier scooted off the crate and led them to the cage. "This was about three times the size." She then assessed the machinery. "That's not the same at all."

Coquelet hurled a wrench across the floor. The clatter could barely be heard above the deafening noise around them. "She's had three years to augment her original design and build. We've had twelve hours. Wasted!"

Frontenac quickly hugged Montpellier again.

"Maybe not," Goüin said. "Duval designed this for four girls."

"Women," Monsieur Vincent corrected him.

"Yes, women. She may have augmented on her end because she's by herself." Monsieur Goüin pulled at his lip.

"But she hasn't had three years," Montpellier argued. "She asked how many days she's been gone, so she's only thinking in terms of days."

The duchess smirked. "With Jacky, three days are the same as three years in someone else's time. Justine, can you describe the machine you saw, and maybe these gentlemen can deduce what changes are needed?"

Montpellier hesitated, then nodded and followed the men, with Frontenac at her side.

Guichet took Montpellier's place next to the duchess. She sighed. "I tossed that pipe," she admitted.

"I know, dear."

"Monsieur Vincent tells me power is something to be mastered," she said. "You learned to master your gift, madame. How can I control what I don't know I'm doing? I'd like to be able to help, too."

Madame Llewellyn took a while to answer, but finally she said, "I had to feel it inside. Sense when my emotions were getting the better of me and I was losing myself. That's when the wolf would take over. Oddly, it was usually when I was happy, not angry; although," she hastened to add, "rage is almost impossible to control. Even more difficult once I become wolf." She smacked the crate. "That's why I'm so frustrated with Têtue running off on her own. She hasn't really had time to learn such control."

Guichet shook her head. "Têtue's more controlled than any of us. She was able to break Mircalla's hold when the rest of us couldn't. I trust her to take care of herself."

"Yes, I suppose you're right." The duchess then smiled at Guichet. "But, Renée, I saw you on Monsieur Vincent's arm. That didn't upset you?"

Guichet caught her breath. Wonder stole back into her thoughts. "I… Well, no." She reflected on the past hours. "It was like walking on Monsieur de Guise's arm, or the duke's."

"And you don't find that curious?" The duchess shifted back on the crate to lean against the wall. Guichet did likewise. "Perhaps you have another gift you don't know you possess."

"Monsieur Blanchet, in Laval's shop, was just as nice. And yet—" She shivered again.

"Watch it, Bardît!" Sançille bellowed from atop the machine. "That hurt, putain!" He gripped his arm.

Bardît's eyes narrowed. He stood more than four meters from Sançille, on a lower level. "And you will set a guard over your tongue, Monsieur Sançille, for the sake of the women here."

Sançille glowered at Montpellier and Frontenac, who merely shook their heads in disdain.

"Oh!" Guichet covered her mouth. She whispered to the duchess, "I did that, too."

Madame Llewellyn grinned. "Let's see if we can find out why. Justine, Adèle," she called. When they came to her she asked quietly, "Justine, what do you see in Monsieur Sançille?"

Montpellier giggled behind her hand. "He's purplish grey with jagged lines of black."

Frontenac sniffed. "He thinks we're morons."

The duchess's eyes widened. "Justine, you learned the names of colors. Aren't you clever? There you have it, Renée. Your gift isn't just moving things about randomly, but delivering punishment to those who deserve it."

They all sniggered except Guichet. She felt her face grow hot. "That's not very useful," she complained. "How can that possibly help find Duval?"

Frontenac hopped onto the crate to put her arm around her. "That's easy, Guichet. Montpellier as much as told us Marteau's ironworks is a pit of death. The wolves already said it stinks of death. Think of it. You might have the power to shut it down. Put an end to whatever evil created those pieces of machinery in there."

"If nothing else," Montpellier added as she climbed up next to the duchess, "you can hit Sançille with a wrench again. He's not very nice."

"That's not very nice," Guichet retorted. "In the tailor shop, Monsieur Blanchet was very sweet." Recalling the moment, she drew a sharp breath. "Oh." She forced herself to control her revulsion. "He wanted to hold onto me. He persisted."

The duchess wrinkled her nose. "Like Mircalla persisted after Jacqueline."

"Selfish. Possessive." Frontenac rolled her eyes. "I've known those men. He wasn't mindful of you, only that he wanted you." She grinned. "That will serve you well if ever you do want to marry again. You can choose someone you are sure cares for you more than himself."

Guichet still frowned. "I suppose it's a comfort to know the key to my power, but I would prefer to know how I can use it for the good of the Order of Duval."

"You know what Jacky says," the duchess reminded her. "There's always a way for the daughters of Bellesfées."

Guichet nodded. "Maybe if I get angry enough, I can throw myself up to that airship to see what secrets it holds."

"No!" Montpellier and Frontenac both cried.

"Please, don't. I felt nothing but horror emanating from that ship," Frontenac said.

Montpellier gripped Guichet's hand. "If you had seen what I saw, you wouldn't say such things."

"But don't you understand?" Guichet insisted. "That's exactly why we should be investigating it. Whoever this Marteau is, his factory is responsible for Duval being snatched from us. Têtue knew that. Monsieur de Guise knows that too. We should be there."

The duchess closed her eyes, pressing her hand to her brow. "In daylight, I would agree. It's late. I know I'm utterly exhausted."

"We wouldn't let you go anyway," Guichet said. "Têtue knew what she was saying."

Frontenac patted the duchess's knee. "Your Grace, I can tell you aren't feeling up to this, but we are."

"But you girls must also be tired. Justine, tell me truthfully. You're still healing. You've crossed the aether twice now, and it took over an hour to revive you this second time. You must feel it."

Reluctantly, Montpellier nodded.

The duchess slid from the crate and began to gather her possessions. "Monsieur Goüin," she called and waved to get his attention above the noise. When he came to her, she asked, "Given your new parameters, how much longer do you anticipate the project will take? Do we women have time for some sleep? I want them rested before they embark on the experiment."

Goüin looked them over and nodded. "There are rooms by my office."

"We have nearby lodgings, monsieur."

He bowed and bent back to the work. The women took up their purchases for the day — mostly stays, corsets, bustles, and shoes along with Guichet's ribbons and buttons. Frontenac didn't seem as disappointed as Guichet thought she would be as they climbed into the fiacre and headed to the park where *Esprit* sat, invisible in the dark. The driver wasn't happy about letting them descend in the abandoned park so close to midnight, but the duchess's louis d'or cheered him, and he promised to return for them by eight the next morning.

"No need, monsieur," the duchess told him blithely. "I doubt we will have risen by then." But she winked to the three women.

Frontenac rapped on *Esprit*'s hull below the gangway. In a few moments they heard Monsieur Claque's heavy tread up the ladder from belowdecks and across the main deck. He lowered the gangplank into place, and they embarked.

"Unmoor us and weigh anchor, Claque," Madame Llewellyn said. "Adele, take us up above the smokestacks."

The young women laughed. They hurriedly stowed their parcels while the duchess brought out the well-stocked basket their housekeeper had provided. As Monsieur Claque opened the hydrogen tanks wide, *Esprit* left the ground. Guichet assisted Monsieur Claque at the capstans to set course for the nearby ironworks. The autonomaton then led her to the revolver-gun turret, a weapon Duval had designed. He tipped his head, asking permission.

"Last resort," Guichet said. She returned to partake of the midnight pique-nique.

"We are not heading into a battle, ladies," the duchess told them. "I wish to get close enough to the factory to speak with Gryffin. He can tell us what he's found, and whether our assistance is needed."

She turned to Guichet, "Meanwhile, Renée, you are going to do some target practice. I believe we're far enough from the P-O factory to avoid hurting any of our workers."

Excitement flushed Guichet's face. "But how?"

The duchess placed an orange on the bench by the companionway door. "In the past, you would get angry, and the anger seethed in you until the energies burst from you because you didn't know they were there." She pointed to the orange. "And now you do. Earlier today, you were able to reprimand Monsieur Vincent, and rightly so, with a dollop of crème fraîche. Now, I want you to focus on a target for this orange. Not someone you wish to punish, though. See if you can direct it, say, over the railing."

Guichet's heart raced, making her arms tingle. "I don't think I can, madame. How do I find the—energies?"

"Maybe I can help," Montpellier said. "I can see them."

Guichet startled. "You can?"

Montpellier nodded. "Têtue, the duchess, the duke—their flux lines are gold. Yours are bright red, but every once in a while, I see flashes of gold. That must be your power showing through."

She moved behind Guichet and held her shoulders, turning her to face the orange on the bench. "Now instead of thinking angry thoughts about something else, think about the problems we face. Think of how much we need you to help us find Duval. Think of Duval, suffering where she is. Watching those children drown. Hearing their cries for help and not being able to save them. Think of—"

A desperate ache for Duval poured into Guichet's heart and flooded her whole body.

"And there's the gold," Montpellier whispered. "We need to save Duval, who saved us from vampires, who saved the life of our king, who will save the three of us from—"

Montpellier suddenly jumped back with a cry as the orange hurtled through the air to splatter on Monsieur Claque's chest. The autonomaton looked down at the pulp and juice, then looked to Guichet and cocked his head to the side. A puff of steam popped from his casque.

They all burst into laughter. Pride kindled in Guichet.

"I felt the gold!" she cried. "The energies, the power. I still feel it."

The duchess turned her to face Monsieur Claque. "Let's try something else. Focus on the mess and send that over the rail."

"Yes," she said, trembling with excitement. "I think I know what the key is. There's something wrong, and I have to make it right."

Montpellier giggled. "Oh, you are so gold right now."

Guichet looked into Monsieur Claque's visual sensors. "I'm so sorry, Monsieur Claque. Let me help you."

A second later, the juice and pulp floated from Claque's bronze torso over the rail. Montpellier and Frontenac cheered. The duchess uncorked a bottle of wine and offered each of them a glass.

"It's not champagne, but it will serve to celebrate." She poured all around and they raised their glasses.

"To the Order of Duval!" the young women cried.

"To my beautiful fairies," the duchess saluted them with tears brimming in her eyes. "Claque, engage the engines, please. Bring her alongside that merdique airship."

Frontenac drank quickly and joined Monsieur Claque at the ship's wheel. The duchess took Montpellier below decks to show her to her berth and help her apply her skin unguent for the night.

Guichet sipped her wine thoughtfully. Her new role pleased her: the one who would set wrongs to right. Solving problems. Maybe fixing what was broken. If nothing else, saving Duval.

Squeals of delighted laughter from below decks drew her down the ladder to find the duchess and Montpellier in quarters near the salon. Guichet stopped in the doorway and gaped in amazement. Frontenac came up behind her.

The duchess had removed Montpellier's bandages. The tortured skin was completely healed.

"Duval said my face was perfect," Montpellier said. "I thought my bandages had fallen off in my fall through the aether. But look at me!"

Then she sobered, knotting her fingers. "I was blind for fourteen years before I woke up in Bellesfées and I could see. Now I'm completely healed. There's only one explanation. My eyesight. My vision. Now this." She blinked back tears. "Tell me the truth. Did you two have your powers before Mircalla? Did we drink her blood?"

Horror struck Guichet. Her heart thudded heavily, and she trembled. "Oh." She thought back to the frying pan. She had felt exhausted. She could barely get through her chores. The strange rash on her neck. Then Monsieur Guichet complained and… "Oh."

Frontenac took Guichet's hand and set it on Montpellier's, then held Guichet's free hand. "Here we are, thinking ourselves victims of Mircalla, when in fact, she gave us the very gifts we need to save Duval. How is that for triumph?"

Madame Llewellyn wrapped her arms around the trio. "I am so proud of you all," she murmured, her voice catching.

"So we won't be vampires?" Montpellier persisted.

"No, we will not," Guichet hurried to assure her. "Frontenac, the master of thoughts. Me, the master of control. Montpellier, the master of the aether. We'll be the daughters of Bellesfées."

Montpellier tipped her head to Guichet's.

Esprit gave a jerk as the engines ignited in the bowels of the ship. Guichet and Frontenac each kissed Montpellier's perfect cheeks.

"Sleep well, little sister," Frontenac said.

Frontenac and Guichet trotted back up to the main deck. The engines engaged the screw-propellers, and *Esprit* eased forward. This time, Guichet climbed up to the fo'c'sle and leaned into the rail at the bow. Ahead of her loomed the black airship of the Marteau ironworks, where there were wrongs to be righted.

12.

As soon as de Guise stepped onto the ironworks factory floor, his eyes narrowed against the bitter, caustic fumes. He loosened his cravate and used it to muffle a cough, then tied it around his face to filter the filth from the air.

Têtue snuffled her agreement and trotted farther in. The factory roof was a grid of glass windows open to the night, but nothing circulated. There was only the infernal heat, well over forty-five degrees Celsius. Têtue panted and licked her lips. She was glad of her thick pelage to shield her from the suffocating temperature.

Têtue had never seen such a massive production setting, and she had seen several in Paris. The long bay housed ten blast furnaces, five to each side. At the foot of every furnace sat a three-meter trough with twelve half-meter molds to either side, resembling piglets suckling a sow—the image behind the name "pig iron." Two men on each furnace operated the huge tuyeres regulating the heat in the furnace. Overhead, a network of charging bridges of steel grating teemed with barrow-toting children running back and forth to the chimney, like so many ants feeding their queen, dumping loads of charge: charcoal, iron, and limestone in turn.

As Têtue and de Guise slid along the wall toward an exit, Têtue heard a high-pitched cry above the roar of the furnaces from the charging bridge overhead. A barrow toppled, spilling its cargo. Têtue recoiled, growling. A man began beating the child who had tripped and fallen even as the little one tried to crawl away. When he kicked him into the pile he had tipped over, something fell through the grating of the charging bridge and landed at de Guise's feet.

An infant's corpse, stripped of skin.

Têtue snarled and ramped, beyond disgust and anger. A dead baby! Headed to the furnace!

A second corpse dropped on Têtue's back. She leapt up. Before rage could consume her, de Guise wrapped his arms around her, holding her maw closed.

"Chut!" He rubbed his chin against her ear and whispered, "Hold on. Hold on, girl."

She couldn't shake him. She whined, then growled.

"Our time will come." De Guise stroked her head, still nuzzling her ear.

With a huff, she slid to the floor subdued and seething. He released her but continued to stroke her head and along her back. Têtue's eyes fixed on the overhead bridge, where the man who had beaten the child now shoved some of the macabre charge back into the barrow. He righted it and kicked the child again, pointing to the chimney. The child slowly collected the remaining corpses and placed them in the barrow. Têtue moaned softly.

"I know," de Guise murmured. "I see it."

De Guise tugged her ruff, and they continued to the door at the end of the wall. As they entered a hallway the air dropped to bearable heat. The first door on their right opened to an unlit stairwell. They climbed, hoping to reach the roof and access the airship moored there. Têtue counted five huge storeys.

She couldn't erase the image of the infants, no matter how much she shook her head. Their cherubic cheeks and rosebud lips skinned. Skinless corpses. What possible purpose could there be in dumping them as charge into the furnace? What kind of monster were they hunting?

Hungry, Montpellier had said. A hungry monster devouring flesh.

The stairwell egressed to a rooftop, but not the one they sought. They descended a storey, and de Guise cautiously cracked the door, then opened it. The hallway was unlit, and no light showed from beneath the rows of doors on either side. Têtue sniffed the air but found no scent of human presence. She trotted confidently forward. De Guise followed her lead.

As they passed the last door, Têtue halted and returned to it. She smelled something different, less soot, more burnt flesh, with a bitter pungency of chemicals. She snuffled at the cooler air at the bottom of the door, then pawed it and whined.

De Guise tried the handle; it was locked. He took an elegant black-velvet etui of lock picks from his inside coat pocket and applied his expertise from years of espionage.

The door opened to what looked like a combination of a physician's office and a laboratory. Overhead, the ceiling windows gaped open, filtered with a fine mesh, allowing cleaner air to circulate. Through the darkness she perceived the hulk of the pestilential airship hovering above.

They entered furtively. Têtue mistrusted every shadow and looming contraption. Tables lined three walls, with a massive clockwork construct along the side wall that stood a full meter wide and four meters tall, nearly touching the ceiling. On the tables, squat boxes with gauges were topped with long clear tubes full of translucent liquids, or with different sized opaque globes. A brass tree suspended flasks at varying heights beside a table of large beakers, retorts, tubes, and hermetic jars containing —

Têtue put her forepaws up to stand for a better look.

— fetuses suspended in a solution.

When Têtue gagged and turned away, she came nose to nose with a severed head in another jar. Beyond it, more of the grisly collection: hands, feet, eyeballs, organs, entire limbs, and small sheets of skin. Têtue whined and dropped to the floor. She shook herself and panted, but tension gnawed at her stomach. She followed de Guise as he explored the room.

Seven reclined examination chairs radiated from a central upright chair, which was wired to each of the others with thick cables. Each examination chair in turn fed cables to a large metal rectangular case that took up the length of the far wall, like a casket with a domed glass cover. All the chairs had restraints for limbs and a metal band to secure someone's brow. All of it stank of burnt flesh.

Above the central chair, a colossal weapon was suspended from an articulated steel arm. Like a spyglass, eight telescoping sections gradually narrowed from six meters across to a fine needle-like pipette directed at the head of the chair. Têtue leapt up onto the chair to sniff at the pipette. She didn't recognize some of the scent she picked up beyond blood. She hopped down to join de Guise studying the preserved fetuses. She growled.

He shook his head slowly. "Look closer," he said, his face intent.

Reluctantly, she obeyed. To her horror, she saw that the fetuses all exhibited a pulse in their tiny chests.

Têtue paced angrily and nosed de Guise away. It was too ghastly to consider. They had to find the bastard behind it. There was no earthly reason for any iron manufacturer to be using the equipment she saw here, and the abuse of unborn babies was an obscenity she swore to avenge.

De Guise instead investigated further, examining each machine, his eyes busy as if he weighed its possible purpose. Finally, he came to the huge case, setting his hands on the glass lid. Têtue caught a whiff of electricity, and her hackles rose.

So did de Guise's curls.

"Têtue," de Guise said softly, his voice even but strained. "I want you to leave. Now. Quickly. And don't look back. Get Llewellyn."

Têtue growled, then alarm-barked. What made de Guise think she would leave him? She glared, but he didn't move. His hands, resting on the lid, trembled. He exuded a scent of fear. Parbleu, she wasn't going anywhere.

"Now," he rasped. "Jacqueline needs you."

Têtue snarled. *She needs you!*

But the air around her was changing, charging. Her pelage tickled and rose from her skin. She whined, inching away.

Sparks danced around de Guise's fingertips. He clenched his jaw. "Get out!"

Têtue yiped and backed toward the doorway.

"Run!" de Guise cried, his voice shrill. "Tell Llewel—"

The door slammed on her snout, shutting her out of the room. A crackle and hum of ignition was followed by the steady rhythm of a clockwork engine.

What was happening? What was de Guise doing?

Têtue whined and ramped at the door. Inside the room, machinery came alive with a buzz, then a growing rumble. She hurled herself against the door over and over, snarling, barking, gnashing at the wood to no avail. Têtue needed help.

"Tell Llewellyn," de Guise had said. *Foute, yeah!*

Têtue raced up the hallway and came to an open, empty workshop. She prowled around the tables and found steps down to a casting room, where again the temperature climbed over forty. Workers bent over the molten metal didn't see her slink along the wall in shadows. She couldn't find an exit. She panted, suppressing a whine. She made her way back to the steps and slipped under them to await some sign to move.

Têtue eyed the work nearest her. The workers poured white-hot liquid metal into cogged molds; from her vantage, she couldn't tell if they were sprockets or gears, but they were larger than she had seen in any foundry she'd worked. She yawned worriedly. Nothing in this infernal abyss was like anything she had seen before, and all of it was wrong.

What was happening to de Guise?

Têtue's ears flicked. Panting couldn't relieve her fears. Every muscle was coiled to leap at something, someone, anyone. Finally, she caught a familiar whiff. She closed her mouth and sniffed again.

The duke! Where? She got up and paced, and other scents reached her: The Order of Duval. And the lavender soap of the duchess.

Pressing to the wall, she padded upstairs again, through the darkened workshop to the door of the grotesque laboratory. Pistons of an engine chomped and hissed within. She pawed at the door, then sniffed the air flowing from the bottom crack. De Guise's scent was strong, but the duke's scent was not there, though the traces of the women were that much stronger.

Têtue flung herself wildly at the door, snarling like a rabid thing, her maw dripping foam and saliva. The image of those fetuses drove her mad. What if Marteau got hold of the duchess? Têtue's barks became furious roars as she pounded ceaselessly against the unrelenting wood. She rammed her shoulder, yelping when she bruised. Couldn't the women hear her? Or worse, were they lying in those chairs, bound by constraints, feeding that machine? Would that monster somehow sense the duchess's child?

Têtue bark-howled for Llewellyn and the duchess. Again. Her cries resonated throughout the empty hall and workshop. She stood hunched in the darkness, her alarm howl calling over and over. They must hear her! Or someone else would, and she could finally rip someone apart.

The pounding of pistons slowed and stopped. The engine stilled to a drone, a low buzz, and finally a quiet hum. Têtue didn't care. She howled for Llewellyn. She howled for the duchess and her child. She howled for the unconscious Montpellier. She howled and ached to hear their answer. She ached for Duval, the first person in her twenty years to show her respect and kindness and understanding. She couldn't lose her, and she couldn't lose de Guise for Duval's sake. Têtue paced a circle to ease her bruised shoulder, bark-howling, longing for a response. What would Duval do?

What a stupid thought. Duval wasn't a wolf.

But Têtue didn't have to be a wolf either.

Têtue sneezed, angry at herself. She shook herself out, then hunched up and released the wolf shape. Naked, she ran back to the workshop to find some sharp, thin utensils she could use. She returned to the laboratory door with two draughting compasses. The scent of the other women of the Order was stronger now. She knelt and applied needles to the lock until the pins surrendered. Têtue burst through the door.

The glass roof shattered in a hail of shots from above. Splintered glass dropped through the torn mesh as lead shot pierced the curtain. Têtue screamed, trying to shield her naked skin from the rain of glass splinters. She bled from a thousand cuts.

Monsieur Claque landed on his feet in front of her.

The cannonade stopped. With one arm, Monsieur Claque seized Têtue by the waist and hoisted her. With the other, he fired his stake revolver upward. A giant blackish-grey figure descended through the roof. The hulk twitched with each hit. It dropped to the floor on block feet, five stakes piercing its chest. It towered over them, undaunted.

Têtue didn't know what she was looking at. It couldn't possibly be human, almost three meters tall, with a sutured patchwork of mottled, necrotic skin and death-grey eyes.

The monstrosity swung a bulky, misshapen stump of an arm at Monsieur Claque. Monsieur Claque deflected it easily and shot again. The creature suddenly reared back with a garbled bellow and whirled. Behind the thing, their backs against the glass-dome case, Guichet, Montpellier, and Frontenac crouched with knives, poised for another attack. Blood stained their torn, sooty daydresses. Frontenac's right eye was swollen shut. Guichet sported a thick, bleeding lip.

Where'd they come from?

Têtue shook her head. Freeing herself from Monsieur Claque, she seized one of the glass tubes, broke its neck on a table, and charged the monster. She leapt onto its back and jammed the jagged glass into its jugular twice.

No blood.

It clawed for her as the other women lunged and slashed, lunged and slashed. The creature caught Têtue's leg, pried her from its back, and threw her into the other three. Têtue rolled and sprang at it again, vaguely aware someone's blade had sliced her leg. The creature tried to pummel her. She jabbed upward and sliced open its wrist before its blow landed. Again, no blood.

What is this thing?

Frontenac dove beneath its arm and stabbed up under its ribs. It grabbed her head in both stumpy hands and hurled her. She crashed into jars and beakers, shattering them, spreading their macabre contents across the tables.

Monsieur Claque kidney-punched with both fists in rapid succession. Têtue counted scores of gashes across the thing's body, but none of them bled. She doubted it even had kidneys to punch. Frontenac's blow to the heart should have killed it.

Têtue's whole body screamed with each splintered cut, and blood made her grip on her weapon slick. "Out," she barked as she eluded another swipe. "Claque, get them out of here!"

Instead, Monsieur Claque clutched the monster's long, ratty hair and shoved his revolving gun into its ear. He fired a stake into the creature's skull. Its thick arms dropped to its side. It crumpled into a mass of flesh on the floor of the lab. Monsieur Claque gripped the thing's head and twisted it from its bloodless body.

Across the room, Frontenac shrieked. Têtue spun about. Her heart sank.

De Guise occupied the chair at the center of the circle.

White hot showers of sparks rained down, as relentless as the teeming storms of the Husker disaster. Electricity shot through Jacqueline's body like bullets from a Colt-Paterson. If agony truly was the gateway to the aether, she would have found it by now.

Her own animal electro-magnetism should have been the only electrical force within the cage. Where had her calculations failed? What element in the mechanics did not want her returning to de Guise?

Not enough power to kill her. Just enough to rattle her brain cells and jolt every muscle in her body. Just enough to overpower her flesh and hold her prisoner in its flaying grasp. Apt punishment for giving away Ada's secrets to Roberts.

Ada King, the daughter of Lord Byron, friend of Shelley, whose wife wrote of animating the flesh. A roundabout poetical scientific justice.

Of course, Mary Shelley's protagonist used chemistry, not electricity, but the concept was the same: outward stimulus of the flesh creating involuntary muscle movement, and some unnamed "essence of life," an author's license.

Unlike Victor Frankenstein's creature, however, Jacqueline's heart was more likely to give out than give life.

It didn't matter that her calculations had failed; Jacqueline wouldn't have a chance to correct them anyway. But she liked to learn from her mistakes. If she survived this experiment, she might retrace her plans, for curiosity's sake.

Curiosity had brought her here. Down the coal chute of the firebox. How could she possibly have done that? Why was it Têtue's voice she had heard?

But no, it was the children. The Husker disaster. Children died. Children died here, too. Is that what had brought her to the Sparks factory?

Sharp's. Not sparks. The shower of sparks would not allow her to laugh at her mistake. Ironic.

Iron. From Marteau's ironworks. The children from Husker molded into the metal from Marteau's factory. How? What connected Sharp to Marteau, other than dead children?

Children died in factories. Their flesh was the price of greed. The governments'. The industrialists'. The financiers'. Like Armand.

Rodolphe Armand. An ugly man, and Angélique would see to it Frontenac did not marry him.

How was he connected to Marteau?

Hammering in her head continued its jarring desultory explorations, circling back to the question of Sharp and Marteau. Goüin was the only shared factor in the equation that steadfastly refused to resolve. Goüin worked for Sharp. Goüin bought parts from Marteau. Goüin called her in because of de Guise.

Alain.

In bed, when her body was excited with pleasure, when her thighs trembled and she clasped his blond curls, his pretty bowed lips closing on her as she fell away to a breathless ecstasy, she called him Alain.

A different spark lit within her, rippling across her flesh, stirring in her breasts and down to her most secret part, where thousands of nerves had their endings, more than any other part of the body, the only part that stirred at a mere thought. The secret part Alain had touched.

Her body responded. Pleasure, not pain. His voice in her head whispered, "Chérie."

"Alain," she murmured. She gasped as electricity sparked a deeper arousal, salubrious stimulus. "Ah, my love!"

"I need you, Jacqueline. You are my life."

She writhed and a soft moan escaped her. "I'll find you, my love."

Instead, darkness descended. The storm funneled about her like a tornado, drawing her upward into a black maw. Lightning arced. Her back arched. A bolt of pure energy pierced her.

Jacqueline vanished from herself.

Têtue fell to her knees in front of de Guise. He'd been stripped to his waist and bolted into the seat with the restraints, and his left eye was pried open and clamped. His eyeball had been removed and the socket cauterized. Wires pierced each breast near his heart and his neck beneath each ear. But Têtue could hear his thready pulse and his ragged, shallow breathing.

"Claque!" Têtue bellowed.

Gingerly she unfastened the speculum, her fingers sticky with blood. De Guise's eyelid sank into the seared hole. She removed the electrodes, the ends of which were bare wire dripping de Guise's blood. Monsieur Claque snapped the restraint bolts and caught de Guise as he slumped from the chair.

The duke appeared in the doorway, out of breath, his face and clothing blackened with soot and oil. "What the devil? Têt—de Guise!"

Monsieur Claque ignited his jets and soared out the roof with de Guise in his arms.

The duke threw his coat around Têtue's bloodied body. "What happened?"

Blood streamed her face. The coat only pressed glass splinters deeper. Têtue shook her head, fighting despair.

"He sent me away. He knew something was coming. He knew—"

Grappling ropes dropped from above as Monsieur Claque returned, wrapping Têtue in his arms and taking her up to the ship. The duke and the others each gripped a rope and were drawn through the ceiling as *Esprit* rose, away from Marteau's airship and the horrors of his laboratory. Monsieur Claque set Têtue down tenderly and turned to haul the duke and the women aboard.

Têtue collapsed to a crouch, her head bowed to the deck. She panted, rage churning in her. "I couldn't reach him. I couldn't get to him. I couldn't—"

She roared.

"You tried," Frontenac cried. "I know you tried. And together we destroyed that thing and got Monsieur de Guise back."

Montpellier murmured, "His colors are all wrong."

Guichet and the duchess knelt beside de Guise. The duchess wept.

"Gryffin, we have to," the duchess said. "We have to!"

The duke pulled off his cravate and cleaned the soot and blood from his face. He said, "Adèle, set course for Bellesfées. Têtue, get dressed. There are clothes in Madame Llewellyn's quarters. Claque, take Monsieur de Guise to the great cabin."

He gently took his wife's hand and held her as she sobbed into his chest.

Babies and body parts. Electrodes. What was that weapon? What the hell was that lumbering mountain of flesh? Why? What was it all for? *What can I do?*

Têtue got to her feet, pulling fragments of glass from her arms and shoulders. "Will wolf blood heal his eye?" she asked, her voice hoarse.

The duke sighed. Têtue then noticed that he must have fought his own battle to the laboratory. His face and hands were slashed and bleeding, with the largest gash along his left cheek. "I don't know," he answered. "Healing is one thing, but replacing the eye—"

"We can try. We have to try," she insisted. Têtue headed for the companionway, but he stopped her.

"Not without his permission," he told her.

Têtue gaped at him, quaking. "What do you mean? He may die! We can't let him die. Duval—"

"Jacky knows," he said. "This is her wish, not ours."

The duchess wiped her tears. "We've had this argument before, Têtue," she said. She choked back a sob. "I don't agree with Jacky, but I do understand."

She took Têtue's hands in hers. "You asked. You saw me change from wolf and back, and you said, 'show me how to do that.' I knew you wouldn't object when I intervened and turned you. De Guise and Jacky have steadfastly refused our offer to make them like us. We can't force ourselves on him."

Têtue pulled away. "It's not right. We have to do something." She paced. "I shouldn't have left the room. He told me to run. I shouldn't have listened to him."

"Not so," the duke said. "You did everything right, Têtue. If he told you to run, he had his reasons. Never question de Guise. Even Jacky knows to listen to him." He kissed her brow. "Go heal and dress," he repeated. "Adèle will need you on deck."

Whining, Têtue trudged down the ladder to the duchess's quarters. Flinging the duke's coat away, she roared again, clutching at her hair. Instinctively, she dropped into herself and became wolf. She howled. Mournful. Aching. Agonized. She had failed Duval. Nothing could make up for that. She howled and whined and crooned her pain.

After a time, the duke came in and knelt, taking her into his arms. She rested her head on his shoulder, moaning, as Llewellyn stroked her and gently caressed her ears.

De Guise's tortured face haunted her. His scorched eye socket. His slack expression.

"Marteau's airship is following us," the duke whispered. "Please, Têtue. I need you. I need you to hold on. See to *Esprit*. I'll assist Adèle at the helm, but the engines have to hold if we're to outrun her."

He was right. De Guise wasn't safe yet. Their enemy was in pursuit, and the duke and the others were wounded. Têtue could heal. Duval needed her.

The duke took a chemise from the duchess's trunk of clothing. He dropped it over Têtue's head as she emerged from the wolf, half-healed and angry.

"Does Duval keep spare trousers aboard?" she asked sullenly.

"If she does, they'll be in her quarters." The duke embraced her. "Hurry. I'll do what I can above."

As he headed back up the ladder, Têtue went to the great cabin. Montpellier applied her unguent to de Guise's chest and neck while the duchess washed him. He was still unconscious. His usual scent was tainted with whatever Marteau had used on him. His pulse was stronger, though, and his breathing more even.

"What happened?" Têtue asked as she rummaged through the chifforobe. "What were you all doing there?"

The duchess sighed. "I was hoping to speak to the duke, so we approached the ironworks. When I sent to him, he was in the midst of a fight with three creatures. He said they wouldn't die."

"In the factory, or the airship?"

"The factory."

Montpellier moaned softly. "Like that monster. No colors at all. It wasn't really alive, just—"

"And that thing was on the airship," Têtue deduced. "Frontenac probably couldn't sense it. Just reanimated flesh and guts." She yanked on trousers and fished around for hose. "So you thought the ship was deserted and there'd be no danger boarding. I'd have done the same." She grinned at Montpellier. "Sheaths was a great idea. You three looked truly ferocious. I was glad to see you." She then nodded to de Guise. "How are his colors?"

Montpellier shook her head and frowned. "They're pale, and they're all wrong. Usually Monsieur de Guise is a quiet blue, except for the white and gold flashes when he's with Duval. But he's mostly grey now. Just a few sparks of anything close to blue."

Têtue nodded. She rummaged a bit more but couldn't come up with any shoes or boots suitable for the deck, so she yanked off her hose again.

"Send to me when he's up," she told the duchess on her way out. "And see if you can get his permission."

Têtue trotted up the companion ladder onto the main deck and closed the door behind her. Monsieur Claque had reloaded the gun turret. Frontenac was at the captain's wheel and Guichet at the capstans that set their course. Already their battle wounds had all but vanished. Têtue grimaced, recognizing the source of their healing.

The duke had extinguished all the lights on deck and climbed aft to keep his eye on the pursuing aerostat. Têtue joined him at the rail.

"Take us up another fifty meters, Adèle," the duke called.

"Belay that," Têtue countermanded. "They'll see the light from the great cabin."

The duke smirked. "I want them to."

Têtue scowled, waiting on an explanation. Frontenac engaged the envelope systems, and the eight hydrogen tanks gasped into the night. Marteau's vessel also began to rise. At fifty meters, Frontenac cut the jets.

"Now we find out if that man truly has some sorcery or necromancy on his side," the duke murmured. "Keep an eye on her."

He headed belowdecks to draw the drapes over the great cabin's window. He returned to the main deck and the capstan gauges that controlled the drive. "Ready, Adèle?"

"Ready."

The duke cut the starboard engines and slowed the port propeller, while Frontenac spun the captain's wheel. *Esprit* yawed to starboard, taking her on a course that slowly curved to the south. The other airship held its course. Relief flooded Têtue. She grinned back at the duke.

"He's awake," the duchess sent, "but incoherent."

The duke smiled wearily. He jerked his head to Têtue, and she jumped down from the aft deck to go below. She took the ladder two steps at a time and headed through the dark to the great cabin only to draw up short in the doorway.

De Guise throttled Montpellier. The duchess lay unconscious on the floor, her head in a puddle of blood.

13.

JACQUELINE SLOWLY OPENED HER EYES. SHE LIVED. BUT WHERE? *WHEN?*

She winced in the dim glow emanating from somewhere behind and above her head. She lay, her upper body raised to a forty-degree angle, on a stark, narrow chaise longue with rails to either side locking her in. A sheet covered her lower body. Her head ached, but when was the last time her head hadn't ached?

Jacqueline closed her eyes again. She became aware of a slow, clockwork ticking, and a steady chirping noise, like a high-pitched squeak of a clarinet.

"Ah!" She groaned. She had yet to finish Angélique's clarinetist. "Zut."

A door shut quietly. Jacqueline blinked. She hadn't noticed anyone in the dusk of the room. She moved to press her hands to her pounding temples. To her horror, she found a thin flexible tube inserted into the crease of her right arm, secured with strips of fabric that adhered to her skin, fed from a gelatinous sac of clear liquid suspended from a metal tree. Her arm hurt.

A wide swath of fabric wrapped her upper left arm, also featuring a flexible black tube connected to a small blue machine with a blank black gauge, on a pole with several blue baskets suspended along its length. A clamp pinched her forefinger lightly, also connected to an electrode hooked to the blue machine.

Her clothes were gone except for her welding cap, gripping her head too tightly. She wore a flimsy, shapeless, cotton pinafore over—she gulped—nothing! Electrodes were stuck to her naked chest, back, ribs, and legs, and the cables ran somewhere under the chaise. Strips of a strange solid fabric, not leather, braceleted her right wrist, one red, one white.

The spartan room had only a chair in the corner and a bed table to her left. Beige curtains on the wall beside her blocked her view from what Jacqueline assumed was a window. The walls featured no decoration but a large flat box mounted near the ceiling, a small round orb beside it, and a plain white square poster board with black lettering and numbers in a code she could not decipher except for the words "Bill," "Fees," and "Doe." That made no sense to her. A bill was a list of fees, which were costs. Doe, English for biche. At the bottom, a series of pictographs. From her position, she couldn't make out their purpose.

Suddenly the fabric band on her upper arm began to inflate. Jacqueline's heart raced as the constriction became painful. Her pulse pounded in her ears and in her arm. Panic overtook her. At the same time, numbers danced up in different quadrants of the black display of the blue machine.

"Poiseuille," she murmured, recalling the physicist's work with arterial flow and blood pressure. Jacqueline winced, certain the band would crush her arm. It had to be squeezing blood from her, which would defeat the purpose of measuring a body's pressure—at least, using Poiseuille's methods of capillary metrics.

At the point of dismay, the wrap just as suddenly released her. Numbers glowed red on the blank display: one hundred twenty-seven, sixty-eight, eighty, ninety-nine. What possible meaning could they hold?

The door swung open. A blinding garish light exploded from large translucent casings on the ceiling. Jacqueline squeezed her eyes shut, then slowly re-opened them.

A man roughly her age dressed in pale green pyjamas swept in and beamed at her. He had short, royal-blue hair in stubby spikes and a close-shaved beard of strawberry red. Where in the world, or when, did people have blue or red hair?

"Welcome back," he said in English as he went to the machine and pushed a button. "Your heart looks good, blood pressure and pulse ox excellent, considering."

He smiled at her again as he strode to her side and pulled out a small blue and white gun. Before she could react, he ran its muzzle across her brow, studied it, put it back in his pocket, then stood at the blue machine and began depressing rows of buttons on a tray, making a light clattering noise.

"How do you feel?" he asked. His accent was North American. He wore a ribbon necklace with a rectangular medallion, like a scapular, that featured his portrait and other information Jacqueline couldn't make out. "Feel like telling us your name?"

Jacqueline shook her head. He flipped the sheet to expose her bare legs. Jacquline gasped and took it back, pulling it up to her chin.

"I'm just removing the leads," he told her.

He evidently thought that would reassure her. When he pried the sheet from her hands and uncovered her again, Jacqueline clenched her teeth, humiliated and angry, but chary of unsettling any of the tubes invading her. She fought to keep breathing as he untethered her chest and ribs. He covered her again, but she still felt things adhered to her. She peeked down her pinafore to see small pads riveted there, though she felt no pain from them.

"Where and when am I?" she asked, her voice barely a whisper.

His eyes widened. He grinned. "That's my line. What year do you think it is?"

She refused to answer. She couldn't guess from any of the technology she saw around her how far she had overshot her target.

He swung the bed table over her and poured water from a squat pink pitcher into a spongy white cup he then placed in her hand. "The EMTs brought you in two nights ago. 9-1-1 dispatched them to the Franklin Institute for a Jane Doe found unconscious in the cab of the Baldwin 60000. Any idea how you got there?"

Jacqueline drank to stall for time, as she had no idea what he had just said other than "two nights ago," "institute," and "unconscious."

"I was on when you came in," he continued as he fidgeted with the sheets, tucking her in. "Looked like you were cosplaying, huh? The boots, cap, goggles, a little steampunk going on? Choochoo!" he hooted, pumping his arm.

His smile was pleasant. Jacqueline barely understood half of what he was saying, but she decided it would be best to cooperate to get the answers she needed.

"I don't know how I got to that institute," she admitted. "I don't know where I am or what year it is. What city is this? Are you a doctor?"

He fidgeted some more, not meeting her eyes. "No, I'm a nurse. Nourrice, right? French for 'nurse'? You sound French. I had a little French in high school."

Jacqueline bit back a bof. She doubted the world could change so much a man could nurse an infant.

"Am I a prisoner?"

He straightened, surprised. "No, you're a patient. I'm sure the police will want to talk to you, find out what you were doing there, how you got there, check for foul play. But you're in a hospital. Le ho-pee-tal. Pennsylvania Hospital in Philadelphia in the United States of America. Les États Unis. The year is 2018."

2018!

Jacqueline's thoughts reeled. The stupid blue machine began crushing her arm again. Tears brimmed in her eyes and she squeezed them back. The past she could reckon with. Passing two centuries into the future was too much for her. She couldn't tell them she was from 1843, nor that she had traveled back across time to 1838 and forward to 1840.

2018.

Why here, and now? How could Goüin, Armand, or anyone from her era have drawn her to this place and year?

"Hey, you're doing fine," the man reassured her. "Dr. Fees is on call, so she should be in shortly, and she's our best. Jenny paged her. Would you like something to eat? I can get you some Jello or Oreos or maybe graham crackers?"

She nodded, but with some trepidation. She had no idea what those three items were. Still, surely a hospital wouldn't feed her anything insalubrious.

He opened a small cardstock box and handed her a soft sheet of pulped paper. "You're going to be OK. My name's Bill. Can you tell me your name?"

She dabbed the pulp to her nose. "Jacqueline Marie-Claire Duval de la Forge-à-Bellesfées."

"That's a mouthful. Jack-leen." Bill managed a passable pronunciation. He pulled another device from under her pillow and set it on the bed table. "Nice to meet you, Jacqueline. Here's the remote for the tv. If you need anything, just press the call button. I'm on until six. Dr. Fees will be in to see you and you two can chat. I'll get you those snacks."

He grinned again and left, and a woman with long reddish hair, though not strawberry red, slipped in and took up the chair in the corner. Jacqueline stared at her quizzically. She also wore the green pyjamas Bill wore. Some sort of hospital uniform, like sisters' habits?

"I'm so glad you're finally awake," the woman said. "I'm Jenny. I'm your tech, just here to make sure you're okay until the doctor does an e-val." Jenny took a small case from her pocket and studied it, tapping it frequently. It didn't open.

Pole socks. The Empties. OK. TV. E Val. Jacqueline was fluent in English, but she had no idea American was so very different. Jenny said she was a tech. She must be responsible for monitoring the machines. Jacqueline sighed and closed her eyes again. Women were polytechs in 2018. Or, would be. That was comforting.

The band on her arm inflated again. Different numbers flashed. Zut, it was annoying.

"Madame Jenny, what is the time?"

The tech tapped the little case again. "Two-thirty-seven. AM."

Morning. Middle of the night, really. Jacqueline was awake and anxious to configure a way back, but she could do nothing at this hour anyway. Unless this new century had the technology to master the aether and carry her back in time, she found no reason to even bother.

Bill swept in again with his affable smile. He set blue-and-silver packets on her bed table. "Here you go. I know you French like your chocolate." And he was gone again.

Jacqueline took one of the packages and tried to figure out how to open it. It wasn't wrapped in paper, and the material stubbornly resisted her efforts. Finally, she tore it with her teeth. Broken layered crisp cakes slipped out onto the table. She ate them, despite their overly sweetened, stale vanilla and chocolate flavors. She pushed the other packages aside with a sigh and closed her eyes.

"Would you like the light off?" Jenny asked her.

When she nodded, Jenny rose and went to a small switch on the wall Jacqueline hadn't noticed. The light behind her head remained on, but the room was mercifully dimmed. Jacqueline murmured her thanks, but Jenny no sooner sat when the door opened and the light glared again.

An older woman with silvering hair, dressed in slate-grey trousers and a long white coat and wearing dark-tinted sun-glasses, came to her side. She lowered the railing that fenced Jacqueline in and took a pen from her pocket. Light flowed from its nib and the woman aimed it into Jacqueline's eyes.

When she could see again, Jacqueline's heart leapt and again tears sprang to her eyes in a rush of joy. "Angélique?" she cried. "Mon Ange!"

Forgetting her tubes, Jacqueline threw her arms around her sister's waist. "Oh, Angélique, I tried to get home. I tried to find de Guise. I tried. How did you find me? Have you truly lived two hundred years more? Angélique, mon Ange, mon Ange!"

Angélique and Jenny both wrested Jacqueline's arms away and pushed her back on the bed.

"Can you tell me your name?" Angélique said sternly. She spoke in English, American. "What's your name?"

Jenny murmured, "Should I get psych?"

"No, she's just disoriented."

Jenny backed away and sat. Angélique repeated, "Madame, can you tell me your name? Comment vous appelez-vous?"

Jacqueline gazed up at her, searching the woman's aged face. The tinted glasses. Those exquisite cheekbones. How could it not be Angélique?

Jacqueline heaved an anguished wail. "Non, non, non!" She tossed her head. "Of course I know my name! I thought I knew yours. I'm Duval. Jacqueline Duval."

The woman was unmoved. "Where in France are you from, Madame Duval?"

Jacqueline set her jaw. "I am sorry. I thought I recognized you. You look so much like her."

The woman brought the chair over to sit beside her. "Like whom?"

Jacqueline turned away. "It doesn't matter. She must be long gone."

"Tell me," the woman said.

Tell her what? Jacqueline guessed the meaning of the word psych. E-val would mean evaluation. They would find her insane if she told them anything. She turned away. She couldn't bear looking at the woman's face, so familiar, so dear, and so wrong.

"Lightning," she said. "I was struck by lightning."

"At the Franklin Institute?"

Bill had also mentioned the Franklin Institute. Jacqueline was found there, unconscious, he said.

"No. I don't know how I came to be at that institute."

"Dans la cabine de la locomotive. Vous vous intéressez aux trains?"

"Oui."

Then Jacqueline startled, realizing the woman addressed her in excellent French with a Tourangeau accent.

"Did you work on trains in France?"

Jacqueline nodded, eyes narrowing suspiciously.

"You're an engineer, correct? A polytech."

"Yes."

"You were working on a haunted train in Orléans."

Jacqueline trembled. How much had she babbled in her unconscious state the past two days? She clamped her mouth shut again. She had said too much. The woman no doubt also understood her claim to be over two hundred years old. Was that enough to put her away in an asylum?

The woman got up and removed Jacqueline's cap — not her welding cap at all, but a gelatinous mesh of some kind. She sat back in her chair. She continued in impeccable French.

"Jacqueline Duval. Polytech extraordinaire. Fought sorcerers and vampires and assassins and mad scientists and ghosts and pirates and revenants and zombies and werewolves, real ones. Flew an invisible airship. Worked on a haunted train in Orléans. Had a sister, Angélique."

Dr. Fees's words pierced Jacqueline's heart. The machine squeezed her arm. Some of the numbers were wildly higher. "Stop," Jacqueline whispered. "Please, stop."

"Loved a man named Alain."

Alain!

Jacqueline choked on the lump in her throat. "I'm begging you."

"With a passion that would burn the ages. Alain de Guise. Who loved her all his life. He gave her two daughters, Dominique and Justine."

Jacqueline gasped and froze, hairs rising on her arms and the back of her neck. She glared at the woman, trying to pierce the tint of the glasses she wore. The woman placed her hand on her breast, as if holding back a secret. Her eyebrow rose, a sly half-smile on her lips.

Her pretty bowed lips.

"Dominique suffered an accident as a child, but she survived." The woman removed her glasses to reveal golden wolf-eyes. "You can guess how."

Jacqueline couldn't breathe. Her heart hammered at her chest.

"Dominique came to America when she was nineteen, here to Philadelphia. Customs officials wrote her name as Dominique Dubell Fees. She was my great-great-grandmother. I was named for her."

The woman leaned closer and gazed back into Jacqueline's eyes. "But she didn't live two hundred years. How did you?"

14.

DE GUISE SLAMMED MONTPELLIER'S HEAD AGAINST THE FLOOR. "YOU! Won't stop me, putain!"

Têtue leapt at de Guise. Her arm closed around his neck as she pulled him off Montpellier and dragged him to the floor.

"Llewellyn!" she summoned.

De Guise clawed awkwardly at Têtue. She shoved his head down, tightening her stranglehold. He squealed and spat, twisting his body, his legs flailing. He was strong, yes, but he grappled like a schoolboy. Têtue thought an agent of the Sûreté Nationale would have been more capable. She kept her face out of his reach and counted — six, seven, eight, nine —

The duke flew to the duchess, shouting his alarm.

Montpellier lay coughing, gulping air, beside the bed. "Not — de Guise —"

— twelve, thirteen —

De Guise slumped, finally unconscious. Têtue relented, but she didn't release him. The duke lifted the duchess onto the bed.

"Rope," said Têtue. "Bind this bastard like a pig."

The duke snatched tiebacks from the drapes across the back window and swiftly bound de Guise's wrists to his ankles behind him. He then put a knot in his own bloodied cravate and shoved it into de Guise's mouth, tying it tightly. He went back to the duchess and examined her eyes. He gently probed her head and cursed when his hand came away soaked in blood. He turned on de Guise, his fist raised.

"It's not de Guise," Montpellier said again, her voice a bare rasp. Lurid welts marked her throat. She huddled, gasping.

The duke gently helped her to a chair and poured water. She tried to drink, but coughed, unable to swallow comfortably.

Guichet halted in the doorway, eyes wide in horror. "What can I do?"

Têtue got to her feet. "Hurry, with me." She hustled Guichet back to the main deck. "Something took over de Guise's body," Têtue explained as she ran to the aft deck. "Knocked the duchess out and nearly killed Montpellier."

Têtue leaned at the rail to spy out the black aerostat. It held its former course. They had eluded it. She sagged, her body buzzing. "Frontenac, set course to return to Orléans. We'll anchor above the P-O works."

"Aye."

With Monsieur Claque's assistance they re-engaged the starboard engines, adjusted the keel, and powered up the drive to speed back to the factory. *Esprit* was losing altitude, but not that swiftly. They probably wouldn't have to ignite the hydrogen tanks again. The duke came on deck as they smoothed out, and joined them on the aft deck.

"Is she awake?" Têtue's brow furrowed.

He nodded wearily. "Thank heaven Jacky had the foresight to keep a brig. De Guise is locked away. We're going back?"

"To finish Duval's work," Têtue answered. She kicked the base of the ship's wheel. "First a body vanishes. Then a body without blood. Now a body with someone else inside it."

The duke gave a mirthless chuckle. "Welcome to Bellesfées."

Frontenac dropped anchor on the roof of the locomotive works. By then, the duchess had regained consciousness, and she couldn't stop cursing, much to Têtue's amusement. Monsieur Claque secured a Jacob's ladder. The duke and the women descended. Monsieur Claque carried de Guise, bound and gagged, as he leapt from the ship, landing neatly and bowing his head to the women. De Guise protested in impotent rage.

Têtue gripped his hair and glared into his eyes. "I don't know where you hid de Guise," she said, "but we'll find Duval and we'll find him too."

They made their way to the factory floor. The men were seated around the table drinking. They halted in stunned silence as the others entered. Léon and Goüin rose.

"De Guise!" Goüin cried. "Têtue, what's the meaning of this affront?"

But Léon took Guichet's arm, his face taut with alarm. "Madame, have you been injured? The blood on your dress… Dresses!" he added as he noted Frontenac and Montpellier. "Léon turned to Goüin. "Monsieur, I warned you Marteau's ironworks presented a danger. Now you see."

"Oh, Monsieur Vincent, you don't see half of it," the duchess said bitterly. "Monsieur Goüin, whoever runs that place is crafting monstrous experiments with living flesh. He invaded de Guise's body with some—personality, or energy, or spirit, whatever the hell you wish to call it. Very nearly split my skull with a candlestick."

"That factory is the source of your haunting," the duke said. "His metal is charged with children's bodies, infants, toddlers. God only knows where he acquires them, but Têtue and I both witnessed the obscenity."

Têtue said, "More. Experiments with body parts and electricity. Unborn ripped from mothers' wombs. It's an abomination."

Goüin took in their words with stony disbelief. He passed his hand up his forehead. Coquelet and the rest of his team joined them, staring at Monsieur Claque with appropriate awe, and at the women's bloodstained dresses with inappropriate disgust. They sniggered at the Llewellyns' and Têtue's lupine eyes.

Têtue seized Coquelet by the collar, baring her teeth. "Do you find our aspect distasteful, monsieur? Do we offend your frail sensibilities? Faint at the sight of blood, do you? Find our stink of sweat disagreeable? You stink of pencil and paper and beer. I can smell your fear of Monsieur Claque and your own scent of inadequacy before the genius of a superior artist."

She rounded on Simon, Sançille, and Bardît, her free hand closed to a threatening fist. "We're the Order of Duval. We fought more battles tonight, against enemies you can't comprehend in your sickest nightmares, than you ever fought in the schoolyards. Who the hell are you to disdain us, you foppish—"

"Enough, Têtue," the duchess said coldly. "You're wasting time with them."

Têtue shoved Coquelet back. "At least I didn't say 'foute.'"

The duke signaled, and Monsieur Claque dropped de Guise on the floor.

"Mademoiselle Montpellier assures me that somewhere inside him, a part of de Guise remains, but he's been overcome by another entity. I'm no expert in electricity or biology or any science that might accomplish such an end, but I'm not beyond belief in the supernatural. Nor should any of you be, at this point, unless you're obstinately stupid. Tetue, hold him."

Têtue knelt on de Guise and pressed him to the floor on his side. He cried out behind the gag while the duke held his head and pried open his empty eye socket, a cone of red tissue.

"I'm guessing Marteau removed the eyeball to gain access to the brain," the duke explained. "He had some sort of weapon with a needle-nose muzzle in his laboratory. I think he used that to slide along the optic nerve."

Frontenac drew a sharp breath and twitched as if stung with electricity. "You're right," she said, searching de Guise's face. "Marteau also uses that weapon to remove people from their bodies so he can— Oh, God!—eat—"

Coquelet's team muttered sullenly.

Frontenac suddenly shivered. "That's Marteau in there. Oh, he's furious. He doesn't know how to control what he's done. He can't even control his thoughts."

Goüin threw his hands up. "What does anyone possibly gain from such profane machinations?"

Frontenac listened. As she relayed the response, her face drew taut. "He says, 'Knowledge is its own reward.' He killed those children, just to see how they would die. Then ate them. He—oh, God!—used their skin to make that creature we fought. 'Carbon strengthens iron,' he says. Used dead bodies in the charge."

Guichet embraced Frontenac as she broke off, choking, and pleaded to Goüin, "Help us, monsieur. Tell me Duval's machine is done."

Coquelet nodded grimly. "It's done. It'll probably kill you, but it's done."

Têtue brushed past him to inspect the machinery. "Duval isn't Marteau."

Goüin and his men followed her.

Frontenac continued Marteau's tale between sobs and groans of disgust, unable to stop his thoughts. "Needed money for equipment. Deal with the devil. Fat pig cheated. Cheated! Parish houses for brats. Brothels for pregnant women. They were going to die anyway. But they don't die, you see. Carbon in the iron. The train runs forever. Your grandfather's axe."

All the while, de Guise grunted and bellowed behind the gag, fury reddening his face.

The duke stood, tugging at his lower lip, studying his friend. "If Marteau is in there, who's flying his airship?" He turned to Frontenac. "Was there anyone else on board besides the creature of flesh?"

De Guise laughed, his good eye creased with venom. Frontenac gave a soft, "Oh!"

"The ship," Montpellier rasped. "Flesh. Alive." She held her throat and swallowed carefully. "Experiment."

The duchess gasped and gripped the duke's arm. "Salaud! Putain! Merdique connard!" She screamed into de Guise's face as he mocked her outrage.

Llewellyn pulled her back. "De Guise is still in there."

Montpellier added, "Fighting."

Têtue called from across the floor, "Lady-knives! We're needed."

Guichet helped Frontenac dry her eyes.

"I just want to slit his throat," Frontenac muttered, glaring at de Guise. "But I know it's not him."

"Do you think he meant an actual deal with the Devil?" Guichet asked worriedly. "He said 'fat pig.' I've never thought of the Devil as fat."

"Who can say?" Frontenac linked arms with her and they crossed the factory floor. "The Holy Scripture says Satan seeks whom he may devour. It would make sense he's fat, seeing how many things in this world he runs."

Then Frontenac frowned angrily. "What I heard was 'fat' and 'cheat.' I heard those two words just yesterday to describe my fiancé. If I learn he's behind Marteau —"

Guichet gave a derisive bof. "Wrongs to be righted."

Montpellier nodded.

As they neared the huge construct, Montpellier looked it over carefully while Têtue and Frontenac inspected the parts for contamination. They completed their rounds at the Faraday cage. It seemed only the disc carried the ghostly traces of the children, but the disc couldn't be replaced. Although they trusted Duval's science, Têtue fretted.

"What if the kids interfere?" she whispered to the others. "What if they take us somewhere else? Damn, we have no idea what we're doing, even if Duval does."

Montpellier shuddered, but she took Têtue's hand. "I'll look for her flux lines in the aether," she said. "I'll find her."

Léon followed them, explaining each step of the process he anticipated. "Her theory is that the electricity will bond to your own animal electro-magnetism. Those forces will merge, forming a vortex in the aether that enables you to transcend the natural static bonds of this plane." His fingers knotted nervously around the wire mesh of the cage. "But it's a theory that hasn't been tested, relying on formulae we've never seen before."

Guichet set her hand on his arm. "We're not afraid to test it, Monsieur Vincent. We trust Duval."

Léon nodded, resigned. He met Têtue's eyes. "You'll be careful, though? No unnecessary risks? What will you do if you manage to cross the aether? How will you find her?"

Têtue clapped his shoulder. "Montpellier will see her colors, Frontenac will hear her thoughts, I'll find her scent, and Guichet will remove any obstacle before us."

Léon smiled. "I believe you." But worry remained in the draw of his face.

"Good." Têtue opened the cage door. "Let's not waste any more time."

As the four entered the cage, Goüin and the Llewellyns joined them. Léon brought a stepladder, and Goüin and the duke helped each woman to climb into the sling.

Têtue looked back to the duke and duchess. "Don't you do anything to put that kid in danger," she warned. "You stay clear of this cage, and if that ship comes back, you take Esprit and you leave. Claque can navigate."

The duchess reached for her hand and clasped it. "We love you," she said, her voice breaking. "Come back to us."

"We'll all come back, once we find Duval." Têtue pointed to her boots, leaning against a leg of the table of food and beer. "I'd like those, please."

Léon retrieved them. He climbed the stepladder to hand them over. "Têtue, I look forward to your return. I feel I owe you—"

The boots flew from his hand and Têtue snatched them from the air. Guichet giggled.

"Ouais, Guichet!" Têtue cheered. She tossed the clothes she had tucked inside the boots to Llewellyn, and she strapped her lady-knife around her thigh. "Can you bring me Duval's coat too?"

Guichet happily obliged, while Coquelet and his team watched in astonishment. "Are we ready?" Guichet asked the others.

"For Duval," Têtue replied.

"For Duval!"

They clasped hands and lay back in the sling. Léon bit his lower lip, his eyes sad. Têtue winked at him. He descended and ushered the others from the cage. As he closed it behind him, he gazed back longingly.

Goüin murmured, "By God, I should be so fortunate to inspire such loyalty and courage."

Sançille sneered. "You mean stupidity?"

A mug of beer flew off the food table and struck his head. Léon laughed.

Coquelet and Léon stayed on the floor to initiate power and monitor the experiment while Simon and Bardît fetched face shields for the onlookers and escorted them upstairs to view the procedure from the shelter of the workshop. Léon headed to the control panel, keeping up a steady monologue in a strained voice raised above the steady drone of the factory. Têtue begrudgingly admitted it was thoughtful of him to try to allay their nervousness.

"Well thrown, Madame Guichet. Sançille can be a real bastard. Mademoiselle Montpellier, I saw those bruises on your neck. Someone tried to strangle you, yes? And Madame Frontenac, you know my thoughts about that, don't you? Of course you do."

Frontenac whispered, "He's crazy about you, Têtue."

"Nah. Just crazy."

"I hear you, Madame Têtue," Léon called. "You laugh at me now, but when you come back, I'll be the one laughing, just to see your face."

He threw the switch. Power engaged with a hum. He closed the panel door. Têtue heard the circuitry come alive as the huge cylinder began to rotate. Beside her, Montpellier cooed; probably watching the flux of forces that Têtue sensed. A few seconds later the wiring of the cage began to glow. Suddenly it exploded into a blazing white light. The hum became a deafening roar. Her body tingled, the way it did after a good fight. Excitated, Léon had called it. He was sweet, she decided. She'd be a different woman if she'd married someone like Léon.

"So beautiful," Montpellier whispered, her head moving side to side. "Oh, I belong there."

Têtue frowned. Unwilling to lose the younger woman, she clasped Montpellier's hand more tightly. Sparks flew from her fingertips, just as de Guise's fingers had thrown sparks when he set hands to that metal case with the glass lid. What the hell had he seen in there? Why had he sent her away?

Now her arms and legs thrummed with excited energies. The sensation was almost pleasurable in places Têtue was not accustomed to being pleasured. She heard Guichet cry out and knew she was thinking the same thing. Frontenac gasped in shallow breaths. Montpellier crooned.

Têtue shouted above the roar of power, "Don't get lost. Frontenac, listen! Montpellier, find a way through for us. Guichet, be ready to protect us."

Léon called for Coquelet, who barked a response. The disc spun faster. Lightning danced wildly throughout the cage. Dozens of blue-white arcs of power forked through the air in a dazzling display beyond any fireworks of Les Trois Glorieuses.

Montpellier sang and laughed. Têtue squeezed her hand. A streak of light shot between them, grazing Têtue's head. The odor of electrified air mingled with burnt hair. The cage was alive, playful, reaching for them. Têtue's heart labored, and she struggled to draw breath. Above their heads, a darkness gathered. It was all backward—first lightning, then thunderheads? But heavy cobalt forces reeled, slowly at first, gathering speed. A maelstrom as vast as the Loire sky descended from the top of the cage.

"Oh, there you are, Têtue!" Montpellier pointed into the center of the whirling blackness. "That explains it. Now I see."

Léon shouted. Coquelet answered. The roar of the disc rose in pitch to a ghastly, ceaseless shriek.

Montpellier squeezed Têtue's hand. "I see it. Everything. Ever. I see it all. So beautiful!" Then she shouted, "There! I found—"

Four bolts slammed through their bodies.

15.

Jacqueline stared out across a jagged, luminous city-scape. Glowing glass towers of unsquared angles and dizzying heights, with messages flashing along their crowns or windows, lit the entire city in a spectrum of colors. Vehicles raced along boulevards at blood-boiling speeds without horses or steam. A suspension bridge almost three kilometers long sailed across a wide river like a Colossus astride the port of Rhodes, with more lights and towers and even a dome on the other shore. Huge locomotives hauled car after car, and every few seconds airships without envelopes glided across the sky like eagles, their aero-jets thundering and sometimes shaking the building. Factory stacks emitted puffy white billows that dissipated in the overcast, orange night.

"Are children still dying in those factories, those machines?" Jacqueline asked.

Dr. Dominique Fees's reflection in the window both thrilled and terrified Jacqueline. The great-great-granddaughter of a daughter she did not have. Yet. And now never would. The physics made no sense. Jacqueline feared at any moment the paradox would resolve and one of them would vanish. She could not begin to guess where or when.

"Not here," Dominique replied. "There are places in the world where children are still worked to death. Enslaved. There are laws in most countries, but not all."

"France and England had laws too." Jacqueline bit her fingernail. "It made no difference."

"It does now," Dominique assured her. "But children still die. Starvation in many countries, even here. Illicit slavery and sex trafficking of young children. Abuse. Disease. Killing each other. Guns, drugs, gangs. We just lost a four-year-old downstairs. A stray bullet. It never stops."

Jacqueline put her hand to the window and leaned her forehead against the glass. She didn't know what she was seeing, and it tore at her. She knew she was being cautiously watched, so she could not explode in the rage that seethed within her. But she also could not hide her story. Not from her granddaughter's granddaughter. Mon Dieu, how was it possible? It could not be a coincidence that she should be swept into the future to be found by her own descendent.

Dominique had listened to her explanation without comment before drawing her from the bed to the window. When Dominique opened the curtain, Jacqueline knew she was lost. Despair pressed her heart like a great stone. She gazed silently across two hundred years of history, the legacy of the Industrial Revolution.

"What's the last thing you remember in 1840?" Dominique asked her.

"I wanted de Guise," Jacqueline murmured. She closed her eyes against the wilderness of her future and searched for Guise's face. "I have to find him."

Dominique laid her hand on Jacqueline's. "Instead you found his distant child. Yours and his, Mémé." Their fingers intertwined. "This must be difficult. You're what, twenty-two? Twenty-three? I'm more than twice your age."

"'Mémé.'" Jacqueline grinned wryly. "I guess I wished too fervidly. I flew right past him and found you."

She glanced up at Dominique and for the hundredth time blinked in disbelief. The hollowness inside was more than she could bear. "I'm sorry. You look so much—I wish I could show you. You are as beautiful as my sister Angélique."

"Oh, well—" Dominique's golden wolf-eyes danced. "Let me show you," she said.

From her lab coat, she pulled a metal case the size of a notebook. When she opened it, half the notebook featured rows of buttons with a seemingly random arrangement of letters and numbers. The other half displayed a detailed, fully chromatic portrait, so much more advanced than a daguerreotype, of a family. Dominique's family: she and her husband, a teenaged son with his father's dark hair and brown lupine eyes, and twin daughters, perhaps twenty years old, with honey-gold hair and green lupine eyes, standing on a smooth pavement beside an over-large statue of a horse-faced lizard, rampant, like something Georges Cuvier had dreamed up for his research on fossilized bones.

Jacqueline touched the display, tracing the faces of Dominique's grown children. The daughters resembled Jacqueline, down to her broad, muscular shoulders. "You're all shapeshifters?"

"We are."

"And no one cares?"

"No one knows." Dominique wrinkled her nose. "People are unmerciful when it comes to appearances. No one suspects what we are, but they have no compunction about name-calling. We wear our dark glasses and claim optical deformity, but children especially can be cruel."

Jacqueline swallowed the lump in her throat. All the arguments she had given Angélique over the years about sharing her sister's healing powers and lupine abilities at the cost of her own vision, her appearance… Here was evidence she would cast those aside to save her own daughter.

Or would her daughter choose it? Or would Angélique do this without her permission? Oh, to know her past's future!

"Do you regret it?" Jacqueline asked.

Dominique didn't answer. Instead, she took back the metal notebook. "Here, this is what I wanted to show you." Dominique tapped, and the display changed. She tapped again, and another, less detailed daguerreotype filled the screen with sepia.

Jacqueline caught her breath. It was Angélique, her own twin Angélique, perhaps close to seventy, seated beside Llewellyn, grey-haired with a sharp-pointed beard and mustache. Behind them stood four sons, tall and dark-haired with wolf-eyes, three women on their husbands' arms, and seven small children seated on the ground at Angélique and Llewellyn's feet.

"1887," Dominique said. "At Harddwch." She smiled wistfully. "And here, I believe these are your housekeepers? It says 'the Benets.' Marthe, Luc, Jean-Paul, Geneviève, and little Michel. And this one…"

As she continued to display picture after picture of a past Jacqueline did not yet know, Jacqueline's mind whirled. Then Dominique brought up a much-faded picture of Jacqueline herself, in her forge, her face swathed in her heat-resistant scarf, casting cogs. The room seemed to spin and Jacqueline's knees quaked. She fell into the chair and held her head.

"When I first saw you in the ER," Dominique said, closing the notebook, "I panicked. I thought you were my daughter Christine."

Again she set her hand to her heart. "The more I studied you, the more I was convinced you were part of my family somehow, a cousin I hadn't met, maybe. So I began researching on Ancestry, and sure enough, there you were."

Dominique chuckled quietly. "I never imagined I was treating my own ancestor. But it isn't so fantastical when I consider the stories I've been told about the mad genius Jacqueline Duval. I'd never have believed half of them if I didn't bear evidence in my own body—and in my children—that some things are beyond simple explanation. You fought vampires and ghosts. You really traveled through time. My great-great grandmother insisted the women in the family keep the name Fees. Perhaps this is why? I wish—"

"I have to get back," Jacqueline said flatly. "Obviously I do get back, or you wouldn't be here. But how? Where can I build another—"

"Electromagnetic trans-aether teleport?"

Jacqueline grunted a humorless laugh. "Is that what they called it?"

"That's what Mémé Dominique called it in her journal."

Dominique sat on the bed and searched Jacqueline's face. "Mémé, how do you feel? You said you were struck by lightning, and you woke up here, in this time, in Philadelphia. Your EKG shows a healthy heart, undamaged. Your EEG doesn't show any indication a billion volts passed through your body."

Jacqueline again waved off the unfamiliar terms. "'Volts'? As in voltaic piles?" She slumped. "It would take me into my old age to catch up with all the polytechnique of the past two centuries." She rubbed her nose. "And my arm hurts. Do I really need this tubing?"

"Your bloodwork was a little off when you came in. It's fine now—I imagine the addition of a little vampire blood is the reason?"

Jacqueline shuddered.

"Still, you need fluids and electrolytes." Dominique smiled an apology. "I think you're handling all this rather well, considering. And I know a bit about these things."

"Trans-aether chronological displacement?"

"No, trauma."

Dominique tapped her own icon pendant. Jacqueline saw the woman's name, but didn't grasp the meaning of the many letters following it, other than Ph.D and M.D.

"My specialty is neuroscience, specifically brain trauma."

"Ah, well," Jacqueline replied, spreading her hands, "traumatic circumstances have defined life at Bellesfées for the past five years."

Dominique chuckled, again patting her chest over her heart. "And many more years to come, Mémé."

Jacqueline gazed out the window again, chewing the inside of her cheek. "I don't see how. I don't know how I got here. How can I get back?"

"My mémé used to say, 'There's always a way for the daughters of Bellesfées.'"

Jacqueline grinned sadly. "I've always said that, too. At least the first part."

"Perhaps this way forward is your way home, Jacqueline Marie-Claire Duval de la Forge-à-Bellesfées." She put her hand on Jacqueline's shoulder. "You said it yourself. You visited the Husker tragedy because those children's blood was soaked into the coal. You visited the Sharp factory and witnessed more children's deaths, and their blood was directly connected to that fat man, Armand. We have to surmise that something in the trains of the Franklin Institute is equally connected."

Jacqueline's eyes widened as she listened to her own voice coming from Dominique, following a logic path she had already traced in her mind in the past hours.

"You said I was found in the cab of a locomotive in the institute. Is that close by?"

Dominique nodded. "The Franklin Institute. It has a huge locomotive on display, and that's where they found you. There's also a locomotive you'd probably find more familiar, a little steam engine called Rocket. No," she said quickly when Jacqueline's eyes widened, "not Stephenson's Rocket, but similar enough."

She leaned forward, and again her wolf eyes sparkled. "From England. Just like your haunted train, Mémé. And it arrived here in 1838. Via steamship. A steamship fueled with coal."

Jacqueline clasped Dominique's hand, silently pleading. Dominique reached under the bed and retrieved a large sack made of a similar substance as the gelatinous bag feeding fluids into Jacqueline's arm. Jacqueline could see her clothes through the gel. Dominique tucked it back and set a finger to her bowed lips, so like de Guise's, so full of mischief.

"Not now. It's almost four in the morning. After breakfast," Dominique whispered. "I'll handle the police reports and get you discharged." She led Jacqueline back to bed. "Fais do-do, Mémé," she said as she tucked her in and raised the railing.

She kissed Jacqueline's brow. Then she tugged a chain behind Jacqueline's head, extinguishing the dim light.

But Jacqueline didn't sleep. How could she? Dominique had shown her a world beyond any design she could imagine. She could still see the tall, multi-colored, lighted towers and giant aerostats in the orange of night through the window. The aerostats reminded her of her conversations with Ada King on the countess's theory of flyology. It made her happy to think someone had listened to Ada at last.

A science institute named Franklin. Probably for Benjamin Franklin, notable in Philadelphia and equally famous in France, and particularly famous at the Polytechnique for his early work in electricity.

And now electricity measured brain activity and blood flow. It summoned people from a distance without the horrid ratchet sound of a Henry doorbell. Jacqueline looked at the device Bill had placed under her pillow, with all its buttons—some round, some square, some numbered, some with pictographs, some with abbreviations she couldn't decipher. Bill had said something about "TV." She found a button with those letters and depressed it.

The large flat box near the ceiling and opposite her bed lit up with moving images of people. Sounds, voices, music emanated from the device in her hand. It was like spying into someone's home: a group of four companions, three men and a woman, arguing about the use of an exclamation point. With every sentence Jacqueline could hear laughter as well, as if others in the room found the conversation equally asinine. Then suddenly the picture changed to display too many flashing words, and a grinning man with huge white teeth shouted at her in capital letters about MEDICARE BENEFITS. Jacqueline hastily punched the TV button again, to no avail. She pressed every button on the device until the box went dark and silent. Jacqueline was glad she was no longer being monitored for her blood pressure and pulse.

Jenny came in and turned on the dim light behind her. "What did you need, Miss Duval?"

Jacqueline blinked at the woman stupidly. Had one of the buttons summoned her? But an opportunity was an opportunity.

"I've been asleep for two days," she said. "May I promenade? Walk?"

Jenny tucked her finger under Jacqueline's odd colored bracelets to read what was printed there. "No, it's not a good idea right now. In the morning, someone can wheel you down to the solarium."

Jacqueline frowned, restless and frustrated. "I'm hungry for actual food. Is it possible to get a meal, and not cakes in a wrapper?"

"Sure." Jenny picked up the device that had initiated the TV. She showed her the yellow rectangular button at the bottom with a pictograph of a fork's tines. "This calls room service. You tell them what you want, and it'll be here in about thirty minutes. Maybe sooner. What would you like?"

Jacqueline did not have to think twice. "Dimsdales," she said. "Do you have dimsdales in Philadelphia? It's a round pastry with a hole in the center."

Jenny returned the device to her. "Never heard them called that before. I think you mean donuts. Or bagels? Is it sweet or bread-like?"

"Sweet." Jacqueline closed her eyes, savoring the thought of Sam's mother's treat. "We called them dimsdales. And maybe strong coffee? With cream and sugar."

"Of course. You gotta have something to dunk 'em in." Jenny patted her hand.

Everyone patted her hand in this hospital as if Jacqueline truly were over two hundred years old, fragile and feeble-minded.

"What about some protein?" Jenny suggested. "An omelet maybe?"

Jacqueline's stomach rumbled, and Jenny grinned.

"An omelet with cheese would be very good," Jacqueline agreed. It would be easier to think on a full stomach. She pressed the fork button, and to her shock, a voice came from the device.

"Room service. How may I help you?"

Voices, coming through the wires, coming through the air. Images of people from far away. Jacqueline trembled. Jenny took the device to place the order for her. Jacqueline lay back, dismayed. She wanted to ask about the TV, but that would give her away as someone missing part of her memory, and the hospital or the police would want to keep her for more tests. She wasn't sure how much Dominique could protect her. Better to stay quiet.

When Jenny left, Jacqueline listened to the sounds around her, beyond the door and the window. Claxons and wailing whistles outside, the regular rumble of an aerostat, but no steady thrum of machinery. Muted bell-like ringing and muffled voices inside, occasionally a sound like her clockwork porters trundling along the hallway.

It was less than twenty minutes when a heavy-set woman with skin darker than Dumas pere's plodded in carrying a tray with a domed charger. She set it down on the bed table and wheeled the bed table over Jacqueline's legs.

"Here you go, Miz Duval," she said as she removed the dome. "Cheese omelet, a pack of donuts, and coffee. Enjoy." Then she waddled out again.

Jacqueline assessed the items on her bed table, perplexed. Yes, a cheese omelet, very plain, unseasoned. How was she to eat it? There were no utensils. Yes, a spongy cup, with a lid made of the same substance as her bracelets, held coffee without cream or sugar. Yes, three very tiny dimsdales, imprisoned in the same wrapping as the little chocolate cakes had been. And another packet with a white cloth inside. When she picked it up to examine it, she found her utensils within. She bit into the wrapping and extracted a small knife, fork, and spoon, a napkin made of pulpy paper, and three little paper packets: salt, pepper, sugar. Peering around the tray more closely, she found two tiny sealed cups hiding under her plate: 'dairy creamer.' The obvious redundancy of the words made her wonder if there was also a non-dairy cream in this century.

In the end, she concluded gastronomy had a dismal future, making her all the more anxious to return to 1843, *Esprit*, and Marthe's cornucopia.

Jacqueline was still covered in the dimsdales' powdered sugar when Bill returned.

"Up and rarin' to go?" he said with his infectious grin. He looked tired though; in fact, he looked worn and much older than he had three hours earlier. He also now wore blue pyjamas, and she pondered how the green ones may have been soiled, given his rôle. The four-year-old gunshot victim Dominique had mentioned preyed on her mind.

"I'll be going off soon," Bill told her as he flitted about the room checking the bag that fed her, removing the food tray to a table near the door, closing the curtains again. He then put the clamp on her finger and wrapped the blood-pressure meter onto her arm once more, and she grimaced as it squeezed and squeezed, though it was much more tolerable now that she knew it would stop before doing any damage. The little gun in his pocket, she deduced, was to measure her body temperature. He seemed satisfied in all things as he entered the information into the blue machine.

He came back and patted her hand. "It was nice to meet you, Miss Duval. I'm glad it all worked out. Dr. Fees says you'll be going home today. Good luck!"

"Thank you, Bill," Jacqueline said.

She knew the man had no idea what 'going home' meant for her. She herself wasn't sure what it meant.

16.

De Guise's one blood-shot eye flashed wildly, the flesh around his empty eye socket twitching. His body spasmed every few seconds and he'd bark random words, but in the main, he kept up a rambling account of Marteau's work.

"But they don't die, you see," he explained, his voice raw, hoarse. "Pils! The flesh goes on. What's flesh but cells? Cells get replaced. Theseus's ship. Grandfather's axe. My body. Doesn't matter. It's all matter. Chérie! Alive or dead. The ship isn't the ship, or the axe the axe, but Theseus lives and so does your grandfather. My ship. Live flesh. Life inside. Thinks, you see. Brilliant! I did that. Wasn't my first test. Wasn't my fiftieth. But I got it right. Vermouth! Kids. That's the key. So active. So much energy. That's where Victor went wrong, you see. He found the elemental source, but he used dead flesh from adults. Used up. Kids. Live kids. Pregnant! Little moldable brains. They die anyway. Buy another one. They die too. They all die. Skull! But they don't die, you see."

The soliloquy took up again, repeating an endless loop.

Gryffin drew his hands down his stubbled face. Monsieur Goüin's men had scrambled down to the floor when the locomotive reappeared on the track at the same moment the four women vanished. Monsieur Goüin remained, looking very much like a man whose world had exploded, pieces flung and falling haphazardly around him. Lack of sleep wore on them all except Marteau. Manic and maniacally smug, Marteau, through de Guise, had been babbling for two hours.

The men were inspecting the locomotive. Angélique watched from the window overlooking the factory floor to shield herself from the strength of the odors. Blood covered their hands, their clothes, their shoes. They looked like they had bathed in it. Nausea roiled, and she felt feverish. Her head pounded. Her eyelids scraped like sandpaper. Her belly cramped, and every time she closed her eyes, dizziness overtook her.

Gryffin had insisted no one explore the firebox to learn Jacky's fate lest anyone else go missing. Monsieur Vincent had argued, but Gryffin said there were more pressing matters. He interrogated Monsieur Vincent and Monsieur Coquelet about the moment the four had disappeared, but they were both adamant: one moment they were in the sling; then lightning passed through each of them and they were gone. Yes, each a separate bolt. Yes, at the same instant. Yes, the black vortex dissipated as soon as the women disappeared. As the locomotive reappeared.

Monsieur Goüin had no color left in his face. He sat with his arms on his thighs, his blood-stained hands dangling, his head bowed as he stared down at the accursed little engine. Angélique would have pitied him if her worries were not so much greater than a hunk of metal and bolts.

First Jacky, now the women. Were they together, or scattered across time and the world? Angélique worried especially for Justine, so young, everything so fresh to her. The others were old enough to take care of themselves, had taken care of themselves for years, but not Justine.

"Fy nghariad," Gryffin called softly, "it hasn't even been twenty-four hours since Jacky disappeared."

The very word—*disappeared*—sent a shiver through her. Angélique put her hand to the window and leaned her forehead against the glass. *Where are you, Jacky?*

Gryffin laid his hands on her shoulders and rubbed with his thumbs. "You must admit, fy nghariad, this is turn-about for the years of torment you gave her."

Angélique hung her head wearily. "If I'd known this was what she was feeling—"

He hugged her.

"Feeling, yes, feeling. Chérie! That's it, feeling." Marteau, inside de Guise, laughed. "That's it! Count! You take that away, anything's possible with flesh, but the brain, you see, the brain poisons everything. The—Clock!—brain wants a reason. The brain wants rules. The brain wants. That's a problem. That's the suffering. That's the failure of the skin. Forge! Remove the skin, you can do anything."

Angélique stifled an exasperated scream. "Can't we put the gag back on?"

"I'm hoping he'll reveal some detail that can aid us." Monsieur Goüin slapped his thighs and stood. "I'm beginning to think he won't, however."

De Guise laughed again. "Hah! Fight!" he barked.

Monsieur Goüin stared down at de Guise's bound and twitching form. "Are you certain de Guise is still in there?"

Angélique nodded. "I trust Justine and Adèle. Both of them have senses beyond ours."

Monsieur Goüin passed his hand up his brow, then rubbed the back of his neck. "I could use some coffee. Your Grace? Your Grace?"

De Guise shouted, "Wine!" Then resumed, "They're not dead, you see…" and droned on.

"I won't waste a good bottle of Bellesfées on you, you bastard," Angélique muttered.

"Language, ma fille! Ah, but the brain, the brain, you see…"

Monsieur Goüin smirked. "We could probably use something stronger than wine, but given the hour, I think coffee is best."

"Wrong! Victor was wrong," de Guise insisted. "So wrong. Clock! He found the elemental principle, but not the—Colt!—right source. Kids. So full of Vermouth! They all die anyway. But they don't die, you see? Wolf! That's the failure…"

Gryffin seized Angélique's arm. "Listen!"

She rolled her eyes, yanking her arm away. "I've been listening for hours."

"Listen!" De Guise shouted. Then he laughed. "The brain wants. That's the problem you see. Drunk!"

Gryffin stooped and stared into de Guise's good eye. "Tell me again about Victor," he said slowly. He signaled to Monsieur Goüin, who paused at the door as Angélique came behind Gryffin, placing her hand on his back.

"Victor was wrong. Drunk! Victor used adults. Corpses. But live kids. Vermouth! Full of energy. Moldable brains, you see. Sherry! He found the principle element, but he didn't know what to—Pils!—do with it. I found it."

Angélique slapped a hand over her mouth. Then she clasped Monsieur Goüin's arm. "Vermouth, Monsieur Goüin. Do you have vermouth? A good sherry or port? Anything stronger?"

Monsieur Goüin looked from Angélique to Gryffin to de Guise. "I'll be right back."

Angélique blew out a heavy breath, patting her chest to still her racing heart. "Two hours we've been listening and not hearing. Do you think it will work?"

Gryffin turned aside so Marteau would not eavesdrop. "De Guise thinks so, and that's good enough for me."

"But they don't die, you see. Knockers! It's the cells. They get replaced. Like Theseus's axe. Your grandfather's ship."

"Augh," Angélique cried. "If he'd only shut up!"

"Pregnant!"

Gryffin spluttered a laugh.

Thunder ceased. The bone-shattering rumble receded to a dim hum, then silence. Guichet opened her eyes. She still clasped Frontenac's hand. They lay in the sling. Guichet's disappointment at their failure welled up in a groan. She blinked and stirred, then realized the sling was smaller, snugger. She sat up and peered about.

A factory, but not Goüin's locomotive factory in Orléans. Her sluggishness passed as her heart pounded with excitement. She shook her companion.

"We did it," she whispered urgently. She gently tapped Frontenac's cheeks. "Wake up!"

A door at the far wall burst open. Guichet hugged Frontenac, trembling, as two men, one fat, one tall and bearded, stalked across the bay followed by a young boy about nine or ten years old. The waddling man yelled in English, but Guichet knew no English. She squeezed Frontenac to waken her, hoping her friend's talents would be able to translate for them.

"Forgive us, monsieur," Guichet answered in French. She hoped the quaver in her voice would appeal to his sympathy. "We're looking for Duval."

The fat man halted so abruptly his belly jiggled. The tall, bearded man set his hand on the fat one's arm, who shook him off to address the women in French. "So am I, looking for Madame Duval. She was right there not two minutes ago. Where the devil's she gone?"

Hope kindled in Guichet's heart. If Duval had lain in this sling moments ago, perhaps she had initiated the same maelstrom, flying back to 1843. Leaving Guichet and Frontenac in her place, but that didn't matter as much as having saved Duval. At least they could find their way to France to reunite with her.

Guichet stammered, "It—it would help if we knew where—We arrived so suddenly, we don't know how—"

The fat man's red face deepened in color. "Beyer, what the hell is going on in this place? What am I paying for here?"

The tall man, Beyer, inclined his head, answering in stilted French. "I am sure I do not know what happened, Monsieur Armand. I am certain this was not Madame Duval's goal. See, the young lady is faint."

As Frontenac moaned and held her head, Guichet pulled her closer, the back of her neck tingling. Monsieur Beyer had said "Monsieur Armand." Of course, Armand was not an uncommon name in France, but in England? The man financing the P-O railway? The very fat financier the duchess had described? The coincidence was too much to ignore. This adipose blob had to be Frontenac's fiancé. She knew exactly what Têtue would say to that. But Guichet had another idea, though only half formed, a way to exact some revenge for her friend's misfortune by getting Armand lose the money he had cheated out of Monsieur Frontenac. First, though, she needed to make sure it was he.

She gasped and squealed in delight. "Are you *Rodolphe* Armand? The famous banker? I've heard of you. My father speaks of you often. Gaspard Frontenac?"

The deep crimson faded slightly from Monsieur Armand's face. He huffed. "Don't know the man."

By now Frontenac had awakened, still disoriented.

Guichet continued blithely. "I am his daughter Adèle, and this is my friend Madame Guichet."

She peered into Frontenac's eyes, willing her to comprehend their circumstances. Frontenac nodded and feigned weakness. Guichet reached out her hand.

"Would someone be so kind as to help us descend?"

At Monsieur Armand's signal, Monsieur Beyer responded hastily, and the boy wore a goofy grin when Frontenac leaned on him.

"Are you hungry?" the boy asked. "Or want some coffee?"

They understood "coffee" and indicated they would indeed like some. Behind them, Monsieur Armand puffed with every breath as Monsieur Beyer escorted the two of them to sit by the table with a huge coffee urn. Guichet was relieved when Monsieur Beyer proved to be acceptable to her prescient sensibilities: a kind, generous, and unselfish man concerned for their welfare.

The boy offered them strange round pastries as well as meat pies. Guichet sighed heavily, and she remembered how exhausted Montpellier had been after descending from the invisible train; crossing the aether must be the cause of their physical weakness.

Montpellier!

Guichet swallowed the rising lump in her throat. Where were Têtue and Montpellier? Frontenac gripped Guichet's hand, her eyes reflecting the same fear.

Monsieur Beyer sat beside Guichet and spoke gently, his soft eyes full of care for them both. "Please, madam, explain how you know Madam Duval, and how you come to be here in her place." He pointed to the cage. "She claims she built this device to save a failed locomotive in Orléans, at Monsieur Goüin's factory. I would like to know how it works, how she could accomplish her task, and just what the purpose of this device truly is."

Guichet chewed her meat pie and drank coffee. She had learned from Duval it was a good way to stall for an answer.

"We work for her," Frontenac blurted out. "We work in her forge, in Bellesfées. We were trying to build a communication system that would send electrical waves to carry a message between Bellesfées and Orléans. But—"

"A wireless telegraphic system?" Monsieur Armand sat, his sizable bottom drooping over the seat like too much ganache on an éclair. He gazed up at the gigantic machine. "That's what I've built?" He pulled at his uppermost chin, obviously contemplating the financial rewards of such an invention.

Guichet feigned a groan. "You have no idea how much money Duval spent putting these machines together."

"*Pfft.* I rather think I do," he said.

"I told her she should find someone to invest in her work. I handle her finances, you see. I thought I could negotiate terms for her, but you know Duval."

"*Hmph.* I know she can be stubborn." Monsieur Armand turned back to Guichet. "But ridiculous at this cost."

"That's what I told her. I hope you weren't thinking of investing in it, Monsieur Armand. Why, the principle would be enormous."

"So would the return," he observed.

"Certainly that's what we hoped," Guichet said. "We built two prototypes in France to test them, one at Bellesfées and one in Orléans, and Duval came here because—the—euh…"

"Because the failed locomotive engine required more detailed information from the base factory," Frontenac threw in.

"Exactly." Guichet agreed. "She was in the middle of relaying that information to us when—" She looked around, indicating the locale. "Here we are. And I don't doubt she is there. Unless she accidentally transported to Orléans and is with Monsieur Goüin as we speak."

Guichet exaggerated a sigh of appreciation for the coffee and breakfast. She wasn't accustomed to lying, and she worried her innate ability would find a way to right that wrong. Her mind, though, was racing.

"I suppose one could count this a fortunate turn," she continued. "We hoped only to send thought waves, but being able to transport a person is quite an accomplishment. I wonder if Duval will finally consider selling the design now that such results have been achieved? She certainly needs the money."

Frontenac finally appeared to catch on to Guichet's scheme. She shrugged. "If Monsieur Marteau gets the funding he seeks, he will likely open that ironworks near the Paris-Orléans factory and cash in on the railroad stock market before Duval can recover."

"Well, Duval doesn't have the finances to try again," Guichet commented. "And with her workshop destroyed, she'll have to wait another two years before she can get the forge up and running to work on it. Ah, well."

She wiped sugar from her hands and drank her last bit of coffee. Setting the mug down, she wondered what Frontenac could glean from Monsieur Armand's thoughts. Had their little plot worked? Would he find a way to align with Marteau and be financially ruined when they destroyed his factory?

"Madame Guichet, we really should be returning to Bellesfées, don't you think?"

Frontenac also sighed, more from weariness. "We should, Madame Frontenac. Perhaps the gentlemen would be so kind as to initiate our electro-magnetic trans-aether telegraphic?"

Rodolphe Armand flustered. "Hold on, hold on, mesdames." He peered into Guichet's face, a sly glint in his eye. "What kind of investment were you hoping for, Madame Frontenac?"

Monsieur Beyer cleared his throat.

"Quiet, Beyer," Armand snapped. "Saxony, remember."

Frontenac offered a forlorn expression. "Alas, monsieur, I'm afraid we are beyond salvaging. As we told you, our workshop lies in ashes, and what, with lumber strikes, you know… Perhaps in another two years or so we'll be ready to put the design up for bids, especially if Monsieur Marteau uses his revolutionary technology to improve his cast iron for the railroad. Such a device allied with the railroad would be financially advantageous."

Monsieur Armand's little piggy eyes glinted.

Guichet and Frontenac stood, thanking Monsieur Beyer and the young boy for their hospitality.

"Please, ladies," Monsieur Beyer pleaded. "From what I witnessed, this machine provides the most painful means of transport I can imagine, based on what I observed in Madame Duval's experiment and your own disorientation when you arrived. The power within the re-generated electrical charges could kill you."

Guichet knew he could be right, but she forced herself to laugh dismissively. "Monsieur, the fact that we are here proves you are mistaken. I know the display is frightful to behold, but as you can see, we're both perfectly whole, if somewhat wearied from journeying such a distance."

They walked toward the cage.

"Wait!" Monsieur Armand cried. He waddled to catch up to them. "What's to stop me from simply taking this machine for myself?" he said. "If you won't negotiate, I can simply take what I've paid for. I financed this whole construction, after all."

Frontenac batted her long lashes and let tears moisten her wide blue eyes. "Oh, monsieur! I would hope honesty and integrity would preclude such an abhorrent action. I beg you, contact Duval at Bellesfées for negotiations. Can you not wait two years?"

His eyes squinted when he smiled, but it was a predatory smile nonetheless. Guichet wasn't sure she was only imagining the saliva dripping from his mouth when he said, "Of course, two years is not unreasonable."

Frontenac squeezed her hand, but Guichet already knew the man was lying.

Monsieur Beyer reluctantly took them back into the cage and assisted them in climbing into the sling. His eyes were sad.

"Is there nothing I can say, nothing I can offer you, to prevent you from subjecting yourselves to this?" he asked quietly so only they could hear.

Monsieur Armand's eyes gleamed in slavering anticipation.

"On the contrary," Frontenac murmured. "That man has been financing a most horrific enterprise that will culminate in the Marteau Ironworks in Orléans in the future. Children will be slaughtered, and their blood is on Monsieur Armand's hands. Our aim is to bring him down. I beg you, monsieur, find a way to balance the ledger. I can sense how your heart breaks for us, who suffer no danger in this. How your heart must ache for the little ones who die in this place, and in other factories like this one."

"The railroad will succeed," Guichet added. "I don't doubt you'll prosper. You're a good and selfless soul. Use your gifts wisely, as we use ours."

She flicked her wrist. An overhead lamp dropped and crashed to the floor behind Monsieur Armand, who yelped and tripped away. She tapped the side of her nose and winked to Monsieur Beyer.

"Trans-aether teleportation," she said.

Monsieur Beyer's brow furrowed. "He has no compunction about stealing Duval's technology."

Frontenac smiled. "He can try. We'll have no compunction about exacting a price. Please, monsieur. Our mission is not yet complete. We must find Duval. Let us go."

He scrunched his beard. "Go where? To Orléans? To 1843? Or somewhere, somewhen else?"

Guichet caught her breath, realizing Monsieur Beyer had not been fooled by their charade. She gazed back sadly. "We simply do not know, monsieur."

She turned her eyes to the control panel. It opened, and the switch was thrown. "Farewell, Monsieur Armand!" she called as Monsieur Beyer pulled him from the bay. "I am so looking forward to seeing you in two years' time."

"My pleasure, Madame Frontenac," Monsieur Armand replied. He yelped again as a stray arc of electricity struck his uplifted hand.

Frontenac snickered. "You're getting quite good," she said to Guichet.

Guichet grinned and took her friend's hand. The two of them lay back with less trepidation than previously, knowing what they would experience.

As the welcome maelstrom began to form, Guichet fretted anxiously. "Do you think we sent Duval home by coming here? And how do we know if we can get—"

Lightning exploded through them.

Angélique and Gryffin descended from Monsieur Goüin's carriage at the Marteau Ironworks. When de Guise stepped down, he crumpled to the sidewalk, laughing until he gave himself hiccoughs. Monsieur Claque gathered him up into his arms. A grin slewed across his face as he clumsily clapped Gryffin's back.

"Good thing I hold my liquor, hey?" He hiccoughed, his head loling against Monsieur Claque's torso. "Took you two damn long enough."

Angélique huffed. "You hit me over the head, you bastard. I was in no mood to listen."

De Guise pouted, glassy-eyed. "S-s-sorry. Didn't—hic—Could—hup—n't stop him."

Angélique had removed her underclothing in case she needed to turn wolf in haste. Likewise, Gryffin had stripped down to trousers and chemise. Sançille had lent a shirt and coat for Monsieur Claque, while Monsieur Vincent found a pair of coveralls for him. Not that he would sufficiently blend in with the others, but it was enough to give him a pass at first glance.

They didn't bother with the back entrance but went straight through the front doors. A new shift of workers was heading in. No one paid the four of them any heed as Gryffin led them up a staircase to the executive offices, where staff would not arrive before eight o'clock. They continued toward the rear of the building and up the stairway Têtue and de Guise had used earlier. They paused; Gryffin carefully cracked the door.

Angélique's heart sank and her stomach lurched when she smelled dead skin, like the creature the young women had fought.

"Two," Gryffin whispered. "Not so big as the huge thing in the lab. Claque, you know how to handle them. Do it swiftly, please."

Monsieur Claque leaned de Guise against the wall and ignited his revolving stake-gun. Once the steam pressure built up, he clomped down the hallway, his arm extended to fire. One hulk went down with a stake in its head. Monsieur Claque chased the other one and seized it, slammed it on its head, and staked it to the floor.

"He's good," de Guise slurred. "Glad Jacqueline ke—hup—him."

Gryffin helped him stagger down the hall to the laboratory. Angélique followed, nausea rising in her throat at the odors. When she stepped into the laboratory, the shambles there overwhelmed her. She doubled over in a spasm and vomited.

"Fy nghariad?" Gryffin called.

She retched again. Monsieur Claque held back her hair and rubbed her shoulders soothingly, little puffs of steam pooting from his casque. Her whole body ached with her throes. She coughed and spat to clear her throat and mouth.

"Just making up for the last few mornings." She dabbed sweat from her face and leaned on Monsieur Claque's arm to regain her balance.

Gryffin placed de Guise in the center chair beneath the needle-nosed behemoth. He followed de Guise's clipped instructions to initiate the huge clockwork engine and engage the metrometometers. As the tubes in each of them took on an electric glow, Gryffin returned to position the pipette. He met de Guise's gaze worriedly.

"Are you sure of this, my friend?"

He burped and hiccoughed. "Hurry. If he wakes up in the middle of this, I don't know what'll happen."

Angélique pressed her sleeve to her mouth and breathed through it to stifle some of the stench of the room. Glass still covered the floor, and the giant mass of dead flesh the girls had fought remained in a heap. Steeling herself, she came to de Guise's side and helped Gryffin place the tip of the pipette into the empty eye socket.

"I hope the cauterization hasn't closed off the optic nerve," Gryffin said.

De Guise grinned. "Me too." He waved his hand to shoo her away. "Out of the room, Angélique. This is—big."

She bit her lip. "Come back for her," she told him, with mock sternness. "No excuses, you cheap bourgeois."

She reached for Gryffin's hand. "My love—"

But she didn't know what to say. She pressed to him as he held her, her stomach weak and cramping, her breath straining against her fear. Gryffin led her to the door and closed her out into the hallway with the deanimated lumps of human skin. She laid her head against the door and listened. A loud hum of electricity erupted, then grew to a deafening rumble that rattled the wood and shook the floor.

De Guise screamed.

She had never heard a man scream. She winced and gasped, her hands curled to her heart as his shrieks rose in pitch. De Guise, the man of equanimity, the man of cool collectedness, screamed for his life. His cries cut through her like the spikes through the heads of those creatures of molded flesh. She dropped to her knees. How long would it take? How long could he hold out? Short, barked shrieks. More prolonged screams. The needle sliding along the optic nerve. Electricity dragging Marteau out of de Guise's brain and —

Then where? How could de Guise be sure he wouldn't be expelled as well?

Above the thunderous noise of the laboratory, she heard running footsteps. With a cry, she peeled off her daydress and crouched to change form. Her skin was so filthy with oil, it hurt when her hair follicles widened to allow her pelage to grow. The shifting of her skeleton, usually a pleasurable sensation, seemed to rip her bones and tear sinew as her musculature fought to find the wolf shape. As soon as her face and tail emerged, a sharp pain cut like a sword stabbing up between her legs. A seizure gripped her, dropping her to her side, panting. She moaned and whined.

No! Please, no!

Footsteps were nearer.

Get up! Get up!

Pain ebbed but remained. Angélique struggled to her feet. Large men in work overalls rushed into the hall from the room nearby. Thank heaven, they were unarmed. She coiled to spring at them, baring her fangs in a snarl. They balked. Then behind her at the far end of the hallway, the stairwell door banged open. She wheeled about with a growl.

Monsieur Vincent led Coquelet and his team, armed with large wrenches or pry bars. Relief overwhelmed her. She collapsed to her side again.

"The wolf's harmless!" Monsieur Vincent cried. "Protect this corridor."

Coquelet, Sançille, Simon, and Bardît pursued the workers out of the hallway while Monsieur Vincent knelt beside her and stroked her flank as De Guise's weakened cries fell beneath the rumble of the machinery.

Angélique's belly throbbed. She yelped. "*Gryffin!*"

"*Not yet,*" he answered her. "*Fy nghariad, what's wrong?*"

She moaned as another slash tore into her. Monsieur Vincent hugged her neck and comforted her.

"*Angélique!*"

She keened as blinding pain ripped up into her belly. Her vision swam and blurred. She could no longer hold on to her wolf form.

Monsieur Vincent gasped. "Ah, madame, no. Not here."

He released her and snatched up her dress to cover her as fur retreated into her skin and her human shape took hold. He wrangled the dress over her head as Coquelet and the others reappeared.

"What the hell, you bastard," Sançille hollered. He ran at Monsieur Vincent, his pry bar raised to strike.

"Stop!" Angélique gasped. She clawed at her dress and pulled it all the way over her head. "Leave him — Ah! — leave him be."

The young men stared, pity and horror in their eyes.

Angélique clutched at her stomach and fell into Monsieur Vincent's arms as blood gushed from her womb. When she saw the tiny blue form in the flow, breath left her being.

17.

Justine Montpellier drifted among stars, a sparkling blanket suspended in the endless night, a spangled canopy over her vast, eternal bed like the one in her room at Bellesfées. Blue, red, yellow, orange, purple, violet, green, brown, black, white. But thousands more. Millions more. Colors no one had ever identified to her called out their names to her, and she knew them. They whizzed around her in all directions. No wonder she could never see them before. She had been too close. She needed distance to understand what it was she was looking at, to hear all their voices, to learn all their names.

She was looking at life. At history. At all of time and existence.

And she belonged.

So small, yet all the universe was contained behind her eyes. There — the moment life began. There — the journey of light across a formless void. There — the beginnings of a swirling mass that would be Earth… that is Earth… that was Earth.

But focus now, Justine. See the children who need you.

Such a spectrum danced up, released from the colorless emptiness of their unrecognized agony. Têtue had sensed them, Duval and Frontenac had heard them, but Justine was the only one who could see them in all their splendor. She welcomed them into herself.

As it always was, and as it must be.

She found the others and reached for them.

The duke's deep rich ungoria had thinned to something close to violet. De Guise, pale eslin, so pale. Almost gone. The duchess's dazzle of purest gold had faded to the sad, lost color of old bronze. A wisp of sacred hol broke away and arose from her, and Montpellier welcomed the child into herself.

As it always was and must be.

There—Maman and Papa. The farm. When she'd run away that night, she had left a note not to look for her. They now glowed happily, summer green and yunor. Without Justine, their blind daughter, life was easier.

And there was Jacques Cezet covered in the colors of mud: fitzel, gurdine, plek, zul.

Frontenac and Guichet floated on frosty, iridescent waves. Their aether flux reached for Duval's, but without sight, they couldn't find her.

And there was Duval. A brilliant flame far afield of its hearth and heart. Justine had always thought her merely pink, the deep amaranth of Bellesfées, but now her eyes were open, and she saw Duval's true colors: gevania, rident, belinep, indeara.

And, of course, in all of them, sacred hol.

Têtue awoke in a chair. Terror seized her when she saw the familiar pipette directly above her eye. She batted it out of the way and leapt up to cast about the room.

"Marteau!" she bellowed. "Marteau, I'll kill you! You won't get me, you piece of shit!"

The room was empty. She smelled nothing else, no one else, in the room. No sound in the room but her own panicked breathing and her pulse in her ears.

Beyond, the building rumbled with the familiar thunder of factory machinery. Another damned ironworks, she deduced from the odors and the heat.

This laboratory was not like Marteau's in Orléans. No clockwork engines. No electrometometers. No metal case with a glass lid. No body parts or unborn children floating in viscous fluids. But the gun above the chair she recognized, a more primitive form of the one in Orléans.

Where the devil was she? No, *when* the devil was she?

From the window, she gazed out over a cityscape on a river. Thousands of rooftops and chimney pots stretched away into the distance on a level terrain. Not Orléans or even Paris, then. The building she was in sat high above the narrow river, grey, green, and rainbowed with grease. Ship-fitting docks and more factories lined the opposite shore, pressed between tottering houses piled one atop the other such that the city huddled in layers of unending back slum. Soot mingled with the dust of horses and carriages and foot traffic. Nothing resembled any city she had seen in France.

England. It had to be England. Everything since the beginning of this damned adventure had centered on England: the haunted locomotive, the dead children, Sharp's factory. Maybe that's where she was: the Sharp locomotive factory. Maybe she'd found Duval at last.

Têtue headed out the door. Following the sound of machinery, she came to a draughting room similar to Coquelet's where a dozen young men sat at tables. She nodded familiarly and passed through the room unaccosted. She went downstairs to the factory floor, a smaller version of the bay in the P-O factory, where sat a locomotive very different from the one in Orléans. Cute thing with four green spoked wheels, a red fender, couldn't have been more than five meters long, maybe two meters high, another meter and a half for the stack. The cabin was a platform with just a railing, and not a sturdy one at that. A polished brass plaque on the boiler said the locomotive's name was Rocket. Another engraved brass tag identified Braithwaite, Milner, & Co. as the engine's maker, and the year as 1833…

The year was 1833.

In the village of Aÿ, east of Épernay, ten-year-old Dominique Durand was hauling the vendange, but couldn't keep her eyes off the handsome, dashing Comte Antoine Villermont, son of Athenase de Villermont who owned the land Messieurs Renaudin and Bollinger had developed into a premier champagne house. Antoine was a scholar, and as an aristocrat he was forbidden anything so menial as working a vineyard, but Dominique Durand still had plenty of dreams in her little head.

A foreman swung at her, yelling, "Hey, you stubborn brat, get to work!"

She dodged his blow, making him angrier. She grinned. "Têtue" — stubborn indeed. Plenty of dreams running around in her head, and she'd stubbornly refuse to let them go no matter who smacked her.

Têtue traced the numbers on the plaque with her fingertips. 1833. Two more years of the foreman smacking her head. Another year married to a wheezing old invalid whose son made use of her as a personal servant and mistress until the old man died of pneumonia. She was sent home with nothing, so back to the vineyard and her dreams until her father found another match: the foreman.

Têtue bowed her head to the boiler of the little engine. Then she slammed her fist against it and stalked away.

No scent of Duval. No scent of Montpellier. But Marteau was here, in the first stages of his experiments. If she killed him here and now, de Guise would be safe. Those kids would be safe, or at least they wouldn't be part of his grisly research. She couldn't figure out how Marteau was connected to the train in Orléans and Duval's disappearance in the first place, but she could think of no better reason for the electro-magnetic trans-aether teleporter to bring her here, separated from the others, and Marteau within her grasp.

She just had to find him.

"Anything wrong?" someone called to her.

Zut. She didn't speak a lot of English. A smattering she picked up in Paris, not enough to pass for fluent. She folded her arms as the older man in a workman's coat and cap neared. "Marteau," she said firmly, hoping to look like she belonged there.

"Marteau?" He looked at her curiously. "He's upstairs. Why would he be down here on the floor?"

Upstairs. Why. Down here. Those she knew.

Têtue shrugged.

"Try the tavern!" another worker jeered. "Probably drinking his lunch again, lousy frog."

They both laughed, but Têtue gave a nod of thanks and headed out the open bay doors. When she reached the street, she studied the shop fronts across the way. A bar named Lavender in Lime directly opposite the front of the factory seemed the most likely candidate for what the man had called tavern.

Têtue ducked to enter the small sitting room and headed to the bar. She bought a pint of beer with coins from Duval's pocket. The barman glared at the currency, but he didn't argue as she sat at a table in the corner where she could study the men in the room. She spotted Marteau immediately—the only non-workman, draughting designs in a notebook, leaning his head on one hand as he gripped and released, gripped and released his long greasy hair. Têtue watched and waited, working out which of the scents in the room was his while she enjoyed her pint. She made note of his drink, a dark stout, almost gone. She polished off her pint, then ordered another along with a stout. She carried them both to Marteau's table.

"Salut."

Marteau startled as Têtue greeted him in French and set the fresh stout in front of him. She was surprised the man appeared to be some sort of aristocrat, judging by the large ring he wore. His shoulder-length brown hair, swept back from his face, curled at the collar. A small, closely shaved beard sat like a triangle on his chin pointing up to his lower lip, and his moustaches formed a perfect downward crescent, all of which served to hide a small mouth. His whiskers sharply highlighted his high cheekbones, and his eyes were set wide above an aquiline nose.

Somehow she'd expected a deranged ghoul to be uglier.

She pointed to his work. "Nobody else understands, right?" She offered her hand. "Têtue. From Épernay. I'm in champagne."

They shook hands. "Marteau. Paris."

They tapped pint glasses. He drank, nodding.

She sat to his right and gulped deeply, then burped and sighed. "I know how that is. Come up with great ideas, nobody wants to pay for 'em."

He bent back to his design. "Bastards. Don't think it through, you see. They die anyway, right? Right? Might as well make use of what's right in front of them."

"Exactly."

She had no idea what he meant, but when he said "die anyway," she twitched, recalling the grisly collection of jars.

"This one, though. This will work. Just needs the right placement, you see."

She nodded, leaning to her elbows. "And who's going to pay for it, eh? I mean, these guys—" She jerked her thumb over her shoulder to indicate Braithwaite, Milner & Co. "They're not going to back you."

Marteau waved her away. "Once they see it work, they'll be begging me to expand it. A self-driving locomotive? Who's going to reject that?"

Her heavy brows shot up. "Zut alors! Can you really? I'd give anything to see that. I love a bit of clockwork."

He frowned. "Not clockwork. Not at all. More like Theseus's ship. Grandfather's axe."

She shook her head, not understanding.

Marteau finished his pint and gathered his notebook and pencil. "I'll show you."

She gulped the last of her beer and followed him back to the factory as he explained.

"You work vineyards, right? Suppose you have your grandfather's grape-picking knife. A harvest knife, right? It's old. The handle gets split. What do you do?"

What did harvesting grapes have to do with throwing children in with the charge? Her hand clenched reflexively. It was her harvesting knife that had set her on the road so many years ago. First she had slashed off her hair. Then…

"Replace the handle," she replied, shaking memory from her.

"Yes, replace it, you see. So, now you have a very good handle, but a few years later, the blade is rusted and pocked. The tip breaks. What do you do?"

"Replace the blade."

The blade coated in blood. Têtue winced, fighting to grasp the man's argument.

"Exactly. So you have a good handle, and you have a good blade. But is it still your grandfather's knife?"

She forced a laugh. "Good one. So how does that make a self-driving locomotive?"

They headed upstairs, then through the executive offices and the draughting room to return to Marteau's small lab. Inside, a little kid about five years old sat in the chair beneath the weapon, his chunky legs swinging, his bare feet lurid purple and swollen. Têtue stared at him, dread turning her stomach.

Marteau wasn't surprised to find the kid there. "Jimmy. Good." He spoke in English. "I heard you got hurt yesterday," he said as he helped the boy sit further back in the chair.

"Fell down 'e 'amsteads," the boy said. "Broke bof me plates."

Têtue couldn't follow the boy's English.

"Poor lad."

Her horror mounted when Marteau began strapping the boy into his accursed chair.

"You'll be running around good as new," he told the boy.

"What are you doing to him?" she protested. "What's that machine going to do?"

He continued securing the boy. "Skin, the largest, most receptive organ of the human form. Cells. Skin cells. Replace each other. New cells every couple weeks. Your grandfather's knife. When do you stop being you?"

"You don't!"

"Oi, wot's 'at fing?" The boy tried to struggle as the madman lowered the pipette closer to his face. "It's me plates, not me loaf!"

The wolf began to rise. She fought to keep it down so she could finally learn the sick bastard's plans.

"Marteau, explain this to me."

He gave an impatient sigh. "The skin isn't really you anymore. *You* are somewhere inside. I can take the you from the skin and place it inside something that will last. The locomotive. Jimmy will be the locomotive. He'll never wear out. He'll be around for the next two hundred, three hundred years."

He tightened another band on the boy, who began to cry.

"Oi! I want me mum! Lemme go!"

"You heard him," Marteau went on. "He broke both his feet falling down the stairs. He had to be carried here. He's no good to his family, no good to anyone. He can't walk, can't work. But the carbon in his cells will strengthen the iron, and the rest—oh, he'll run, you see."

He straightened up. When he met Têtue's face, his expression fell. "You don't approve." He shook his head at her, glaring like she was stupid. "It's just useless skin."

She snarled and snatched her knife from her sheath. "I can't let you do this."

"Cut 'im! Cut 'im!" the boy pleaded. "Don't let 'im hurt me!"

She stabbed and sliced, just like the duke had taught her.

Marteau yiped and grabbed his arm. "Putain!"

He swung out of her range as she stabbed again.

"They're just kids. They die in here anyway. What's the difference if they die by accident or for science, for the greater service to humanity?"

"What do you know of humanity!"

Têtue stabbed once more, into his back. Marteau reeled away from her, shouting curses. She held him at bay as she took a moment to free Jimmy. The boy flopped, unable to stand, wailing and sobbing. She hoisted him over her shoulder and escaped the laboratory. She stopped at the draughting room and set Jimmy down on a man's table.

"I want me mum!" he wailed.

As the confused draughtsman hastened to attend to the boy's cries, she returned to the laboratory with caution; she had given Marteau time to defend against her assault.

She listened at the door. When she heard harsh breathing on the other side, she kicked the door in. As she had guessed, Marteau had also pressed his head to the door, but he hadn't figured on her strength. Blood streamed from his broken nose, and he held his face in pain as he fell back against his table.

As she advanced on him, he slapped his hand around the work surface. Têtue came around the row of tables and leapt at him, cutting deep into his ribs. He seized a flask and threw it at her. It shattered on her chest.

Acid exploded into her face and eyes and across her breasts.

Têtue roared. Blinded, she beat at herself, screaming, screaming. Searing fire ate into her breasts, her cheeks, her jaw. Screaming wasn't enough. The torturous burning increased, digging deeper into her flesh and her eyes. Agony overwhelmed her senses.

Marteau tackled her to the floor. He grabbed her arm to wrest the knife from her hand. She jabbed upward, striking him, and kept pushing, forcing him off her, she couldn't see where.

Still she screamed. It burned. Everything burned. She saw nothing but fire. She couldn't breathe, but screamed nonetheless.

The wolf would heal her, but she had to get away while she could still walk. Blind, she staggered to her feet, shrieking, flailing the blade wildly. She bumped against the damned chair. Caroming away, she crashed backward into a cabinet.

The glass door shattered as her head broke through. Glass splinters slashed her arms and wrists. Gasping, she stared up through a bloody, burning haze at a large shard above her like the blade of a guillotine.

The blade dropped, slicing her carotid.

The smell of her own blood and burning flesh enraged her, but she couldn't find the wolf. She couldn't do a damned thing. The wolf couldn't do a damned thing but keep her alive. She slipped down into a pool of blood fed from her opened arteries.

"Foute."

Justine Montpellier raised a finger. The aether opened at her bidding. Rident from Duval touched the rident in Frontenac's purple. Their frays entwined and knotted as they found one another.

As Guichet soared and reached for her, Justine showed her amaranth and bleu-de-France and gold.

You're needed elsewhere.

She laughed and sent Guichet on her path.

Ho, là, Marteau, so sickly and broken, a sputtering grey, just grey, dead inside, clawing at the void, vainly clutching death to wield against Têtue's gold, yunor, white, and sacred hol.

Ah, but Têtue! Majestic, glorious, magnificent.

Justine stretched out to welcome Têtue into herself, as it always was and must be. The frays knitted and received her colors, all but sacred hol. Alarmed, Justine reached again, opening wider, to no avail.

Têtue was lost to her.

Marthe Benet kneaded bread first thing while the sky was still dark. She found it relaxing, pounding and shoving and folding and shoving until every lump was smooth and gleaming. By then the fire was up and hot, ready for the brioches and boules for the day.

Jean-Paul brought in the fresh milk and put it on to boil. "They're not home," he informed her. "The airship isn't here."

She grumbled to herself. "They didn't send word about staying. What are those two up to now?"

He shrugged. "It's not just those two anymore. First time the ladies have seen the city. Probably stayed to shop some more."

She nodded. "Without a doubt."

She took up kneading again, but her brow furrowed. Angélique had not mentioned morning sickness the past two days, and in Marthe's experience, that was not always a good sign.

Lisette came in to fetch her apron for eggs. She yawned and rubbed her red eyes.

"What's wrong, ma fille?" Marthe said. "I don't give you enough work to make you sleep at night?"

The girl coughed a few times. "Too noisy upstairs last night to sleep. I'm afraid to see what it looks like."

Angélique had hinted something about the upstairs servants' wing, insisting everyone keep clear of the noise and mess until her return. Again, and for the thousandth time, Marthe wondered what the twins had been up to.

"You can sleep at the cottage tonight. Have a hot coffee with boiled cream before you go out."

"Yes, Marthe."

Geneviève and Gaudin joined them just as brioches were coming out of the oven. Luc followed Geneviève inside, his face grim.

"Something's coming. Not very soon, but it doesn't look good."

He pulled off his cap and washed his hands as she waited for him to decide what to say. She handed him a towel, her brow raised.

"Big airship, fouler than dung. Heading our way. You girls stay inside. I'll keep an eye. Jean-Paul, get the new guns."

"Right away, Papa."

Jean-Paul left the kitchen juggling two hot brioches while Luc went back outside.

Marthe glared at the three wide-eyed girls. She put a fist on her hip and waggled a finger. "Don't you even pretend to be scared," she scolded. "You've been in worse and come through. Hurry your breakfast. You've got chores."

She heard them stifle laughter when she turned her back, but what was the point of being a housekeeper if you couldn't let the girls get away with a little fun? Heaven knows she couldn't tame the twins, and they turned out all right.

Mostly.

She tossed her towel across her shoulder and went out to find Luc. He stood in the western courtyard with a spyglass trained east against a dark blue sky.

"It'll spoil the last of the harvest," Luc said in disgust as he handed her the glass.

Marthe *tsk*ed. She couldn't see much detail, but whatever it was, it spewed who-knows-what from its tail end onto the fields on the horizon. But she wasn't thinking of the harvest.

"What have those girls done now?" She fretted. "You know this has something to do with why they're not home."

Luc shrugged. "Well, we're home. It's up to us."

Jean-Paul brought out the guns the mistress had re-fashioned and handed one to his father.

"Don't miss," Marthe said, and Jean-Paul snorted.

The two headed to the west turret to await the ship's approach.

Marthe shielded her eyes against the sun, glaring balefully at the distant pestilence. "How do those two get into such trouble?

18.

ANGÉLIQUE KEENED. SHE HAD RETURNED TO THE HEALING FORM OF THE wolf, but the wolf couldn't heal a wound that would not close. She snuggled around her lost little boy.

Gryffin removed the dress that encumbered her. He ripped away the bell sleeve and used the patch of fabric to swaddle the tiny form that he cradled in one hand while he caressed her. He murmured in her ear, but she didn't hear what he said. She stared into the sightless gaze of deep blue set in a featureless face but for a vague arch of the brow that indicated lupine eyes.

De Guise sagged between Coquelet and Simon, barely conscious, too weak to stand on his own. Vincent had traced the cabling of the macabre system Marteau had constructed and concluded that whatever part of the madman had inhabited de Guise now resided in the dome-lidded case, excitating the air within.

"But from there, I don't know where it can go," he said worriedly. "Whether he can do this again..."

At the moment no one cared, Angélique least of all. Grief consumed her. Llewellyn's tears fell into her ear, and she didn't twitch them away. She tenderly lapped the baby's head and nuzzled him. Têtue had guessed aright; wolf blood had advanced the development of the child in the womb.

Had wolf blood also expelled him?

The men had followed them to the ironworks in a wagon still laden with leftover parts from Jacky's machine. Monsieur Claque swiftly shoved the huge hunks of iron aside to make a place for her to lie in Gryffin's lap. Gryffin cupped the infant in his hands, and De Guise lay beside them. She could smell nothing but anger, terror, and grief.

She wanted Jacky.

She needed her sister, her twin, her other half. Surrounded by men and metal at that moment, she felt alone and lost. Not even her husband's shared pain could assuage the ache overwhelming her.

But why was she mourning? She would not have suspected pregnancy at all except she'd been sick every morning since the day her flow should have arrived and had not, a mere week after the wedding night. Reason said there was always a risk of loss, and so she had made no fuss. "Wait," Marthe had told her, "wait a few months to be sure." She had given no thought to her condition. Women became pregnant all the time; it was not a condition to be feared. She'd felt no anticipation of gender, had no list of possible names, planned no interviews for nursemaids. It had never seemed real until the flutters began, too soon, too soon. Then the delightful movements here and there. Still not real.

Her love for the unborn child, though, was real. How could she have so loved a child that didn't wholly exist? Yet, there he was, a tiny boy cradled in the palm of Gryffin's hand. Their son.

Love bled from her, and she grieved in quieter whines.

"It happens, fy nghariad, fy anwylyd," Gryffin murmured. "My beautiful golden angel, my Anyel, it will be all right. You'll be all right. I have you. I have you. I'll never let go of you."

Monsieur Goüin's men were grimly silent as the wagon trundled through the city, Monsieur Claque keeping pace alongside them. Her weeping eventually ceased. She pressed her head to Gryffin's chest, heaving tremulous sighs. By the time they arrived at the P-O factory bay and the first hints of indigo colored the pre-dawn sky, the wolf had healed her body. She consigned herself to the hollowness that filled her.

De Guise said, "Why don't you two go back to Bellesfées? There's nothing you can do here."

She protested with an angry snarl.

"The girls," Gryffin told him. "Angélique won't leave the girls and Jacky."

"Angélique, my dearest girl, you should be in bed." He chucked her chin.

She barked her response. Gryffin clenched his jaw, but he nodded.

"She has lost one child. She will not stand by to lose the others. By God, de Guise, you should realize that."

De Guise turned away. Monsieur Claque helped him descend from the wagon.

Vincent wept quietly. "Quel malheur. Quel horrible malheur," he murmured over and over.

Angélique recalled the words their esprit frappeur had left them: *les fleurs du malheur*. She whined. Where were her flowers? Where were those blossoms of womanhood? How could any joy come from this night if they were lost as well?

Monsieur Goüin met them, his face drawn. "Coquelet is fetching a doctor. Come quickly. There's—a development."

Angélique sensed the man's anxiety. She groaned and hunched down. Gryffin set the bundle in Vincent's hands and removed his coat for her as she changed form. When she stood, shaking, Gryffin wrapped the coat around her. Vincent returned the precious bundle to her arms. Gryffin held her as they followed Goüin to the bay and the locomotive sitting smugly on its track, refusing to give up its secrets.

But the air smelled different. Angélique lifted her head to sniff.

"The blood is gone."

She cuddled her child to her cheek as the others hurried to the locomotive.

The cabin gleamed as if freshly polished. The glass gauges were clear and clean.

Gryffin asked, "When did it disappear?"

"Not long after you left," Goüin said. "But there's more." He climbed up to the cabin and opened the firehole door.

Giggled laughter spilled from the firebox.

They stared at one another, perplexed. Despite their torn spirits, the infectious peals of laughter brought smiles to their faces.

Angélique smelled the wave of relief brought by the sounds of children of all ages playing in the sunshine, whooping and calling, giggling breathlessly. For herself, the hollowness within only deepened; she would never hear those sounds from her own child.

She held him closer.

Goüin hopped down again, leaving the door open. "'They that sow in tears shall reap in joy,'" he quoted. "I don't make suppositions, de Guise. I'm a man of facts. But the fact is, their mourning has turned to joy, as the psalmist promised. I never heard their cries of anguish, but I do hear their laughter. Do you believe, as I am persuaded, Madame Duval has accomplished her quest?"

"I don't," Angélique said flatly. "If she had, she would be here."

She sat on the bottom rung of the ladder to the cab, drinking in the laughter, all the sadder for the incongruity of the sound with her own grief.

"Jacky would be here. Têtue, Justine, Adèle, and Renée would be here. But they're not. Their particles are scattered across the universe and all of time. Without them, nothing's been accomplished." She bowed. "And so much has been lost."

De Guise leaned against the engine, his head tipped to the railing of the cabin. "You have to admit, though, it sounds a little more hopeful, dear Angie," he said. He sagged, and Monsieur Claque caught him up, scolding him with a puff of steam.

Gryffin pulled at his lower lip, frowning.

"What is it, my love?" Angélique reached for his hand and brought it to her cheek. "Something still worries you."

Gryffin indicated the firebox and the cheerful giggles. "How do the children of Husker figure into Marteau's devilry? 1838. Coal. How can that be related to the iron industry today, other than the willful abuse and careless slaughter of children? Why did this locomotive take Jacky to Husker? Why not to London, to stop Marteau in the first place?"

She rested her head against his leg. "I'm too empty to fathom it."

Gryffin quickly responded, lifting her up and wrapping an arm around her. "Goüin, I need to tend to my wife and my friend. Please excuse us for now. We'll return to the question of your haunted train when we've all recovered."

"The doctor—"

"Can do nothing for us," Gryffin finished. "Understand, Goüin, we've given you twenty-four hours without rest and with tremendous loss. You and your team must be exhausted as well. We're returning to our ship above to heal and mourn. If any new developments arise, you can summon us there."

A shout from Simon and a sudden loud hum halted them.

Goüin jerked around. "What?"

He hurried back to the Faraday cage and the attached engine, which had powered itself up.

"No one touched it, I swear," Simon said.

"Close the cage. Now!" Goüin ordered.

Bardît complied just in time as the engine engaged and power coursed through the perimeters of the Faraday cage. Angélique pressed into Gryffin's breast to shield her eyes, holding the bundle to her bosom, while Vincent snatched up face shields and tossed them to everyone, then helped her don hers.

The cage burned white hot. No sparks, no arcing, no bolts of electricity. Just the thundering roar of pure power coursing through the cage, excitating the air within its containment. Angélique covered her sensitive ears, as did Gryffin. Her freshly healed body rocked with every revolution of the gigantic Faraday disc.

Just as suddenly, the entire machine—engines, cage, disc, voltaic piles, cylinders, capacitators, everything—vanished. The bay floor was bare except for a glowing figure standing where the trans-aether teleportation device had stood. The glow faded.

Renée Guichet opened her eyes. She looked around wildly, then found Angélique.

"What are you doing here?" Renée cried. "We have to get to Bellesfées!"

Jacqueline stood aghast at the derangement of traffic whizzing in front of her. Philadelphia's streets were narrow, pocked, and uneven; and the vehicles rushing along them pressed too tightly together. How could they avoid collisions at such speeds? How could their blood not boil? In the shadows of the towering buildings, some forty or fifty storeys at least, hot winds pushed at her. People hurried by like so many busy ants. No one could take time to sit for coffee because there were no places to sit. In a shop opposite her, people queued to buy coffee in tall paper pints they carried away with them and apparently tossed into the street trenches when they emptied them.

Beside her, Dominique threw her arm up to flag one of the vehicles. Jacqueline hesitated. Automotion was her specialty, but automotion in the hands of such reckless direction was downright deadly.

"Franklin Institute," Dominique told the driver, and Jacqueline understood this was Philadelphia's version of a horseless fiacre.

Jacqueline climbed cautiously inside, and Dominique followed. The door closed and the car accelerated with such force Jacqueline fell back against the seat. Dominique grinned at her. Jacqueline tried to return the smile, but her teeth were too tightly clenched.

Raucous music blared too loudly from somewhere in the front seat, a miniaturized orchestrion hidden under the cover of many dials, playing instruments she couldn't identify, and voices singing about dancing on an ocean and liars in love. The driver shouted along with the orchestrion, slapping his hand against the side of his vehicle as he rested his arm on the open window. Jacqueline tried to take in every detail, but it was all so dizzying.

"You'll like Haddonfield much more than Philadelphia," Dominique assured her. "It's much like a faubourg. I live in a house that's older than you." Her eyes crinkled merrily. "Café dining, small boutiques. We'll head home after the Institute. The family is excited to meet you."

Jacqueline's stomach twisted, not just from the crazed ride through Philadelphia's harrowing streets.

Home. The family.

"Dominique," she said, "if I don't find my way home to Bellesfées, will there even be a family?"

The doctor's smile faded. She gazed distantly ahead through the curved window that stretched across the front of the vehicle.

"You know," she said, "so many scientists, philosophers, and writers have theorized about time travel and the spacetime continuum for centuries. There's what they call the Butterfly Effect, from a short story about how one simple change in the past can modify the future. If you stay here and don't have a daughter Dominique, will I simply vanish?"

Jacqueline's jaw tightened.

"But I'm of the belief that I am here," she continued, "therefore, I will still be here. You'll go back. Your return has already been established in photographs. It happened, so it must happen."

Jacqueline tried not to think about the alternatives. "Sicut erat in principio, et nunc, et semper, et in saecula saeculorum."

"Amen," Dominique responded. She chuckled at Jacqueline's surprised expression. "Yes, I was raised in the Church, although the Mass isn't in Latin anymore."

The vehicle halted. Jacqueline pitched forward, catching herself on the seat in front of her. Dominique paid the driver and they descended onto a place that evoked a little of Paris. A circle for traffic, the streets like boulevards, a fountain with statues, a church, and across the way, huge low buildings of classical architecture.

"I'd show you the remains of Haddonfield's dinosaur over there in the Museum of Natural Sciences," Dominique said, pointing to a building with a large banner hanging in its doorway, "but first let's solve the mystery of Jacqueline Duval in the twenty-first century. You can learn about our dinosaur once we get home."

"Dyno-saur?" she mused as they walked. "Power lizard. Owen's dinosauria."

"Hadrosaurus foulkii. The first complete fossilized skeleton found in North America, and practically right in my backyard. Important especially because it proved dinosaurs could be bipedal."

"That portrait you showed me, in front of the statue of a strange horse-faced saurian. That's the dinosaur?"

"It is." Dominique's face lit up. "And my family. Oh, I can't wait for you to meet them."

They climbed a long flight of steps to a building that resembled the Pantheon in Rome. Jacqueline wanted to run up, but she deferred to her great-great-granddaughter's age, yet another irony. They entered a rotunda where Benjamin Franklin was enshrined in marble over six meters high, set upon a pedestal three times the mass of the statue. The whole rotunda was brightly skylit, although she noted subtle lighting above the pilasters. Families, couples, and large groups, crowds of different nationalities all perambulated the huge chamber of twenty-five meters in circumference and height. Several people pointed at her, smiling or laughing. Some rude ones shoved their thumbs up at her, smirking. Others held up their little devices, like the little case Jenny owned, which Dominique insisted she should not concern herself with.

"Otherwise, we'll end up with a bootstrap paradox," she had warned, "and I know you don't know what that means, but, please, let's not risk a temporal calamity."

But the crowd's treatment of her bothered her. She was accustomed to blending into the background.

"Is something wrong with my clothes?"

When she looked down at herself, she realized the answer was "yes." No one else was wearing gogglers around their neck or sturdy leather boots or a simple chemise and vest.

"Yo, steampunk," someone said to her as he passed. "Noice. Wher's yer corset?"

She whispered, "This isn't an institute of learning, is it?"

Dominique laughed. "It's a public museum. Don't get too caught up in what you see along the way, and don't read any of the informational material. Bootstrap paradox," she repeated.

But Jaqueline's mind was already overwhelmed. She wasn't even curious to know how one's bootstraps could affect a timeline. Displays more dazzling than the 1840 Exhibition at the Royal Academy tempted her, but Dominique rushed her past these, as well as food venues and a bouquiniste. Hastening down a flight of steps, they emerged near a planetarium.

Jacqueline's body tingled as they followed the corridor around the planetarium theatre. It was not the smells or the sights, but something here felt familiar, comfortable. Drawn by an organic magnetic force, she knew her presence here was somehow preordained.

As they came to the end of the corridor, she caught sight of a colossal locomotive, more massive than she could imagine any engine needed to be. She slowed, awed and apprehensive. The majestic 2-5-1 engine numbered "60000" stood in a small cage of fencing like a stallion in a sty.

"Sixty thousand?" she murmured. "Someone built sixty thousand locomotives?"

Dominique squeezed her arm. "Many more than that, Mémé."

She drew her around the front of the engine to the other side against the wall where a small flight of metal stairs led up to the cabin. They waited in a queue. Little ones of all ages leaned out the window of the enclosed cabin and danced around inside before moving on while the line slowly shunted Jacqueline and Dominique up the steel steps and into a cabin large enough to accommodate four or five adults, or — as the case was — two adults and seven children running from side to side playing with inactive valves, gears, switches, and pull chains.

Jacqueline caught her breath as the visceral magnetic force dragged her to the bolted firebox. "I crawled out of this firehole," she said in a hushed whisper.

Dominique set her hands on one of the steam valves and gazed around the huge cabin. "That's what the police said. I think they may have presumed you were inside somehow. Certainly, no one was here to observe it. But, Mémé, if you were inside, who let you out?"

She ran her hand along the firehole door in wonder. Why had the aether led her here? And indeed, who had opened the firehole door? She felt no 'intimation of correspondence,' as Angélique's bohemian friend Charles would have called it.

The tingling vibration throughout her whole body remained; however, it didn't emanate from this titan of a train engine. It pulled her instead out of the cabin. Below, like a rude toy beside the Baldwin 60000, sat an old 0-2-0.

Hair rose on the back of her neck and a shiver ran through her. She was familiar with the design from her earliest studies in engineering, before her years at the Polytechnique.

"Is that more your style, Mémé? It's almost as old as you are."

But Jacqueline's eyes were fixed on those gathered at the exhibit, on the young blonde in a sooty, blood-stained daydress standing at the fencing that guarded the 0-2-0. Jacqueline trembled; beside her, Dominique drew a sharp breath.

Frontenac turned and found her.

Jacqueline cried out in joy, but grief and horror filled Fronenac's large blue eyes, and she choked back tears, shaking her head. When she leaned weakly to the informational display case, Jacqueline's heart burst. She hurried down the steps and fought through the crowd until she could seize Frontenac in a fierce embrace. The young woman fell on her, weeping.

"Tell me." Fear closed Jacqueline's throat. "What's happened?"

Frontenac clung to her desperately, voiceless "oh's" escaping between sobs. When Dominique came up beside them, Frontenac stared at her for a brief moment before weeping again. The crowd around them eyed them curiously, some with fond smiles as if witnessing a joyous family reunion, others with amused grins at the costumed figures.

"Where did you arrive?" Jacqueline prompted.

The younger woman wiped her face on her sleeve and sighed with the weariness of one who had traveled a great journey. "Here," she said, her voice breaking. "Right here. Only a moment ago. Ah, Duval. It's—"

Again she buried her face in her mentor's shoulder.

Jacqueline's dread rose once more, crushing her heart. She couldn't bring herself to ask, and Frontenac wasn't ready to speak. When she looked to Dominique for help, the woman led them out of the exhibition hall to the quiet corridor outside the planetarium where they sat on a curving bench. Dominique took a clear bottle of water from her large handbag, twisted off the cap, and offered the bottle to Frontenac. Once the young woman had calmed, she sat with her head bowed.

"We searched for you," she said. "The four of us went into the aether together, but—" She shook her head and pressed her eyes closed. "Only Guichet and I landed in the cage of your Manchester machine in

1840, with Rodolphe Armand." She shuddered. "A disgusting pig. Then we used your machine to go back into the aether to find you and Têtue and Justine. We searched, Duval. We tried. Justine—" She choked on tears. "She's merged with the aether. She—she *is* the aether."

Jacqueline hugged her, almost as much for her own comfort.

"When Guichet and I left 1840, we drifted in the aether looking for you, listening for you. Suddenly, I could feel waves of—how can I say it—completion? I heard Justine laughing, and I thought I'd leap for joy. Then Guichet was gone. Suddenly I was here. And then I heard—"

She shuddered in great sobs. Finally she choked out, "Duval, it's Têtue!"

Panic seized Jacqueline. She held Frontenac at arm's length, gaping in fear of what words would come next.

Frontenac lifted her sorrowful eyes. "You could hear the children, Duval. You could see the blood. I think you'll be able to hear her. In the little engine where you found me."

Dominique caught her breath. "The Rocket? That's the key?"

She nodded to Dominique, then gave a weak smile. "I can guess who you are. You resemble the duchess."

When Jacqueline introduced them, Frontenac's lips quivered.

"'Dominique'? Oh, Duval." She sobbed again.

Jacqueline put her arm around her. "We're almost home. I can sense it. Come show me what I need to see."

As they got to their feet, Dominique tugged her arm. Her gaze had lost its twinkle.

"Mémé, I have a feeling you're going to vanish on me as mysteriously as you appeared, and I won't see you again."

She struggled to find words, then surrendered in a sad smile. Jacqueline threw her arms around her and kissed her cheek.

"You'll see me again when you kiss your daughter. And again in twenty years when you kiss your granddaughter."

Dominique hugged her so tightly Jacqueline squealed and chuckled quietly. "I would love to take home a souvenir, but somehow I think you'd say 'bootstraps' again."

"Oh, Mémé."

Dominique caressed her head and kissed her brow. She set her hand to her heart again, debating. Then she reached back and unclasped a necklace, drew it from beneath her blouse, and clasped it around Jacqueline's neck.

"Keep this," she whispered. "Pass it to your daughter Dominique. This is your bootstrap."

Clutching the pendant, Jacqueline could feel the flux of the aether that surrounded it swirl about her hand and curl up her arm, pulling her to the past and future at the same time. The other women caught her as she faltered in the dizzying sensation. Together, the three of them entered the train exhibition hall again.

Jacqueline scanned the informational display for the Rocket. Twenty-five horsepower; wheelbase of four feet, ten inches; two cylinders ten and a half inches in diameter; forty-two-inch wheels, later replaced by fifty-inch wheels. A passenger train in America in 1838… What made this engine different?

"It was built in 1833," she noted, "five years before Husker. What could they possibly have in common?"

The answer resounded in her head.

"*Me.*"

Têtue's voice startled her, and she looked around the crowded hall to find her. Frontenac began to cry softly and pointed to the Rocket.

"*It's all my fault, Duval. All of it. From the beginning. I went back to stop Marteau from hurting all those kids, from hurting de Guise and the baby.*"

Jacqueline clasped Dominique for fear her legs would give way. "De Guise? The baby? Têtue—"

"*Duval, I'm so sorry. I had him, damn it. I had him. I failed.*"

The tingling in Jacqueline's spine drew her to the plaque on the boiler: Braithwaite, Milner & Co. 1833.

"*Marteau stuffed me in here with his merdique machine. After he skinned me alive. Foute, that hurt. I felt it. The wolf kept me alive, and I felt it all, stuck in that machine. Then he stuffed my body into the charge, and I could still feel it. The fire. Pieces of my body falling into molten pig. It hurt, Duval. Sometimes I still feel it.*"

Jacqueline choked with a rush of shock and fury. "Têtue! My Têtue. I didn't know. It's all my fault."

"*No, Duval. Don't you dare. Don't you dare regret the gift you gave me. It's what brought me here to you.*"

"How—"

"*Sat in this engine for five long, lousy years. Then coal from Husker shipped me to Pennsylvania in 1838. All those Husker kids, I heard 'em. On the ship, I could hear them crying. Begging for help. Then I heard all the kids who died building this thing — working the foundry or Marteau's experiments. All the way over, crying and calling for help. That's what we do, right? The Order of Duval. We fight the evil in front of us.*

"So, I tried to get back to you. Jumped ship at the dock, but they dragged me out of the river. Ended up hauling more coal, more kids crying. Then passenger cars. Damned engineer whipped me with rawhide, me and all those kids. So I told the kids how to find you. My body was already in the pig iron, and Husker coal fueled the hot-air blast on their casting. All the iron went into the Orléans locomotive. The steam valves, the firehole door, that was us. That was me, calling you. Just searching for you, waiting for you. And I knew you'd be there because I knew you were already there."

She heard Têtue's muted pride. She could envision her, folding her arms, assuming her stolid stance, her defiant sneer. She pressed her sleeve to her face to stop her tears, but Frontenac openly wept.

Têtue caught, flayed alive, burnt alive in a molten fire of over a thousand degrees. The stubborn, vengeful victim who had defied Mircalla, impaling herself rather than slaying Jacqueline. Her triumphant sneer as she lay gasping for life.

The black wolf, launching herself at the vampire to defend Jacqueline. Romping across the hills of the parc at Bellesfées, frolicking with the Llewellyns, the three of them howling across the pond, chasing one another through the forest.

And Têtue, the woman, learning swordplay from Llewellyn, monitoring the engines of *Esprit*, tossing back glasses of Pilsner with her in the courtyard. Jacqueline had anticipated years of having her kindred spirit beside her at the forge.

She leaned against the little guardrail and stretched out her hand, but she couldn't reach the plaque. She stared at the date until her eyes blurred with tears. She blinked.

When her vision cleared, she stood in a vineyard. Nearby a little girl with long black curls hefted a wide harvesting basket onto her shoulder.

"Eh, Dominique Durand, putain têtue," a man nearby hollered, and he took the basket from her, dropped it, and punched her head, knocking her to the ground. "What'd I tell you about wandering eyes? Têtue!"

He kicked her where she lay and stalked off.

Jacqueline gasped. She suddenly stood in a cottage watching the same man beat an older Têtue. He then seized her by her long black hair and dragged her barely conscious body across the kitchen.

"You won't think yourself so fine when I drop you off the roof, têtue!" the man said as he hauled her up the stairs.

Têtue held onto her hair with one hand to ease the strain. With the other, she drew her harvesting knife from her boot. She slashed at her hair until the man dropped her. Then she slashed again, and blood filled Jacqueline's vision as Têtue fled.

Again she was swept away to a mill where another man raped Têtue, face down in a corner so close to the machinery that if she moved she'd be shredded. Her hair was short, but not short enough to escape the razor-sharp fullers.

Then in an ironworks, where a foreman whipped her to the floor. Then a mill where a large young woman held her down while another woman crawled between her legs. Then a wheat field, where a scorched and haggard Mircalla in desperate need of blood found Têtue sleeping as *Esprit* sailed overhead.

Finally, she watched Têtue slip to the floor of a rude laboratory surrounded by bloody shards of glass, blood streaming from her neck. A young man with a broken nose, his arm and his chest coated in blood, approached her with a scalpel.

Jacqueline wailed in horror, returning in seconds to the Rocket.

She reached with her whole body. Around them, the crowd murmured. Someone asked if she was all right. Dominique Fees assured them it was a family "thing," as she put it. Jacqueline longed to caress the train, run her hand along the boiler, embrace Têtue with her very being. Her heart broke for the little girl Dominique Durand, and for Têtue, a daughter of Bellesfées.

"No, no, no. It's backwards. *I* heard them crying, not you. *I* went back. You followed me. How could you—before I even—"

Dominique Fees set her hand on Jacqueline's shoulder. "How can you be here with me before your daughters are even born, Mémé? Why do you think she waited to bring you here, to Philadelphia?"

Jacqueline did not know the answer. She understood what Têtue had said, but the circumstances defied logic. How could Dominique just accept Têtue's explanation? How could Dominique have even heard the explanation? She searched the woman's face, pleading.

She put her arm around Jacqueline, a mother patiently comforting her daughter. "I'm part of you, Mémé. Of course I heard it all. Têtue searched for you and found me. You searched for de Guise and found me. And Têtue traveled to 1833 to make certain you could get back to 1843. Bootstraps, Mémé. It's time to go home."

Jacqueline burned with an ache that crossed too many centuries. She wept on Dominique's shoulder.

"I don't know what that means. Help me find her. Please! Help me save her."

"You already saved me, Duval."

She could hear the grin in Têtue's voice.

"You saw what I did to the Beast. I was meant for Madame Guillotine. You know it now. But you saved me. You're the best thing ever happened to me. My fault you're here. I brought the kids to you. I just didn't know it yet. They sent you here to find me. Doesn't matter which time you're in," Têtue said. *"Time to go home."*

Jacqueline could imagine the woman's characteristic shrug, and she laughed through tears. Frontenac did as well, folding her arms and imitating the constant curl to Têtue's lip.

"Marteau said I'd run forever, but I was only here to save those kids. Now I'll get you home. And I'm so ready. Climb aboard."

Jacqueline gripped Frontenac's hand and they nodded to one another. Dominique stopped them before they took a step. She embraced her on both cheeks.

"Bon voyage et adieu, Mémé. Kiss de Guise for me when you see him."

Jacqueline didn't know how to answer her. She would never see Dominique Fees again, unless it was in the faces of her daughters and granddaughters.

Dominique stepped back and blew her a kiss, with her pretty bowed lips. "Such a handsome man." She winked. "So sexy with that eye patch."

She melted into the crowd.

Jacqueline turned to Frontenac. "What did she say? Eye-patch? What does 'sexy' mean?"

Frontenac tugged her along, and together they stepped around to the rear of the engine. People closest to the train clapped and laughed as the two of them climbed into the cabin. Many took out their rectangular devices and held them up. Some of them gave off tiny flashes of light. Across the hall, security agents moved toward them.

Jacqueline opened the tiny firehole door. "How will we—"

"Just like Orléans, Duval. I'll catch you. Like me and the Husker kids caught you before. I'll make it work."

She stepped back to let Frontenac peek inside the tiny firebox. To her astonishment, Frontenac poured through the opening like water through the drift. She vanished. The onlookers gasped, then laughed and applauded. More flashes came from their devices. Security agents called harshly for her to halt. Jacqueline searched the crowd one last time. Dominique was gone.

Cheers followed Jacqueline as she knelt.

Justine finished stirring the night sky for Van Gogh, turning her attention to little Pluto lost out among the stars. When she heard the lonely laments from the third planet, she returned, sending a spark to Maxwell Anderson so no one would be forgotten out there. A burble of confusion erupted near Andromeda, so she pushed a wave of plani-cialus to soothe the upheaval. She exhaled the floral name of a planet whose language was fragrance. She nodded to Einstein as he swam past her in three different directions at once, and sighed wistfully over the duchess's broken friend Charles cursing the stars, crying for the darkness in his morbid obsession.

Joy suddenly swirled up from the twenty-first century in a blinding display of white and gold and rident, and along with the brilliant burst, a long-awaited wisp of sacred hol. Justine cupped joy in her hands and carefully set Duval and Frontenac down where they belonged, above a little vale just off the Loire in 1843.

Sacred hol she held to her cheek a moment more before taking Têtue into herself.

As it always was, and as it must be.

Tears spilled out across the aether behind her. Justine sent them off in aethereal flux across the universe.

Marthe faced down the hideous aerostat that slowly, frustratingly slowly, passed over the distant vineyards and bore down on Château Bellesfées. The gunports opened, the cannon aimed at the château.

She shook her rolling pin. "Not my house, you don't!"

When at last the black ship came into range, the two Benet men opened fire. The revolving mechanism the mistress had designed and installed allowed them fifty shots each, but the men required only twelve to shred the fabric of the envelope's bullet-nose within a few seconds.

The ship lurched backward and tipped. Cannon fired, but the shots flew wide. The envelope began to collapse, and the entire ship drifted to the grounds of Bellesfées almost soundlessly.

Marthe wrinkled her nose. "Something not right there."

She headed around to the back of the château as Luc and Jean-Paul came running out. They planted themselves and took aim to subdue anyone escaping from the wreck. The three waited, Marthe and Luc more patiently than their son.

Marthe shook her head, her heavy brows bristling. "Something not right," she repeated. "No smashing noise? What's it made of then, clay?"

Luc didn't answer. His right hand fidgeted on the trigger.

"Not natural," Jean-Paul grumbled. "Nobody inside?"

There was no sound of engines. Whatever pestilence fueled the machine exhausted itself in clouds of soot puffing up from the black mound. As the tattered envelope flapped in the breeze, it slowly peeled away, freeing the boxy gondola…

… which was moving.

19.

Jacqueline landed in darkness. Her head spun. She reached again to hold onto Têtue, but she was gone. Montpellier had taken her and given her to the aether. Jacqueline was left with a cameo in her hand: twin girls.

She hunched on all fours at Frontenac's feet between the two engines of *Esprit*. She tried not to vomit, gulping air. She no sooner managed to pull herself up when Frontenac said, "They're coming."

She leaned weakly to the engines. "Who's coming?" Then she peered at the gauges and focused. "Why is my ship so low on fuel?"

At that moment, the boiler ignited.

"And who's stealing my ship!"

Frontenac slipped between the engine and the hull and got to the companion up to midships.

"I have her," she shouted as she disappeared up the ladder.

Jacqueline did not recover from the trans-aether teleportation as swiftly as Frontenac. She managed a few steps before her legs gave way and she flumped on the deck, her arms resting on her knees, her head hanging between them, as she watched the twins on her cameo swing.

Têtue. Montpellier. Gone.

They'd been hers to shelter, to lead, to guide. She had saved them from Mircalla only to lose them to her sad misadventure. What made her think she could be the one to give them a better life? That she could hold on to them all and see them bloom and flourish? She had never been able to hold on to Angélique, the spectacular performer, the savage wolf, the dissolute bohémienne, and now lost to her for good, given over to a husband and a child on the way. What arrogance to assume…

Dominique and Justine.

Jacqueline gazed stupidly around the hold. Why here? Why *Esprit*? Why not return her to the haunted locomotive?

The ship was in motion. So, they were already aloft. That would explain her imbalance. What could possibly explain the engines being engaged?

Engaged. Like Frontenac to Rodolphe Armand.

No. She would not lose another girl. Not to cruelty, not to harsh law, not to brutality and indifference, not to greed and appetite, not to any supernatural fiends or unnatural madmen. She would not lose Bellesfées. She knew that now. But what choices would lead her to that end, and who else might suffer for them?

And why would de Guise have an eye patch!

"Jacky!"

Angélique's cry shook her from her stupor. She lifted her head. She couldn't find her voice.

Angélique knelt and hugged her fiercely. "Jacky, m'amie, crazy, silly, mad…"

Angélique's voice, too, was broken. Her heart, torn. She held Jacqueline too desperately for her to believe her twin was all right. She combed through her sister's hair with tender strokes.

"I lost them, mon Ange." She buried her face against Angélique. "I found the children, but I lost our girls. And I don't even know how. Any of it. I—I lost Têtue and Montpellier."

Angélique cupped her face. "No, Jacky." She kissed her. "You were the one who was lost. They found you."

Bleakness clouded her sight. "I'm still lost."

Angélique gripped her hands and pulled her to her feet. "I'm sorry, Jacky, but you can't stay lost. Marteau's airship is headed for Bellesfées."

"The black ship?"

Despair and self-doubt drained from her as anger rose up and filled her. Galvanized by grief and pure rage at the man who had slaughtered Têtue, Jacqueline released Angélique and clambered unsteadily up the ladder. She staggered across the lower deck and took the ladder to the main deck, into the pale-violet morning sky, straight into Llewellyn's arms.

He kissed her cheek. "Welcome back. No time for the full tale."

"De Guise?"

"Safe below in your quarters, sleeping. Marteau's ship—"

"I know."

He caught her arm. "No, you don't know. The gondola, the command decks, all made of Marteau's animated skin."

"Anima—"

Had Jacqueline dreamed of Mary Shelley's fictional creature, or had some transcendent correspondence from the aether intimated a prescience of Marteau's evil?

"Claque destroyed a few of his demons," Llewellyn said, "but this… You saw it yesterday. Monstrous."

"Yes. With gunports."

She headed to the captain's wheel where Frontenac had taken command. Guichet monitored the gauges on the capstans, assisted by a young man Jacqueline didn't know.

"Who are you?" she demanded.

The man looked up, and he flashed a wide-eyed look of amazement as he saluted her.

Frontenac answered quietly, "That's Léon Vincent, one of Goüin's men. He's a good man."

Jacqueline stomped away as Monsieur Claque came on deck. "Claque, are there any fuel stores?"

Monsieur Claque shook his head.

She sighed, frustrated. "Llewellyn, how much of a lead does this ship have on us?"

His face, somber and drawn, made her wonder how long they had waged this battle while she had bounced around in the aether. How long since Têtue had drawn her into the firehole?

He said, "I don't know if it spent any time looking for us after we eluded it, but by now it will be closing in on Bellesfées."

"With gunports."

Jacqueline drew a deep breath, contemplating her boot tips. "I don't even know this man. I've never even met this man. Why is he bent on my destruction? Is he somehow connected to Armand? I'd never met him either before—"

Before yesterday. In 1840. The machine, the apprentices, the cost—

Jacqueline whirled on Guichet. "1840. You met Rodolphe Armand. What did you tell him?"

Guichet flinched at the sharpness of her tone. Reddening, she confessed, "I told him I was Adèle Frontenac. And we told him Marteau—"

Jacqueline ripped her cap off and slammed it to the deck. "Ha! That's it."

Her laughter was less jocular than contemptuous.

"You led him to Marteau. Of course he would be upset if the dynamic re-generator didn't function after you left. He said it vanished." She tugged her lip. "Justine took it. That's why he went after— why he demanded… All of this one temporal circle."

She tugged at her lip. "So, bringing down Marteau brings down Armand. Where's my coat? My spyglass is in my pocket."

Their fallen faces implied the sad answer.

"Têtue took my coat." She kicked the wheel. "Well, foute."

"Language, ma fille," Angélique scolded as she came up the ladder. Pain had etched years into her weary smile. "We're together again. What can we not face together? What is to stop us?"

"Empty tanks, for one," answered Guichet. "Claque's rockets are near empty, and *Esprit*—"

Jacqueline frowned. "I know. What about the hydrogen tanks?"

"They'll hold to Le Bardon," Léon Vincent said.

"And we need to go a bit beyond. With the wind against us."

She set her fists to her hips and bowed her head, drawing calculations in her mind. "All right. Give us altitude. That'll shorten the trip."

"Aye." Frontenac signaled to Monsieur Claque, then turned back. "Why? I thought the hypotenuse—"

"That's plane geometry. This is—" She waggled her hand. "Oh, call it flyology. We go up, the round earth spins toward us, and when we come down we'll be closer to Bellesfées. Right now it's easier to go up than forward."

Frontenac's mouth quirked. "But," she said, "you haven't reckoned with Guichet."

She glared. This was no time to spring surprises. They all turned to Guichet.

The young woman's eyes slowly widened, and a grin tugged at her lips. "I can. I can do it."

"Do what?"

She spun about as Guichet ran forward, Vincent with her.

"If the corkscrew propellers spin faster than the engine is driving them, will they damage the engine?"

Before she could answer, Frontenac replied, "I'll disengage the engines and lay in the course. You do what you can."

Jacqueline followed the pair's movements with annoyed curiosity as Guichet climbed to the fo'c'sle and stood at the bow with her arms spread behind her like a swan, her head high and her auburn hair wild in the wind. Jacqueline couldn't help a grim smile of pride. she looked fierce and majestic sailing the skies, a Valkyrie charging to a field of war.

"Altitude twelve hundred," Frontenac sang out. "Cutting engines. Full steamless ahead!"

Jacqueline pressed her fist to her mouth to keep from belaying the orders of her first mate. To her shock, Esprit surged into the wind at almost twice the speed of her engines.

And their blood didn't boil.

"What have you done to my ship?"

Angélique stood beside her. "That's Renée. Power to move things at will. Isn't she glorious?"

She stared, incredulous. "And Frontenac hears thoughts." Her voice broke. "Justine—" She bowed her head. "I saw her. I called to her. She danced away on the aether."

Her twin nudged her. "Like a mermaid sporting in the waves. Justine is home at last."

She raised her eyes to Angélique's. "Do you think so? Do you think she's happy, really?"

"I do."

Jacqueline doubted. She needed more than reassurance. She needed—

"De Guise." She released Angélique. "I have to—"

"Filth ahoy!" Llewellyn sang out from the aft deck.

He seized a cable and swung across to the fo'c'sle, where Jacqueline and Angélique joined him.

"I make it two nautical miles."

Vincent suddenly shouted, "Madame!"

Guichet fell back into his arms, drained. "I—thought—I—could—" She fainted.

Frontenac reignited the engines to catch them up to the failing propellers and engage them. "Full steam ahead!"

From a distance, cannon thundered. A moment later, a crash below decks shook them off their feet, all but Frontenac who held to the ship's wheel. Above them the envelope whistled, losing air from a cannon-ball-sized hole.

"Everyone belowdecks!" Jacqueline cried. "If we go down, midships is the least vulnerable. Now!"

Vincent didn't hesitate to take up Guichet and follow Angélique down the companion.

"Frontenac, you too," she ordered.

"With respect, Duval, no. I just got you back. I'm not leaving this wheel while you're on deck." She lifted her chin, defying Jacqueline's glare. "I heard that. I'm cutting the jets."

As she did so, distant gunfire drew Jacqueline to the rail.

Llewellyn clambered up crown lines to find the tear in the envelope. He quickly swung down again.

"It's too wide to close by hand."

"Not your hand, anyway. Claque!"

"No," he argued. "Claque's weight on the crown lines will expel the air more quickly. Let it go. We're nearly there, and the other ship is down."

The black monstrosity plummeted to the ground behind Bellesfées.

"Luc and Jean-Paul must have taken it out. Hopefully they're able to fend off—"

"They're not. Not unless they get lucky like we did. As I told you, it's animated skin. It doesn't die."

She snorted. "Everything dies."

"No, ma belle Jacky, it doesn't," said a beloved voice behind her.

De Guise seated himself wearily on the bench by the ladder. Elation filled her and she ran to him.

"Gently, ma belle," he warned with a half-smile. "I'm a bit diminished, you see."

She stared in horror at his drooping eyelid. Dominique's voice— "eyepatch"—rang in her head.

"What happened to you?"

He pulled her closer and laid his head on her bosom, nuzzling her with delight. "Ah, my clever girl. My sweet Jacky. I'm so happy you're back. I can't wait to hear about your adventures." He playfully slapped her derrière. "But you have more important worries, my little cabbage."

Jacqueline shivered with a glacial chill. She leaned back and stared deeply into de Guise's face. Those beautiful bowed lips twisted wryly, making his eyelid slip into his mutilated eye socket. A shudder seized her down to her bones.

"Tell me what you learned about the ship," she said sharply. "What do you mean, this skin thing doesn't die?"

He gave her a sly grin and tapped the side of his nose.

She released him. When she glanced up to Frontenac, the younger woman's eyes narrowed, and she slowly shook her head. Jacqueline's stomach knotted as she clenched her fists. She had no time to dwell on it, but de Guise wasn't going anywhere soon.

"We're coming in fast," Llewellyn warned. He raced to the fo'c'sle.

She hurried to join him. "We're coming in guns blazing as well," she said. "Claque! The turret."

"Hold fire, Claque," Llewellyn cut in. "I can see people on the lawn. Luc, Jean-Paul, Marthe." He pointed them out as she joined him at the rail. "We killed his creatures with stakes to the head. How would a ship of skin have a head?"

"We have to find the conning tower and take that out."

At that moment, the polluted ship's blackened envelope slipped away into the wind. The mound advanced on Luc and Jean-Paul like a horrid gastropod, shoving fleshy appendages forward and dragging itself along.

Jacqueline growled and cursed. "Oh, I am going to crush this thing."

She leaned into the wind as the ship descended with accelerating speed. As they closed, she shouted, "Fire!"

The rotating guns sent a round of fifty shots into the giant coal-polluted mass as *Esprit* swooped down on it. The grisly ship shuddered but did not cease its slow progress toward Bellesfées. Monsieur Claque swiftly reloaded.

"Brace for a collision." Llewellyn took her into his arms.

She freed herself and grabbed the rail instead, poised to launch herself upon impact. He laughed heartily and assumed the same crouch. Behind them, de Guise also laughed, a high-pitched titter that scraped along Jacqueline's last nerve.

Esprit struck the ground twenty meters short of Marteau's ship and slewed toward it. Monsieur Claque kept the guns firing into the mass. In the moment *Esprit* rammed it, Jacqueline and Llewellyn leapt over the rail and dropped atop the monstrosity. Llewellyn pulled his knife and began slicing into it, gripping a flap of bloodless skin to hold fast when the thing began to buck. Jacqueline spread her feet wide to keep her balance.

"Jean-Paul!" she called. "This thing is covered in grease and oil. Fetch an igniter."

The young man ran off. Marthe, standing arms akimbo as ever, straightened up and stomped back into the kitchens, muttering to herself. Luc kept up a steady fire, focusing on the fleshy projections that propelled the creature, while Monsieur Claque continued his broadside. Jacqueline scoped out its exterior.

"No doors," she cried. "No way to board it. If there is a conn—"

Llewellyn shouted and lost his footing when a flap extended itself to seize him by the neck. He hacked himself free, but a gap opened below his feet and folded over him, smothering him.

"Gryffin!" she screamed.

A tawny streak flew from the deck of *Esprit* and landed near where he had vanished. Angélique tore into the mass and ripped it away until he emerged again. She snarled and turned her attack to another meaty stalk as it began to burgeon. Llewellyn peeled away his clothes and changed form. Together, the wolves gnawed chunks of skin and tossed them aside so they could not reincorporate, digging to break through to the center of the mass to find its conning deck.

Luc bellowed. A gastropod appendage had lashed around his leg. It hurled him into the table and chairs of the kitchen courtyard.

Jacqueline lurched, wobbled, and regained her balance before another appendage sprouted before her and flailed at her. She ducked under it, then leapt over it as it swung back at her feet. Another arm erupted behind her and shoved her face down into a gap opening beneath her. She rolled to her side, wedging her feet against the side of the gap, fighting to keep it from closing on her.

From the corner of her eye, she caught sight of de Guise leaning on the rail at the bow. When she glanced up, a placid grin plastered his face. He nodded happily and waved, his grin sliding to a self-satisfied leer.

Fury exploded in her, but before she could roar, Frontenac appeared behind him raising a belaying pin. She struck de Guise over the head.

As he dropped to the deck unconscious, the mass of filth stilled.

Jacqueline rolled to her knees on the surface of ship, waiting for the mad pounding of her heart to slow. In the sudden silence, she and Frontenac exchanged grim nods, and Frontenac dragged de Guise away.

The wolves broke off their assault once the appendages ceased moving. Jacqueline jumped to the grass to see to Luc. Stunned but conscious, he got to his feet, waving her off. Jean-Paul reappeared with an igniter just as Marthe came back from the kitchens with a filled pig's bladder strung shut.

"Ignite this," she said with a *hmph*. "And get your aereo-thing out of the way."

Jacqueline's shoulders sagged. She groaned. "I can't. The envelope's torn, the engines are—"

But *Esprit* edged back, seemingly of its own accord. Monsieur Claque leapt from the main deck to the ground and clomped around to the bow. He pushed, and *Esprit* picked up speed, sliding down the hillside a dozen meters or so. Jacqueline saw Guichet on the main deck wrapped in Vincent's arms, her trembling hand upraised. Frontenac stood guard over the unconscious de Guise, belaying pin at the ready.

The wolves rejoined her, circling her and nuzzling their ears to her legs. Jean-Paul took the bladder from his mother, ignited the string tie, and tossed it onto the obscene mound.

"It's gonna stink," he said, blowing his hair out of his face.

"I put some rosemary in the oil." Marthe tossed her towel over her shoulder. "Might help."

Flames burst up. The odor of burning oil made their eyes tear.

"Pouah! I'd better make sure the girls are all right."

He trotted into the château. Scowling, Marthe followed him.

"Breakfast is ready when you finish cleaning up," she called back to the others. "Angélique, go get decent. You too, Your Grace."

Jacqueline watched the fire char away Marteau's creation. Once the soot had burnt off and the skin caught, the odor abated to that of burnt rancid meat. The stink didn't bother her so much as the madness it represented.

She was aware of the wolves boarding *Esprit* to change form and dress, what Marthe called "decent." Frontenac, Guichet, and Vincent made their way to the château with congratulations for Guichet's powerful accomplishments. Finally, Monsieur Claque jetted up to the ship, picked up de Guise's unconscious body, and soared up the hill to await her orders, tiny poots of steam revealing the automaton's own exhaustion.

Jacqueline gazed sadly at the man she cherished more than her life. She wanted to kiss those lips that had taught her the meaning of love, of trust, of pleasure. She tenderly combed back his wild blond curls.

"I'll find you, my love." ·

Jean-Paul took charge of Monsieur Claque's refueling; Jacqueline trusted no one but the bronze autonomaton to guard the possessed de Guise. Once she saw him secured and Monsieur Claque up to steam, she joined the rest of the household in the dining room. Gaudin brought a pitcher and bowl and proceeded to wash Jacqueline before she sat down. Glum silence and the ambient noxious odor dampened their appetites.

"Marteau." She spoke the name as a curse. "Murdered Têtue. He *slaughtered* Têtue. With his own hands. He captured her spirit and entombed her in a locomotive, then skinned her alive and dumped her body in the charge to make the iron that he used to manufacture the parts for Goüin. And wolf blood kept her alive throughout. She suffered every agony until her flesh and bone had melted into the iron. My Têtue. Our Têtue."

She lifted her eyes to Angélique. "Did you know? You never told me if you did." She swallowed tears. "All those years poisoning yourself. Draganov's shot. My God, you were utterly ravaged, you died, and you never told me you felt it all. Did you tell Têtue?"

She didn't accuse; she pleaded. "Please tell me she knew what I'd chosen for her."

Angélique wept into Llewellyn's shoulder. He answered, "She knew. I trained her. I taught her." He folded Angélique into his arms and wept with her. "She knew."

Jacqueline thought of Dominique Fees, her family; of her prophesied twin daughters and the decision that would turn one of them wolf. How desperate would she be to make such a choice, knowing what Têtue had been forced to endure? She bowed her head to her hands.

"Coal fueled the ship that carried Têtue to America," she continued bitterly. "Coal drove the engines that made the Orléans locomotive parts, parts made of iron charged with Têtue's body. Coal from a mine where twenty-six children died at once. Not that others hadn't died there, or in any of the mines where children are stuffed into dirt coffins to await their summoning like souls on Judgment Day."

She "dunked" — as Jenny had called it — her brioche into her coffee, wondering if Sam Varnay had survived the past two years at Sharp's factory. She swallowed the lump that rose in her throat. She ate her brioche and drank her coffee, fighting back every memory that assailed her.

"That was the source of the screams. Têtue gathered them to herself and brought them to me. And I brought Têtue to them. It's all on me. Dominique Durand and Justine Montpellier gone. De Guise consumed. All my fault."

Llewellyn's voice broke. "Yours is not the only loss, Jacky."

She looked around the table as the others somberly shook their heads. One by one, they told their tales. Babies thrown into the charge. Skins reformed and animated. Fighting for their lives against creatures that would not die. Each detail struck her heart like the shards that had killed Têtue. When she thought she could endure not one more blow, Angélique closed with her sad news. Jacqueline staggered from the table, broken.

"No, Jacky, that wasn't Marteau." Angélique spoke through tears. "I lost him days ago. I just didn't know it." She again clung to Llewellyn and sobbed. "Now we've lost both our children."

Utterly drained of purpose, Jacqueline trudged out of the dining room. Her workshop, gone. Têtue, Montpellier, gone. Angélique's child, dead. De Guise, a grisly guignol, a reanimated cluster of cells manipulated by a man behind a curtain of obscenity, a shroud of ungodly power, Marteau.

That monster, at least, was within her grasp.

Jacqueline stormed upstairs. Monsieur Claque tipped his head and puffed a greeting as she approached the bedside, her heart in turmoil. De Guise's wrists and ankles were bound. He lay still as death. Those precious curls, those lips, the beloved face, now the face of a creature out of Victor Frankenstein's laboratory.

Not de Guise.

Jacqueline had lost de Guise. How could she now suffer this monster to live, wearing his flesh? If Marteau had erased all that was de Guise, was that not murder? Did she not have the right to murder the madman?

She wanted to slap him. She wanted to beat him until he surrendered to her. She wanted him dead. If de Guise no longer lived, neither should his body.

"Wake up, you obscene waste of flesh."

De Guise twitched. One eye opened. He grinned, then winced. "Ma belle Jacky."

She knotted her fist into his cravate and lifted him. "Flesh burns, Marteau. Can you smell it?"

When she hauled him off the bed, he struggled feebly. She dragged him out the window to the balcony and shoved his head over the wrought-iron railing so he could see the fiery heap on the lawn.

"It burns, Marteau, and I swear, you will burn too."

He grunted and spasmed. Then he vomited. She yanked him back and shook him, slamming him against the window frame.

"Yes, you have a cracked skull, Marteau. But it doesn't equal the pain you have inflicted on so many others. Do you even know the agony she endured? I swear by her precious memory, I will skin you alive and dump your body on that pyre."

He dribbled the last of his vomit down his chest. "I don't even know who you're talking about," he said. He coughed and spat, then groaned.

"Dominique Durand. Têtue."

He slowly grinned. "Têtue. I remember Têtue. The little liar. Tried to kill me." He coughed again, though it sounded like a laugh. "She'll run forever."

Rage swelled to madness. Jacqueline bellowed, and her roar rose to a screech. She kicked his ribs and pounded on his head. He knotted up, shielding his head with his bound hands.

"You won't kill me, my little cabbage. I'm the man you adore."

"Watch me."

Jacqueline heaved him up and shoved his body half over the railing. "You're nothing, Marteau. And you will burn."

She wrapped her arms below his hips and readied to hurl him to the pyre below.

A shriek stopped her. "Don't, Duval!"

Frontenac rushed onto the balcony and met Jacqueline's furious gaze with firm assurance. "He's still in there. Monsieur de Guise is still inside. That's why I didn't kill him when I had the chance." She tugged her sleeve and pleaded. "He loves you, Duval. With a passion that would burn the ages."

Her words pierced her heart. Dominique Fees's words. Were they de Guise's words? Dominique would probably say "bootstraps."

Doubt overtook her. She released de Guise and he collapsed on the marble, gasping and gagging. Monsieur Claque retrieved him and dropped him back on the mattress. Jacqueline sat heavily in the chair beside the bed and buried her head on her crossed arms.

Frontenac laid her hand on her shoulder. "I can hear his thoughts, Duval. I can hear Monsieur de Guise. He's far down inside, but he's calling your name over and over. He loves you so, and he's fighting to come back. We just have to find him."

She saw only the warped face mocking her. "How? Llewellyn said he used Marteau's extractor, and it failed."

De Guise cackled. "Failure. That's you, Jacky Duval."

Frontenac restrained her before she could throttle him. When De Guise tried to rise, Monsieur Claque put his massive hand on his chest and held him down. His single eye bulged as he laughed.

Frontenac stared at him intensely, then tipped her head, listening.

"There's a storehouse, Marteau says. In his laboratory. The elemental chamber, he calls it. I bet it's that metal case with the glass lid."

Jacqueline's heart raced. "Is that where he put de Guise?"

"There's nothing in there!" he shouted, straining against Monsieur Claque's hand.

Frontenac continued. "No. There's only a piece of Marteau in de Guise's mind, but that's the conn. The rest of Marteau is in the elemental chamber, keeping this piece alive, keeping de Guise buried deep, deep down in his consciousness. But if we extract this piece here—"

"He dies." De Guise sneered. "You can't do a thing. This body is alive only because I own it now. Remove me and he dies."

Jacqueline leaned over him, glaring. "And what happens, I wonder, when I send a telegraphic to Orléans and have Goüin's men dump that case?"

De Guise clubbed her face. She fell back into Frontenac, and the two crashed into the side table, knocking over the lamp. He thrashed and kicked his bound legs, beating at Monsieur Claque's arm and tossing his head from side to side, shrieking.

The others appeared, and when they saw the struggle, the men hurried to subdue de Guise while Guichet and Angélique helped Frontenac and Jacqueline stand. Angélique put her arms around Jacqueline's shoulders and held her close.

Vincent sat on de Guise's legs while Llewellyn wrestled his arms over his head.

"What are we doing? What's wrong with him?" Llewellyn demanded.

Jacqueline gingerly palpated her cheek and jaw, seething. She wanted to drive the heel of her palm into de Guise's nose as he struggled and cursed them all.

"Have you ever heard de Guise call me 'Jacky'? 'Ma belle'? 'My little cabbage'?"

Angélique gasped. "He's still Marteau?"

De Guise spat at her and crowed when Llewellyn slapped him.

"I live or he dies. I live or he dies," he cackled. "You can't do anything."

Jacqueline wrapped her arm around her twin's waist, holding to her as a grounding line. "Oh, there's so much I can do, Marteau. Unlike you, all of my choices trouble me deeply. But I've killed evil before now; I can kill again to protect those I love."

De Guise crowed again. "Ah, you see, you see? What am I? What are you? What was that Têtue girl? Murderer!" Again he flashed a smug smile. "But you won't kill *him*. You won't let *him* die."

But when she studied the contemptuous curl so foreign to those lips, and the wild, desperate menace of his eye, she saw no sign of the man she loved.

"I am so sick of death," she murmured, "but I can't allow Marteau to live. Even if de Guise is buried within his own body, I don't know how to begin to find him."

Guichet cautiously approached. "Let me try, Duval."

De Guise laughed at her. "Oh, yes, let the little girl try. I'll eat you too, little girl."

But Frontenac's eyes widened. "You think it will work?"

Guichet drew a deep breath and waggled her hands. "I think it will. The two of us together."

Jacqueline looked from one to the other, trying to understand what would "work." Frontenac could hear thoughts. Guichet could manipulate the engines and had moved the airship with her newfound power.

"Ah, mon Dieu!" Her heart leapt, sparking tears in her eyes.

De Guise scowled. "Bah. I'm your grandfather's axe, stupid putain. Trust me. You can do nothing."

"De Guise says..." Frontenac's lips twitched. "He trusts the daughters of Bellesfées."

With those words, Jacqueline's doubts hardened into resolve. "As do I."

De Guise thrashed against Llewellyn and Vincent as Frontenac put her hand on de Guise's head.

"Claque, hold his eye open."

De Guise shouted again, "I live or he dies! I live or he dies!"

He bucked beneath them, trying to roll. Monsieur Claque pressed his chest down with both hands while Llewellyn wrapped an arm around his neck and opened the empty socket.

"No," Frontenac said. "Marteau burnt out the optic nerve there. That's why you couldn't extract him. The other eye."

As Llewellyn obeyed, de Guise shrieked, "No, no, no! She's lying! Filthy liar!"

He screamed in short, desperate, craven rasps. Jacqueline wanted to cover her ears, but a deeper need drove her to observe, to make certain Marteau was truly gone.

Guichet held her hand above de Guise's face and closed her eyes. Her eyelids flickered as she searched behind them to find the source of Marteau's being. Her breath grew shorter, more rapid, as she wrestled through the darkness.

Then Guichet gasped in a sudden, deep breath.

"It's Justine! I see her! Oh, little sister. Oh, she's so—so—vast!"

Surprise shifted to concentrated awe. "She's showing me the flux lines of Marteau's essence."

Jacqueline brushed away tears. Angélique was right: Justine was not lost.

De Guise's screams trailed off to a string of obscenities. He writhed in Llewellyn's grip. "I'll eat you! Eat you all!"

Guichet's eyes narrowed, wincing in pained effort. "And now I see you, Marteau."

She shuddered. Her arm quaked as she strained to reach some unseen mass. "And—I have you—now, you—disgusting—"

She clenched her hand and yanked it back. "Feculence!" She shook her fist in triumph.

"Is that it?" Jacqueline cried. "Is it done?"

Guichet opened her hand again and raised her palm as in an offering. "It's done. Justine has him now."

Frontenac smiled at Guichet. "Justine says, as it always was, and as it must be."

De Guise sighed and stilled so suddenly, Jacqueline choked back a sob of fear.

Frontenac bent over him, listening. She tipped her head. "He says, 'To the Order of Duval.'"

Jacqueline put a hand to her mouth to still her quivering lip. The Order of Duval. They had saved him. They had saved them all.

Résolution

Ernest Goüin passed a cheque for fifty thousand francs to Jacqueline as Gaudin brought them each a sherry.

"I don't know how you did it, Duval," he said, saluting her with his glass. "First you disappeared along with my train. Then the girls disappeared, and my train reappeared. Then the colossal machine we spent eighty man-hours building vanished into thin air of its own power. Can you tell me how that happened?"

Gaudin sniggered as she returned to her post. Jacqueline contained her own amusement much better as she thought of the two gigantic electro-magnetic trans-aether teleportation devices, with their unique dynamic regenerators, that now squatted near the forge, hidden away in the forest.

Justine Montpellier had the oddest sense of humor.

She returned his salute. "And I'll gladly repay you for any of the equipment that was lost."

"Not at all." Goüin's eyes gleamed. "With the education you gave my team, I'll make up the losses soon enough."

"And I have plans for Marteau's foundry," she said, "so perhaps we shall be in business together again soon."

They drank.

Goüin cleared his throat. "Hmm. Yes, the explosion in Marteau's factory. If I hadn't seen your airship flying off to the west, I'd have my suspicions, but the inspectors say it was the sinister machinery in the laboratory that shut the building down that morning."

When she didn't comment, he regarded her with all the suspicion he had withheld. "Hold on, did you really build a machine at Sharp's, and were your two apprentices transported there?"

Jacqueline protested her innocence. "I promise you, monsieur, two years ago, Madame Frontenac was in a convent and Madame Guichet was being tortured by a vicious husband. I met them only a few short weeks ago. As for building a machine—did the King's investigators find any sign of a machine in England in 1840 as Monsieur Armand claimed existed in his lawsuit?"

His eyes crinkled. "No more than they can find a machine at the P-O factory."

He gazed at her with respect and amazement. Then his bright eyes dimmed as he noticed the white armband over her coat sleeve.

"I am so sorry for your sister's loss. And the terrible loss of Madame Têtue and Mademoiselle Montpellier. So young, so strong, and so brave."

Jacqueline still fought the ache of grief, but she responded with a soft smile. "Two powerful, great-hearted women. I will miss them. They will not be forgotten here at Bellesfées. Dominique and Justine."

"I do begrudge you Léon Vincent, though." Goüin shrugged. "But he's quite taken with Madame Guichet and insists on staying with her."

Jacqueline waggled a finger. "Madame Clément now," she corrected him. "Her divorce was granted immediately, three weeks ago, once the evidence of her husband's abhorrent cruelty was established and he confessed it to the church."

His brow rose and he smiled. "I see. To the happy couple, then."

Gaudin quickly refilled their glasses. They drank to the conclusion of a harrowing adventure neither one of the engineers could scientifically explain.

Goüin rose and took his hat. "I wish you happier days, Duval. I will not soon forget the great favor you've accorded me, nor the weight on my conscience of the pain you suffered, the cost to all of you."

She offered her hand, and he took it warmly.

"I ask one thing only, Goüin," she said. "Here and wherever your future takes you. Dismiss every child under the age of eight from your factory. Observe the legal limits of working hours for those under sixteen. It's the law. It has been for two years now. Enforce it. Obey it. If families need the money, find a way to assist them, but save the children. Help end the slaughter."

Jacqueline held his gaze firmly until he nodded.

Once Goüin left, Jacqueline went upstairs to Frontenac's room. Angélique was there, assisting the young woman with her new evening gown and dispensing advice more maternal than the bohemienne Angélique had ever given Jacqueline.

"Oh, Frontenac, you look beautiful." She came around behind her to admire the cascade of curls Angélique had given her.

Frontenac grinned at herself in the mirror, a wicked gleam to her bright blue eyes. "I am so looking forward to meeting my fiancé tonight."

Jacqueline hugged her. "Good. You deserve all this and more."

"Hey, hey, take care." Angélique pushed her out of the way. "I still need to adjust the shoulders."

Jacqueline tweaked the ribbons, the tri-color of Bellesfées, securing the knife sheath Clément had fashioned for the Order of Duval to wear openly on their upper arms.

"Oh, this draws the blue of your eyes. You will have him melting."

Angélique sniffed. "Ho, là, That's a disgusting thought."

Chuckling, Jacqueline went to her own rooms where Gaudin had laid out her gown of royal blue silk. She sat at her vanity, and Gaudin dutifully began brushing out her hair.

"Is Madame Frontenac really going to let that man court her?" she asked, her disapproval evident in her tone.

Mischief lit Jacqueline's eyes. "She has no choice, remember."

The maid *hmph*ed. "But he tried to take Bellesfées."

"And he lost. He'll have to reimburse my expenses for the Assizes and the appeal to the court, and tonight he'll have to reckon with *us*." She tapped the side of her nose and winked. "Never underestimate the Order of Duval. There's always a way for the daughters of Bellesfées."

Jacqueline left her rooms just as de Guise closed his door. He smiled at her across the hall. She caught her breath at the sight of him in his evening cutaway, and his beautiful smile warmed her. Long gone was the repulsive sneer of the maniacal Marteau. Though de Guise had spent almost a week recovering his strength, he had erased the bitter memory of his possessed features from her mind. His voice as he greeted her, deep and thrilling, filled her with hope anew.

Dominique Fees was right; the eyepatch gave de Guise a roguish look. Jacqueline instantly knew the definition of "sexy."

But she didn't know how much she could trust the brief vision she'd been shown of their future together. The Butterfly Effect, Dominique had called it; one decision could destroy that future, and she would never know it.

De Guise fingered the cameo of twin girls that adorned her bosom. Although she had said nothing to him of her adventure through time, he seemed to understand its significance to her: Dominique and Justine. She had yet to figure out how a bootstrap was involved, but she knew somehow the necklace her great-great-granddaughter had given her would one day be returned, only to be given to her again. Yet another dizzying paradox she could not resolve.

De Guise took her in his arms and kissed her lightly before touching the edge of white crape that covered her coif.

"Don't think poorly of me," he said, "but your veil of grief reminds me of Queen Victoria's white bridal veil." He kissed her again, then suddenly seized her in a desperate embrace. "Jacqueline, there's so much—"

He stopped on the verge of saying more. She answered his fear with a more ardent, longing kiss, then wrapped his arm and leaned on him contentedly as they descended the worn marble staircase, pressing against him to let the spice of his skin arouse her, reveling in the sensation of his touch on her arm, shivering in delight at his quiet laugh.

"Tonight," he promised.

She cooed softly. "Oh, yes."

Marthe brushed by and swatted Jacqueline with her towel. "Fine example you set for these women," she groused.

Jacqueline and de Guise exchanged sly glances.

Jean-Paul leaned in the entrance gazing out into the evening sun. De Guise set his hand to the young man's shoulder. After a silence, Jean-Paul asked, "You think she's watching?"

"I know she is," he assured him. "She sees us all, just as we are a part of her. Let's make her proud of us. Let's make them both proud."

He straightened the white armband on Jean-Paul's livery and clapped his back.

Jacqueline and de Guise joined Llewellyn and Angélique in the drawing room. Léon Vincent and Renée Clément—Jacqueline reminded herself of the happy change of the young woman's surname—soon came in, and de Guise poured apéritifs. Clément glowed in her lovely peach gown, her face flushed with excitement. Jacqueline did not need to guess why. It didn't take long for the news to reach Frontenac's perceptive mind, and she rushed downstairs to embrace her companion, while Llewellyn and de Guise congratulated Vincent.

Yet, their joy moved in subtle currents, with none of the explosive electricity of Jacqueline's electro-magnetic trans-aether teleportation device. Grief was yet close, as attested by the white veils covering the women's hair, the grey mourning fans they held to their bosoms, and the white armbands on the men's dinner jackets. They spoke in murmurs, and their eyes glistened in the silences between.

Jean-Paul appeared to announce Rodolphe Armand, who strode in before he had finished presenting him. The women stood and curtsied. Armand eyed them all with seething disdain. His piggy eyes narrowed on Jacqueline.

"We meet again, Duval," he said with a contemptuous smirk.

She displayed the appropriate shock at the affront of his address, and Angélique led the women in a furious application of their fans. The gentlemen regarded him coldly as the women sat.

Jean-Paul, however, refused to allow the insult to stand. "Monsieur, you may address the mistress of Bellesfées as Dame Jacqueline, Madame Duval, or madame. Or I can show you out if you can't behave with civility in our time of mourning."

Armand faced down the icy tableau. "I beg your pardon. Madame." The curl of his lip belied his words.

Jacqueline smiled stiffly. She invited him to sit in one of the Louis XVI chairs she'd brought from Angélique's music conservatory concert hall expressly for his discomfort. As they were all likewise accommodated, he glumly took his assigned place. The chair groaned beneath his avoirdupois, and he struggled to balance on the delicate seat.

"I am glad to have the opportunity to see you again, madame," he reiterated with more decorum although he maintained his disdainful tone. "I quite feared for your life the last we met."

She refused to look at him, not for his effrontery, but for fear of bursting into laughter in anticipation of his impending fall.

"Your concern is appreciated, monsieur, but the court firmly established the flaws of your account."

Before he could protest, she indicated Angélique. "I believe you have met my sister, however; Angélique Laforge, Duchess of Singlebury, Glamorgan."

Armand huffed. "Your Grace. Yes, we are acquainted."

"Oh, I know you quite well, monsieur." Angélique dipped her chin. "My husband, the duke."

Llewellyn dipped nothing. He merely held the man in his cryptic gaze, daring him to give any further insult.

Armand glanced at the others and scoffed when he saw the decorated knife-sheaths on the women's arms. His eyes glinted when they settled on Renée Clément. He grinned toothily.

"Madame Frontenac, I remember you too. Which is why I requested your hand in marriage when I had the opportunity."

Clément gave a soft cry of alarm.

Frontenac batted her eyelashes, wide-eyed. "Monsieur, do you mean to say you wish to marry Madame Clément, not me?"

Vincent and Clément conferred in whispers, and Vincent frowned. Frontenac fanned herself slowly, her face reflecting abashed sorrow.

Armand reddened, sweat beading on his bald pate. He glared at Clément, then back to Frontenac.

"I—You said—" He gulped. "You told me you were Madame Guichet."

"Really?" Jacqueline raised a brow. "And was that also two years ago?"

The women tittered behind their fans.

Vincent cleared his throat. "I am surprised, monsieur, you gambled for a bride you obviously hadn't met. May I present Adèle Frontenac, daughter of Roland Frontenac. She's the reason you've come this evening, isn't she? To claim your prize in consolation?" His words dripped with loathing. "You may have won her hand in a card game, but this is certainly a poor start to winning her heart."

The dinner bell sounded, preventing the man's flustered protestations.

Jacqueline stood. "Madame Clément, as Monsieur Armand seems to have been taken with your charms, would you allow him to escort you to dinner?"

Clément reluctantly offered her hand. Scowling, Armand tucked her hand on his arm. She shuddered and gave a quiet "oh," shaking her head to Frontenac.

Jacqueline and de Guise led them to the table. She beamed as they took their places. This was turning out exactly as she had hoped.

After a dinner tainted with constrained animosity, Gaudin poured brandies in the salon, where again the delicate chairs had replaced the comfortable divans and bergères. Monsieur Claque greeted them with puffs of steam, answered by a shocked oath from Armand at the sight of the imposing autonomaton. Monsieur Claque then clanked to the corner to stand sentry behind Gaudin's chair.

When Angélique brought out the cribbage board, Frontenac's somber face brightened.

"Do you play, Monsieur Armand?" She flushed with excitement. "The duke taught me the game just after I arrived at Bellesfées in August. It's such fun. And the duchess bought me a brand-new deck of O. Gilbert cards. Aren't they beautiful? Look, the royals are printed upside-down on half the card, so they're plainly seen by both players." She fanned the deck out on the table.

Armand didn't appear impressed with the cards. "August, you say. So you deny you visited the Sharp factory in 1840 when you told me you worked for Madame Duval?"

Frontenac blinked up at him in surprise. "Why, monsieur, I was in a convent school in 1840. Fleury." She allowed some sadness to color her voice. "Do you mock me, monsieur?"

Jacqueline caught her twin's eye; they exchanged winks. Angélique had coached Frontenac very well.

"Come, madame, you and I will play," Llewellyn offered, setting up the pegs.

They sat, he shuffled, and Clément raised a finger; Frontenac cut an ace of hearts. She dealt.

Armand observed with a shrewd eye as the two played a lively game. The women squealed in delight each time Frontenac scored fifteen or thirty-one, or pouted when she cut a valet for Llewellyn. Her peg languished behind the double-skunk line for two rounds as Llewellyn's edged ahead, but Frontenac then followed a scoreless hand with the coveted rare twenty-nine-point crib of three fives and a valet in suit with the five that Llewellyn cut.

Llewellyn gave a hearty laugh. "I knew I'd regret throwing you that pair, but they didn't suit my seven, double eight, nine run."

Frontenac made a very pretty moue. "Confess it, Your Grace, you pitied me, tossing away fives. Now you'll pay for it."

The comedy continued without Armand observing Clément's slight gestures manipulating the shuffles, not realizing Frontenac could hear

Llewellyn's thoughts reveal his cards and coaching her play, being utterly oblivious to the machinations that brought the two pegs closer to the end of the board. It came down to Llewellyn's deal, giving him two hands to score, his peg closer to the winning hole. But Frontenac would score her hand first, and twelve points between hand and the play would win her the game.

De Guise, keeping to his part as the inscrutable agent of the Sûreté Nationale, had maintained a disinterested silence most of the evening. As Llewellyn shuffled for the final hand, he quietly spoke for the first time.

"Two thousand francs on Madame Frontenac."

The women gasped on cue. Llewellyn paused mid-shuffle. His jaw clenched. "You know I don't gamble, de Guise," he said curtly.

Armand shifted in his chair, eliciting another groan from the fragile frame. "I do," he said. "But only when I play."

Llewellyn set the deck down and stood. "As you wish." He stalked off and poured another brandy.

Frontenac's large blue eyes widened. She again batted her lashes with naïve innocence. "You would wager against me, monsieur? Have you so little regard for me?"

Armand took Llewellyn's seat and resumed the shuffle of the cards without looking at her.

"You, madame, along with your friends, have conspired against me, to my great financial loss." He began the deal. "So yes, for two thousand francs, I will bet against you. You don't fool me. I know what happened, I know what I saw, and what I didn't see once you left. You and that grisette over there. You somehow stole that machine built with my money. You—"

The card he dealt flew off the table, landing face up—the king of pikes. He tried to bend over to retrieve it but could not. Clément recovered it, glancing up at Frontenac. Frontenac's eyes narrowed. Jacqueline smiled wickedly behind her fan; she understood that Clément had not rigged the errant card, and this was Armand's opening cheat gone awry.

Armand thanked Clément for the card and resumed the deal.

"Misdeal," Llewellyn declared sharply. "Shuffle."

When Armand muttered, de Guise spoke again. "Ten thousand on Madame Frontenac."

His impassive face fanned Armand's temper. He puffed as sweat trickled along his cheeks. Again he shifted in his chair, this time responding to the groan of the chair with his own flatulent squeak. The women plied their fans, and Frontenac lowered her big blue eyes, blushing. Armand rubbed the back of his neck, then began the deal again.

"Monsieur Armand," Jacqueline said, "you must know the king's agents inquired hereabouts when you first pressed your claim two years ago. The good sisters of Fleury gave testimony that Madame Frontenac was indeed in their convent, and Monsieur Guichet swore his wife was at home with him, where, as she can attest, she was cruelly mistreated."

Armand's head tipped back and forth dismissively. "I know what I saw, madame," he said with scorn. He dealt his last card, and a second card slipped from his sleeve with it. He froze.

"Twenty thousand on Madame Frontenac." De Guise raised his glass to Armand.

Llewellyn took the deck from Armand and shuffled yet again, glaring so fiercely Armand reached for his handkerchief to mop his brow.

Three aces from an American Cohen deck fell from the folds of the linen.

"Damn you all to hell, you futtering bitches!" Armand blurted as he tried to stand.

The obscenity evinced immediate outrage. Jacqueline jumped to her feet, aghast, and Angélique turned away, fanning herself. But the Order of Duval whisked knives from their be-ribboned sheaths and poised to strike.

Vincent stepped forward and backhanded Armand with force, knocking him into his chair. The chair gave out, dumping him to the floor.

"How dare you, monsieur?" Vincent cried. "I have forborne, for the sake of the mistress of Bellesfées, while you called my fiancée a liar and a cheat and a grisette! I have received your whines and complaints against Madame Duval with the patience she herself has evinced. But your actions, your gross affront I will tolerate no more!"

He threw the aces into Armand's face, where his handprint deepened the scarlet already there.

"I will see you on the field tomorrow, monsieur, to redress the egregious insults with which you have abused the honor of these women. Else call yourself a coward."

Frontenac brought the tip of her knife closer to Armand's protuberant, rhinophymic nose. "Redress the insult to your fiancée and to the daughters of Bellesfées, if you will, Monsieur Vincent. I will avenge my own honor."

Vincent bowed to her. "As you wish, madame. Leave a piece of him for me to reckon with. Will you second me, Monsieur de Guise?"

De Guise didn't answer. After a tense silence, he strode to the card table. Frontenac relented. De Guise offered his hand and pulled Armand to his feet.

"Madame Clément," he said, "has Monsieur Armand anything further to add?"

For answer, two O. Gilbert cards shot out of Armand's cravate at the back of his neck. Armand clutched at his chest, wheezing.

"Monsieur Vincent, I understand your choler," de Guise said with a wise nod, "but it would not be fair for such a slender target as yourself to take on this side of a barn. Nor would it be fitting, as he is no gentleman. Monsieur Armand has revealed himself to be worse than a coward. A conniving, crude, and vulgar villain with no honor to defend."

Frontenac pressed her knife to her "fiancé's" throat. "You cheated my father out of twenty thousand francs. Are you not ashamed of yourself, monsieur?"

He stammered, "I know what I saw. I know what I saw."

She *tsk*ed and wagged her head with a scolding frown as if gently reproving a child. She jabbed lightly, just enough to draw a trickle of blood.

"I'm sorry, monsieur, but I do not think I heard you correctly."

He squealed. "I did! I did! I cheated to win you."

She smiled sweetly. "And now you try to cheat me." She wiped her blade on Armand's lapel. "Renounce your claim on my person, and you are free to leave."

Jacqueline signaled Gaudin, who hopped up and rang for Jean-Paul. Armand stumbled forward to lean on the card table, gasping for air. His request for a drink was met with frosty disregard. Jacqueline took her seat again, and the other women followed suit. Frontenac and Clément sheathed their knives and helped each other adjust their ribbons, graciously suppressing smirks.

"Now, monsieur," Jacqueline said, "despite irrefutable evidence amassed in the past two years, you pursued a case against me without so much as preamble or dialogue. Monsieur Armand, I would see you in court myself for reparations but for two reasons. First, I know with the fall of the Marteau factory, you haven't a spare sou to your name. Nor do you have the twenty thousand francs for Monsieur de Guise's wager, so you have no choice but to renounce Madame Frontenac's hand."

He said nothing. He dared not look at any of them.

Then she softened slightly. "Second, despite all evidence to the contrary, I did indeed build a trans-aether teleportation device in Sharp's factory in 1840. However, I didn't know that until I myself was transported back through time some days ago. I also built a device in Orléans that carried my two protégées back to 1840, where they took the opportunity to seek their revenge for your cheating Monsieur Frontenac, which you would not have done had they not traveled back in time."

Armand gaped at her, his face reddening further. She could see the confusion in his eyes as he tried to work out the contradictions she presented.

"I cannot explain how the machine vanished upon their departure," she said. "Perhaps the build-up of such electro-magnetic, re-generated dynamic power caused an implosion into the aether. But I do promise you, monsieur, I did not lie then, nor did the young women. We were not there in 1840. We were there three weeks ago."

Armand stammered, unable to voice his thoughts.

Frontenac explained, "We tricked you because you cheated my father for my hand in marriage, which you did because we tricked you. A temporal paradox." She took Clément's hand. "In hindsight, it was a grievous mistake, as it led to an escalation of Monsieur Marteau's monstrous experiments. But you tried to ruin my father, Monsieur Armand. I take satisfaction in ruining you."

Armand quaked with suppressed rage. He mopped his brow, his eyes red.

Jacqueline stood with an air of finality. "If you recall, in our encounter I bade you come to Bellesfées to present me with the bill. Had you done as I asked, you would have spared both of us much grief and animosity. Instead, you filed a suit despite all evidence against you. You're a rude, deceitful, scheming, vulgar coward, Armand. But I do pity you. With interest."

She drew Goüin's check from her bodice and offered it to him. He snatched it and read the figure, dumbfounded.

"So," she finished, "rather than suffer the guilt of having you die of your shame here in my salon, I will ask you to take your leave. This matter goes no further, but you will go."

Jean-Paul appeared at the door. She dismissed Armand with a withering look as he gulped like a landed fish.

"Inform Monsieur Armand's footmen that he will need assistance," she told Jean-Paul. "He will not be returning to Bellesfées. For any reason. Claque, see him out."

Armand babbled in terror as Monsieur Claque clomped toward him.

Champagne flowed as easily as their relief, although Frontenac pouted she didn't get to beat Armand at cribbage.

"I could hear every pusillanimous thought in his piggy head," she boasted. "I could have won, even without Guichet's help."

"But that would be cheating, my dear," Llewellyn observed, feigning shock and disapproval.

She giggled behind her fan.

"You have won, my darling Frontenac," Jacqueline reassured her. "You've won your freedom from both Armand and your father. Now I need to know, do you and Clément still wish to stay on with me at the forge?"

The young women both tapped the badges on their sheaths, then folded their arms defiantly.

"We are the Order of Duval," Clément said.

"Three of us, if you're willing," Vincent reminded Jacqueline, though his eyes were on his future bride. "I haven't battled any vampires myself, but I would swear allegiance to the Order of Duval, if I can earn that privilege."

Jacqueline raised her hands. "It's not for me to say. It was all Têtue's idea, this so-called order. As you have seen, in Bellesfées, 'order' is not the order of the day. Of course, you're all welcome to stay. But, my friends, I'd like to offer you another course of action, if you'd hear me out."

The three sobered at her serious tone. They seated themselves together on the couch as she nestled back in her chair. She glanced at de

Guise, and he nodded encouragingly. She sipped her champagne, giving them time to measure the gravity of the topic.

"The decision belongs to you women," she said, nodding to Frontenac and Clément, "but the weight of it falls on the shoulders of Monsieur Vincent, so take all the time you need to think over my proposition. Marteau's laboratory lies in ruins. His foundry, however, is quite operational, while I am an engineer in constant need of parts and other resources."

Frontenac gave a quiet laugh. "You're buying the foundry."

"I will buy the foundry," Jacqueline amended, "if you three will manage it. Monsieur Vincent, as chief engineer, will guide Madame Frontenac in the appropriate sciences to accomplish a degree in engineering, while Madame Clément will learn the economics of industry to keep the business running smoothly and growing as necessary. On the condition that you hire no children under the age of twelve, and then only if they wish to be employed, not whipped, not chained, not stripped, in no way abused. I think we've all had enough of tainted metals to last a lifetime."

The three gazed at her, stupefied. Jacqueline waited, then pursed her lips.

"Having no such talent as Madame Frontenac, I'm afraid I can't know your thoughts. But as I said, take what time you need."

Vincent stood, his cheeks flushed. "Madame, I'm deeply honored by your faith in me. In us. I will devote my life to honoring the sacrifice made by Madame Têtue and Mademoiselle Montpellier."

Clément rose and hooked her arm in his, gazing up at him with glistening eyes. Frontenac seemed to be calculating. Jacqueline waited her out.

"We stay at Bellesfées while I teach mathematics to Clément, and you instruct Monsieur Vincent on operations," the young woman stipulated.

Jacqueline grinned. "Soit."

"You'll teach me your poetical science."

"Soit."

She offered her hand to Jacqueline, and they shook on it.

Gaudin poured more champagne. Jacqueline raised her glass.

"To the Durand-Montpellier Ironworks," she said.

"Salut!" They drank.

"Salut?" said a voice from the doorway. "What have I missed now?"

Jacqueline and Angélique whirled. "Papa!"

They hastened to greet their father, home from yet another of his business journeys.

"My girls, my girls, have pity on an old man!" He kissed them each. "My faith, was that Rodolphe Armand here? The man has a lot of nerve."

Llewellyn laughed. "No, I think we stole the last of that."

"We did," Jacqueline said. "The king ruled in my favor."

"Of course he did." Monsieur Duval grinned happily. "Well, it's nice to still have a home to come home to. I knew I could trust you to hold it, Jacqueline. No presents, I regret to say. Another revolution, but with a more hopeful outcome this time."

He stood back and eyed Vincent with feigned suspicion. "Adèle, Renée, my sweet girls, would you care to explain who this gentleman is?"

The young women fanned themselves, blushing. Vincent quickly introduced himself as Renée's fiancé and a new associate of Madame Duval.

Monsieur Duval's eyes widened and twinkled. "Oh dear, oh dear," he said, clapping Vincent on the shoulder. "Clearly these men haven't told you what that means."

Monsieur Duval dipped his head to Llewellyn and de Guise, but he lost his joviality when he saw de Guise's eyepatch.

"What—"

Then he noticed the tokens of grief. As he searched the room, his grey eyes lost their joy. He stumbled to a chair as his legs gave way.

"Tell me. Tell me all."

"No, Papa." Angélique knelt beside him and laid her head on his lap. "It's not a tale for the telling. Not yet. Too much lost."

Llewellyn set his hand on her shoulder. Monsieur Duval looked from one to the other.

"Oh." His voice caught. "Angélique—"

She gripped his hand and kissed it. "It's all right, Papa. It happens."

He hugged her, trembling. "I'm so sorry. I'm so sorry."

Looking around again, he gasped. "Têtue? Justine?" He shook his head in disbelief. "No, no. My girls."

Angélique sobbed, and Jacqueline bit her lip.

"They're both at peace now," she said. She seated herself beside Angélique and wrapped her arms around her. "They truly are, Papa."

He caressed both their heads and kissed their brows. "And are you at peace? My little polytech? My little angel?"

Frontenac and Clément came to stand behind him to rest their hands on his shoulders.

"We fight the evil that confronts us, Papa Duval."

"We right wrongs."

Monsieur Duval considered de Guise's tortured face and Llewellyn's drawn frown. "At what cost? My girls… All my lovely flowers."

"It has been a terrible loss to us all," de Guise said.

Jacqueline stirred. "The harvest cuts the vines back to nothing, and yet the spring brings a richer bounty for it." She stood and pulled Angélique to her feet. "It's not a consolation, but it is a promise."

Gaudin broke the heavy solemnity of their silence by offering Monsieur Duval a glass of champagne. Looking around at their encouraging smiles, he took the glass.

"To my family. To Têtue and Justine, and the peace you say they found."

But he hesitated, pondering his glass, then raised it. "To the daughters of Bellesfées."

The card table flipped over. More than fifty-two cards swirled around the drawing room, followed by champagne caps popping off two bottles, all of which swept into the cold hearth where the hearth stand tipped over with a noisy clamor and a fire roared to life. Monsieur Claque reappeared in the doorway and pooted a loud toot of surprise.

While de Guise and Llewellyn laughed, Gaudin, Clément, and Frontenac hurried to mop up the over-bubbling champagne. Monsieur Duval gaped about the room in shock, stammering, "W-who—wha—"

Angélique heaved a rueful sigh. "Ah. Yes, Papa," she said, tapping her glass to Jacqueline's. "I suppose I should mention our little knocking spirit…"

Acknowledgements

Much of this book is created with *Handwavium* and a lot of time spent on Google images, old maps, and Wikipedia. It's amazing what information is out there on the Wide World of Websites, and it's all free!

But no one writes alone, and I have to thank the following people for their insights that have guided me in creating *The Order of Duval*:

My husband Jack — yes, Jacques d'Ile, the flugelhorn extraordinaire — Alas, I have forced him to resign himself to being "married to a liar," but he has embraced the role and has given me unremitting support and encouragement throughout. I love this man with my life.

My amazing son Buddy Deal is an electrical engineer who provided me with all the electro-wonderful engineering assistance. I had fun taking his knowledge and creating "punked" designs *(what the heck is an electrometometer?)*, but my special nod to him is that he designed the lighting of the Franklin Institute rotunda described in the novel, and I'm just so proud of him that I had to include it. *(Don't worry, Jesse, you're in book 4 because I'm equally proud of you!)*

Three longtime friends — Debbie Souder-Pelaez, Jenny Davidson, and Bill Yingst — talked me through all the details I needed on nursing, nurse techs, and how to handle a Jane Doe.

My dear French friend/adopted son Yann Matthieu and Bucks County Writers Workshop member Daniel Dorian gave me a lot of good French tech assistance *(although I still don't know why pig iron is called "salmon" in France).*

One of the changes that I experienced while writing this novel was a deepening relationship with my own two sisters. As a young teen, I worshiped my older sister who probably didn't want me hanging around her; and sadly, I resented my younger sister, as I suppose my older sister resented me. Children grow up, but don't always grow together. We didn't. But as each of us grew into womanhood, we learned more and more about each other's strengths and power. Teri and Donna, I love you more than I've been able to say.

My beta reader was LCW Allingham, one of the editors at Speculation Publications with whom I'm pleased to also publish. Her understanding of women and the relationship between mothers and daughters *(alas, I had only sons)* helped me bring my four wayward victims to life to create the Order of Duval.

Gregory Frost *(who refuses to accept the title of mentor, so I'll call him my role model)* gives me constant lessons in narrative writing through his own works and in our conversations. He says that's not true, but his enthusiasm for *Aéros & Héroes* was the impetus for my efforts to make *The Order of Duval* equally worthy of his approval. And I'm sticking my tongue out at you, Greg.

Most of all, Danielle Ackley-McPhail has taught me so much, pushed me so much, encouraged me so much, and loved me so much that I could not have written this book without her. Sent by God to be my friend, my sister. Thank you, Danielle!

About the Author

Ef Deal is a musician, a poet, an editor, a video editor, and an author of science fiction, fantasy, and horror. She's been writing and composing since she was nine years old. Her short fiction has been published in numerous online zines and print anthologies including *The Magazine of Fantasy and Science Fiction*, *A Cast of Crows* from eSpec Books, *Dangerous Waters* from Brigid's Gate, Chris Ryan's *Soul Scream Antholozine*, two anthologies from Speculation Publications, and most recently in eSpec Books' *A Cry of Hounds* and *Other Aether*. She is currently public relation coordinator for *eSpec Books*, assistant fiction editor at *Abyss&Apex* magazine, and video editor for *Strong Women ~ Strange Worlds*.

Her novel *Esprit de Corpse* from *eSpec Books* is the first in a steampunk paranormal romance series set in France, featuring the gifted Twins of Bellefées, who tend to show up in other eSpec Books anthologies as well. When she's not writing, she plays bugle in the Blessed Sacrament Golden Knights drum and bugle corps, and is a member of the Buglers Hall of Fame and the New Jersey Drum Corps Hall of Fame, honored for her contribution to playing, teaching, directing, and arranging. She lives in Haddonfield, NJ, with her husband Jack and her chow chows Corbin and Rory. She is a member of SFWA and HWA. Her website is www.efdeal.net. Follow her blog *Talespinner* at efdeal.blogspot.com.